MW00526812

We love you guys
John you have a
great family and I
am glad you are back
home ~~7~~ 4/3/21

M Adams

Hunter
Adams

"The Lottery Ticket 2035"

Marshall and Hunter Adams

-A Novel-

All Scripture quotations, unless indicated, are from the Holy Bible: New King James Version

Printed in the United States of America

ISBN: 978-1-7366523-0-5

Second Edition

"The chances you take, the people you meet, the people you love, the faith that you have. That's what's going to define you."

--Denzel Washington

Introduction

The year is 2035. The story is about love and survival. Christine Conder, by her own actions, yet against her will, is a contestant in the most serious lottery game ever played.

Money generated by this new lottery supports the advancement of government programs throughout America, and millions of people, young and old, are buying tickets for a chance to enter *The Hunt for Money*. Signs flash along freeways and in downtown parking lots: "The Hunt for Money—$493,940,076—Enter to Win—Hunt for Money!" And the dollar amount changes daily.

There is a growing lack of morality in America. Some say it was caused by the promotion of violent video games, others blame it on a new level of violence accepted in television programming. Most say it is caused by smartphones with unlimited access to the internet in the hands of children. What is known for sure is that these children will be America's leader's tomorrow.

It is a desperate time in America. If you win a chance to hunt in this lottery, you may become rich, or you may lose everything.

There is a difference in belief between two sisters. One believes in God, that we must return to those values, the other does not. Yet they love unconditionally, and that bond grows stronger during Christine's struggle to survive.

Portland, Oregon

October 2035

A new office of government has been enacted. Children's Learning and Advancement (CLA) began during those difficult years following nationwide political protests in 2020. Their primary responsibility is to track families with children and charge those families on a per child basis. The goal, however, is twofold. The first, to limit the size of families. The second, for government to gain a window into the lives of children they might otherwise not influence. Children taken from families are taught to follow without question. By charging oppressive fees CLA takes children from poorer families. The resistance began with families who believed in the original intent of America's constitution—and CLA's goal is to change that.

When fees cannot be collected, children are taken from their homes and placed in Step Homes. The facilities are Step I, Step II, and Step III and are operated solely by CLA. Children are tested and placed in the homes accordingly, and accidents have happened in the Step 1 homes.

Dana is Christine's sister, and CLA has taken two of her children. David and Karly were taken after Dana's husband died in a boating accident on the Columbia River. Now Dana works full-time. She is older than Christine. They both possess loyal, loving, tender natures, but will always say what they think.

David was five when CLA took him. He was not a fast learner, but there was nothing wrong with him. He was among thirty-two children who died in a Step 1 home. Television stations reported it to be a tragic accident, stating the cause to be a chemical leak at a nearby substation. The news segment lasted less than a minute and was never aired again.

Karly is ten and currently in a Step III home. Liam is Karly's cousin and has sworn revenge against CLA. Not only for David's death, but for CLA's actions against families.

Americans have lost confidence in the once great American system of government. Homes once owned by the rich and famous have become dens and lairs of the most aggressive attorneys this nation will ever see. And soon, I have a feeling, a generation without political interests will rule the land. They have grown up in a time where morality was not a requirement but a choice. While we worked to buy pleasures, they learned to trade violence for money.

"It is a dangerous world," one contestant said. "Everyone who leaves their house or watches the news knows it is—yet there is still love if you look in the right places and compassion if you are old enough to remember. My name is Christine."

This book is written under the strictest standards of fiction. With the exception of known historical places and persons, the characters herein are purely fictional. Any resemblance to actual person's, businesses, or companies is coincidental.

This book is dedicated to all of the families who have been impacted seriously by the COVID pandemic.

May your imaginations run wild and your actions forever be in authority to God, family and country.

"The history of Government on this Earth has been almost entirely . . . rule of force held in the hands of a few. Under our Constitution, America committed itself to power in the hands of the people."

--Calvin Coolidge

One

A mosaic of brightly colored leaves fell onto a country styled yard and began to cover the narrow two-lane road in front of a large, single story home. Unlike a true country home, however, its covered porch extending the full width of the house was less than seventy feet from a paved road. Shadows from limbs on a Norway Maple moved rhythmically over a flagstone walkway leading from the house to NW Cimarron Street and the mailbox of Frank and Christine Conder. On days like this the eastward-facing hills above Hillsboro, Oregon might well have been 100 miles from the nearest city. One might have expected to see Glenn Ford, Anne Baxter, Maria Schell and Harry Morgan poised in the movie 'Cimarron' from the year 1960—but this was certainly not that time.

Christine was on the front porch with her two sons, Liam and Jeff, waiting for the school bus. At fourteen and twelve they could catch the bus alone, but Christine traveled in her job with the SunDay Travel Agency and enjoyed seeing them off to school when she could. It was mid-October. A chilly wind was blowing from the north, but the sun would be high within a few hours. Christine was dressed for a warm, fall day. She was wearing a pair of shorts designed by Kuhl and a thin-strap tank top with a pair of Keen's hiking boots. She was what Frank's friends described as breathtaking. Especially on this morning, as she stood on the porch with goosebumps on her legs from the early morning breeze, her natural blonde hair blowing gently in the wind. At five-foot 8 with a face and body blessed by God she showed the well-defined shape you would expect in a gregarious, outdoor tour guide who hiked for a living. The SunDay Travel Agency would always send Christine on their most rugged wilderness adventures.

The school bus came and went, but in one of the back seats another story began to unfold. There was a strong, handsome boy on the bus. He was a quarterback on the varsity football team and had not been seen without his letterman's jacket in two years. Steve Polarano was embossed over a zippered pocket, and he had the world by the tale, so to speak. He had the prettiest girlfriend in school and came from an affluent family. But everyone knew he had lost his driver's license for driving while under the influence too many times. Obeying the law was probably the one thing Steve failed to do well.

Before the bus pulled away, he stood and walked back to where Liam was sitting, "Your mom is pretty hot Liam. Is that your name—Little Liam? I think I'll take her out this week. What would your daddy say about that? Steve laughed, a puerile type of laugh that indicated a weakness in his character. Liam didn't answer. He knew that before this day was over, the popular Steve Polarano would have more to think about than what he had just said. His life would be changed, and Liam already had a plan. Today would be anything but normal at Wesley Jackson Academy.

Liam was relatively thin, not husky like his dad and brother. But that should not be confused with his ability to settle scores. He was like his dad in the sense that they were unwavering when faced with what might be an obstacle to another person. With dark hair and blue eyes like his dad, he was quite different than his brother. In temperament also.

Frank was five foot ten, sturdily built and strong. But he seldom worked out in the gym. He was technical in his thinking and smart.

Jeff had blue eyes and blonde hair like his mom, yet was husky like his dad. Where Liam would think through a number of ways to get Steve Polarano, hurting him for the long term, Jeff would be more likely to come swinging.

If you didn't know where Jeff lived, and if you were old enough to remember, you might think of the original Muscle Beach on the south side of the Santa Monica Pier. You might expect to see Jeff walking on the beach, tanned in the sun, his shoulder length hair blowing in the persistent breeze that comes from the ocean.

***

There was something else about to happen that the family would not be ready for. Frank's birthday was on October 28th, and he would receive the worst birthday present of his life.

It was a perfect fall day in the Pacific Northwest. Frank was up early to prepare for a business meeting, but as he often did, he had fixed Christine's favorite breakfast-in-bed. Complete with a caramel macchiato of his own design. They were always close to being like the real ones, but sometimes he didn't have all of the right ingredients.

Frank's meeting would be with two senior NASA officials who would ask if he had ever worked privately for the mega company, *Jackson, Trimmer and Bach.* They were well known for providing information in a Supreme Court case against T-Con International when the company used another satellite provider's transmission band to spy through a popular screensaver. The case ended in a multi-million-dollar settlement to a political candidate who had been the victim.

T-Con was charged with using xBand satellite communication frequencies in the range 7.25GHz to 7.75GHz (Space to Earth) in a manner illegal in the United States. The company offered no proof but said they received information on how to enter into the xBand frequencies from someone within NASA. The satellite they illegally used belonged to Sardac Global Technologies, and Sardac easily had the resources to put T-Con out of business.

NASA did not suspect Frank of wrongdoing but wanted to know if it was possible to separate and copy specific information from the Space to Earth xBand frequencies. Frank was their best hope to answer that question.

Sam Morrison, a best friend to the Conder family, had called Christine to say he would like to go to the mall with her and find a gift for Frank's birthday. It would have to be after ten o'clock, as he had been asked to furnish documents for one of his bosses at work. Christine knew that meant NASA where he and Frank both worked. He assured her that all he had to do was deliver a file containing information about how he had been able to break into Frank's most sophisticated program. He would tell his boss that no one else could have done it, that he was only able to by knowing Frank well enough to understand how he reasons—and that a certain amount of luck was involved.

Christine said okay to the shopping trip. It was true that Sam had learned to think like Frank in some ways. As a programmer, Frank's job was to write code. Sam's job with NASA was to break it if he could. Over several years he had only been successful once. Frank was clever enough to not use colors that could recognize various elements of the code. He also would never use the systems code editor or the Integrated Development Environment.

NASA's system offered Intelligent Code Completion, but Frank chose never to use that either. He spent more hours at his desk than someone else may have, but he had only been partially broken into once in 11 years, and that was by Sam. In his defense he told his boss that Sam was still not inside the program where he could see classified information. He had only been able to enter the first layer and that layer had been designed deliberately to be misleading.

Sam arrived to pick up Christine at a few seconds before 10 AM. She was sitting on the front porch in a Veranda Teak Rocking Chair. She had scolded Frank when he paid $1,070 for it, but it was worth every penny. It was more than 11 years old yet worked and looked like new.

Sam was driving his 1972 Chevy Cheyenne 4x4 truck. It was a shame to risk someone scratching it, but he had no problem changing suits between working and playing. And he loved to drive the truck. Today he was shopping for his best friend and wanted to bring the truck out before winter fully set in. He was wearing a pair of Dan Post riding boots with levis, a light blue T-shirt with a pocket and a white PBR Gleason straw hat. Sam was the farthest you could imagine from being a bull rider, but the hat and boots stood him out in any crowd.

Christine, however, had not received the memo. She looked more like a model who might be seen in a Hollywood movie. It was the end of the season for summer clothes when she agreed to the shopping trip, and she wore a modest pair of shorts with one of several light colored tank tops she owned. But if you really knew Christine, you might think of the song, “She Don’t Know She’s Beautiful,” by Sammy Kershaw. Christine seldom dressed purposely to attract attention, unless, of course, she and Frank were going out and he invited her to wear something pretty, maybe even daring.

***

As Sam and Christine entered the parking lot at Westman’s Adventure Outlet, a large scrolling, LED billboard flashed: “Enter The Hunt for Money—$503,000,000—Win—Win—Win…” And the dollar amount changed several times each day.

Christine mentioned what it would be like to have that much money. She brought up the subject of her niece, Karly, being in the Step III home. Sam was aware of it and had been very close to the family after Dana’s husband was killed in a boating accident three years earlier. With the cost of payments to CLA for three children, Fred and Dana had not owned a life insurance policy. After that time things were hard for Dana. The year after Fred was killed CLA took David. He was placed in a Step I home and the year after that they took Karly. David was seven when he was taken and Karly ten. Children were interviewed and tested when they were taken, then placed accordingly in the Step I, II or III homes. Dana’s oldest son,

Jeremiah, was fifteen. CLA never took children above thirteen years of age or under five.

"Sam," Christine said, "what if I won a ticket to hunt in that lottery game and made enough money to bring Karly home and keep her away from CLA?"

Sam's look said he did not appreciate what Christine said.

"Christine, I have offered to loan Dana enough to keep Karly out each year. But you know she would not accept that."

Christine looked at the flashing sign as they drove by, then Sam parked a fair distance from the store where no vehicles were likely to park by his truck. He pressed the alarm button and closed the door.

It had been several years since Frank and Christine met Sam. They still did not know much about his personal life—but soon would. One of the many skills Sam learned as a SEAL Commander was surveillance. His security subscription would send aerial pictures to his phone if anyone entered within a distance he could preset around the truck. It was an expensive system, yet more and more people were using it. The platform was powered by satellite imaging. When Sam entered a position, the program would ask for the size of area to guard. Today Sam chose a 30-foot circle and would be notified if someone or something entered into that circle. He would be able to see the assigned area in live video.

The subscription included surveillance of his property

and the outer-fenced area around the home. The area around his home was guarded additionally by a 12-foot metal fence and gate that could be electrified from any location if Sam needed extra security. That would mean locked outside, or locked inside if anyone had been able to get in.

"I'm going to the sporting department," Sam said. "I'll call you if I need advice."

"Okay, I'm looking for a small tent. Something just Frank and I would use and a pair of boots like yours. Then I will find you."

Sam answered, "You won't find my boots here—wrong store."

After entering the main doors Christine went one way and Sam the other. That is when she saw a kiosk with the same flashing sign she had seen in the parking lot, *The Hunt for Money—Buy Your Ticket to Win—$$$$$.*"

Thinking it would be a priceless joke to play on Frank's birthday, Christine put her card in the slot and chose $50 for one ticket in the beginner's category. She was required to enter the zip code of her primary residence and her phone number or email address. Dropping the lottery ticket into her purse she went to find tents. Christine did not know that while purchasing the ticket she was live on video at a place called the Induction Center. It was not a matter of scratching the ticket and winning or losing, but contestants were chosen according to their appearance and sometimes location. They were chosen according to what type of contestant the Induction Center was looking for.

When their shopping was finished Sam and Christine left the store. As they drove by the large billboard again Christine said, “I bought one of those tickets.”

“That’s not funny, Christine. You couldn’t kill anyone.”

“I did buy one. I didn’t scratch it and I’m not going to. I think it will be a classic to show the ticket to Frank at his birthday party and tell him I am going to be a contestant in *The Hunt for Money* lottery. We could pay for Karly in advance till she is old enough to not be part of CLA’s program.”

Christine didn’t realize there was not a scratch strip on the ticket. In the window it had simply read: *Winners will be notified*—but someone at the Induction Center in San Francisco had watched her buy the ticket.

***

Three men walked toward Aaden Bradley as he signaled them over. There were twelve large screens mounted on a curved wall in The Induction Center and Aaden was watching one of them. “Wow, where is she from?” one of the men said as he approached Aaden.

Another said, “She is exactly what we have been looking for. Count me in. I would hunt her myself—but not to kill her.”

Each of them laughed, and Aaden said, "Seriously, she is the one we have been looking for. Can you imagine her as the featured contestant in the coming PPV event? Wow doesn't even describe her."

She could not know it then, but in just days Christine would be in that same room, talking to Aaden Bradley. There were six men working there who looked like they had been cloned from characters in the video game, *Conquer The Gladiators*. Each had black hair and dark shadows at 11 o'clock in the morning. They wore black suits with white shirts, black ties and polished black shoes—and had handguns on their belts.

After the shopping trip Sam let Christine off at her house. His trip home took him from busy, crowded streets to country roads. There was not a head that didn't turn as his beautifully restored Chevy truck turned through intersections and past curb-side homes making its way from Cimarron Street to a large house at the end of Camelot Drive. From Sam's house he enjoyed a magnificent view of Mount Hood, and on many mornings the orange glow of sunrise would set his mood for what he hoped would turn out to be a nice day.

Camelot Drive was a single-lane, paved road leading only to his house. His property covered 61 acres of gentle, eastward facing grass covered fields dotted with established oak groves and scattered pines. The outer fences were built with creosoted railroad ties and 2x6 lumber spaced 4 horizontally in each span. He had painted the fence white and repainted it every few years. The heavy wire fence around his house encompassed 4 acres. That area was cleared of brush and shrubs, offering no hiding places. In Sam's type of work security was important.

With the Chevy securely locked in his barn, Sam unlocked the back door to the house and went in. It appeared that he did have a little bit of cowboy in his personality. A four-foot by ten-foot table built of five-inch thick redwood planks sat in the dining room. Its decoration was that of a single man's house. The chairs were massively built, also from redwood planks, and on the back of one hung a level III bulletproof vest. On another a level IV. On the table in front of the level IV vest laid a lightweight ceramic, rigid plate able to be attached inside the vest for extreme protection. Farther down the table were six boxes of 10mm cartridges. They were the 140 grain Extreme Penetrator round.

The home was built of large diameter logs. The windows, although appearing to be modern grid style, were reinforced with steel flat-bar that had been painted white. They were attractive and at a distance looked like factory windows. Sam got a beer from the refrigerator and walked to a door between the living room and his bedroom. This door took longer to unlock. It was a heavy, steel door and had been locked in the most unusual way. Also, it was covered with rough-sawn boards and did not look like a steel door. Once inside the room, a small closet next to the door encased an electric gate opener. The rod from the gate opener extended through the closet wall and attached to a piece of steel, half-inch flat bar. There were three pieces of the flat bar. They were three inches wide and four feet long. As the rod extended from the closet, each of the metal bars lowered into steel cradles bolted along each edge of the door. The bars were spaced three feet apart across the width of the door when closed. It was safe to say that no one would ever get through that door when it was locked. The opposite action raised the bars, moving them clear, and the door could be opened.

As he walked into the room there were four large monitors on the wall ahead of him. He pulled his chair back from a heavy wood-built desk and sat down. He sat his beer on the desk and unlocked a top center drawer. Inside that he pressed a button and the monitors came to life. Sam leaned back and began to watch the monitors. As he reached for his beer one monitor showed the inside area of the President's Diplomatic Reception Room. No one was in the room, and from a small control board in the desk drawer he changed the picture to see the President's private meeting room. The President was with two other men. Sam raised the volume. Not being anything he needed to hear he lowered the volume and looked at another screen. Satisfied that nothing had caught his interest he left the room and locked the door.

"Those in power need checks and restraints least they come to identify the common good for their own tastes and desires, and their continuation in office as essential to the preservation of the nation."

–Justice William O. Douglas (1898-1980)

Two

Christine was standing on the front porch when Frank walked up and put his arms around her.

She said, "Have you noticed that Liam seems to be in deep thought most of the time. Yesterday he was on his laptop reading about surveillance cameras, or maybe he was writing about them. I couldn't tell. He writes like you. I don't think he knew I was standing there."

Frank answered, "I don't know what he is doing, but right now the boys are not here, and I have their mom in my arms. I am going to get the truck and take my amazingly beautiful wife to enjoy some fresh, mountain air. Frank had taken the day off work. He and Christine would cross the river at the Interstate Bridge and drive eastward up SR-14 to the Dog Mountain trailhead, then take the steep hike leading to one of their favorite views of the Columbia river. There is a choice between difficult and more difficult along the course, and they would readily take the more difficult climb to the top. They would gain 2,800 feet in elevation from the trailhead. In October many of the wildflowers would be gone, but the beauty of the trail would still be nothing short of spectacular.

Frank's job kept him at a desk most of the time, but he

and Christine had a gym in the pool building behind their house. At a distance the building looked like part of the house. The difference was that this deck led to a large in-ground pool and gym. The deck was a covered breezeway and sheltered a well maintained arboretum. A rushing stream like one you would picture flowing through an opened meadow somewhere near John Day, Oregon ran through the arboretum and dropped into the pool to be recirculated through a twenty-inch underground pipe back to headwaters of the stream. The stream flowed from a rock feature built close to the end of the deck, and as the water traveled through the covered area, it wound through a stand of dwarf, white-barked birch. Its manicured stream banks were covered with bear grass and several other species of native grasses. Frank had added the pool and gym several years earlier as an anniversary present when he knew Christine would be gone for a month guiding tours in Australia.

***

When Frank and Christine arrived at Dog Mountain it was still early. Frank parked the truck, and they set out on the trail. During times when the trail was narrow, Frank would let Christine go ahead. He said it was because she would set a pace he would have to work for, but more than that it was because watching her walking ahead of him was something he had never stopped enjoying. It had been fifteen years since they were married, yet Frank could hardly keep his eyes off of her and told her that often. They had been high school sweethearts but were not married till Christine was twenty and Frank was twenty-two.

When Liam arrived at Wesley Jackson Academy that morning, a private school for grades seven through twelve, he went straight to the library where he sat down to use a computer located in one corner of the room. He created a black and white flyer with the word WARNING in bold type at the top. In a section below that, he set a picture of Steve Polarano with pictures of two other people he found online. He put Steve's name below his picture and fictitious names below each of the others, making sure those two pictures were not of anyone local. Before Steve returned to his seat that morning Liam had secretly taken his picture. He edited the picture to remove any likeness of the school bus and in a following paragraph listed the name of a well-known Medical Disease Center and a contact number should anyone see one of the persons suspected of carrying a deadly, contagious disease.

In the same paragraph, he identified the Marburg virus, asking all people to stay away from the infected persons. The flyer stated that anyone seeing one of these persons must by law report them immediately and restrict them if possible from public areas. After printing the flyers Liam posted them in several places throughout the school. He deliberately listed the correct phone number for the Center for Contagious Disease Control (CCDC), knowing they would not easily know if the flyers had come from a department within their own system. Liam had found an article that morning discussing contagious diseases in the United States. It was written by CCDC, and he used their own letterhead. It was a professional looking flyer when he finished. He was sure that with the Marburg virus shown it would go straight to the principal's office and would result in Steve Polarano being removed from school. Liam hoped Steve would be subjected to extensive testing and quarantine. The same virus, had been responsible for more than two-hundred and fifty thousand deaths in the United States years earlier.

Things happened exactly as Liam planned and faster than he expected with the exception of one thing. Every person in the school was restricted to quarantine, not just Steve Polarano. What few masks the school had in the health room were given to Steve, his girlfriend, and students who had been around them. Two vans from CCDC arrived within thirty minutes of Liam posting the flyers. Channel 2 News set up a good distance from the school to report what was already being called an outbreak of the Marburg virus in Portland, Oregon. Steve Polarano was sent to the school health room where he was quarantined with seventeen other students who said they were feeling sick. One of them was Steve's girlfriend Angela Perry. They had been seen in a classroom kissing that morning and now were in what seemed a serious fight. Angela accused Steve of knowing he had been close to someone who carried the virus. She said he hadn't cared enough about anyone but himself, and from what else was said in the room it was certain she was not his girlfriend anymore. A few others said they hated Steve for doing this to them.

It wasn't long till catering vans arrived with food and drinks, which they left outside in an area of the parking lot restricted to bus parking. Workers from CCDC wearing Tyvek suits and masks loaded several pallets and moved rations inside the building.

It was not part of Liam's plan to be grounded at school for an unknown period of time, but one thing was certain. When his brother Jeff got home from his school there would be no one there. Jeff was 12-years-old and also attended a private school. It was small compared to Wesley Jackson Academy and accepted only students who had graduated with high marks from fifth and sixth grades in the greater Portland area. Jeff attended Naylor School of Wildlife Conservation (NSWC). The school had opened in 2022, sponsored by a local icon and pioneer in *Partners for Wildlife and Habitat Conservation, PNW*. It was known for graduating students who would go on to impact areas of Geographic Information Systems relating to obscure relationships in wildlife populations and habitat diversity.

Most of the graduating students from NSWC went on to attend Wesley Jackson Academy where they would continue studies in conservation, including the use of satellite imagery related to surveillance systems applied to public trespass. Jeff was interested in the reasons for declining species within both terrestrial and aquatic conservation plots. Liam had graduated early from NSWC and gone directly into *Surveillance Recognition and Data*, and with help from his dad and Sam, he quickly earned special recognition for authoring two papers. They were titled, 'Entering Guarded Data-1,' and 'Entering Guarded Data-2.' In the first paper 'Entering' was related to Recording, while in the second 'Entering' was related to hacking, or breaking into guarded data.

Liam found as quiet a place as possible with all that was going on at Wesley Jackson and called his dad. He knew he was going to be grounded but told him everything. To his surprise his mom and dad already knew of the situation. Another hiker on the trail heard the news through an alert on her phone and told everyone she met of a Marburg virus outbreak that was taking place in Portland.

Frank told Liam that he and his mom had been near the old fire lookout at the peak when they heard the news and quickly turned back for home. Then as if something funny had been said, Frank could not contain his hearty laugh. He had put the phone on speaker, so Christine knew exactly what Liam did. Frank told his son that he would have Sam go to the house to meet Jeff in case they didn't get home early. He also thought they should have a barbeque later in the week to celebrate the way Liam handled Academy's All-Star football hero. Christine, however, was not ready to applaud her son's disrespect for the school. What he did had caused a great inconvenience to other students, their parents, and teachers. She and Frank would have plenty of time on the trail to discuss that. Frank reminded Christine that they were encouraging their boys to be leaders and to be creative.

He had always told them, "If something needs to be done, do it. Get permission if need be, but otherwise just do it."

Knowing there was not a Marburg outbreak, Frank and Christine turned again toward the lookout. They would be home early enough to enjoy time with Sam.

It was almost five o'clock before Liam got home from school. Sam was there and in the gym with Jeff. Jeff was only twelve but had been lifting weights for about a year. He was the one in the family who most appreciated the gym. Sam knew Jeff's drive for working out and brought his own gym clothes along. They had used the gym many times together. Frank and Liam would go to the gym occasionally, but Frank had built it primarily for Christine. She enjoyed a workout every day when she could, and it kept her in shape for hiking the steep trails she traveled in her work.

Sam had once kept a membership at Gold's Gym in Vancouver, Washington but let it go after Frank built the gym. Sam had helped during the construction, and Frank, of course, said he had earned a free life membership.

Sam was the one who spurred Jeff's interest in lifting weights, and also was the one teaching him that being dedicated was more important than pushing hard, especially when he was young. Sam's six-foot-one physique looked plenty tough, but he didn't have the exaggerated build of a hardcore lifter. Jeff had teased him saying he had the advantage being black, that muscles just looked better on him. But Sam was like an uncle to the boys. He assured Jeff that he would look good and even better if he stayed with it. There was no question that Sam was tough, and very soon, because of the lottery ticket Christine had purchased, the Conder family would realize how tough and loyal to their family he really was.

Frank and Christine arrived home, and the conversation went straight to what Liam had done to Steve Polarano. Then they began to make plans for Frank's birthday party the next day. He would be thirty-eight years old, and this one put him awfully close to that over-the-hill forty mark. But at sixty-one himself, Sam was hearing none of it. He left for home and promised to be back early the next morning to help with things and get the barbeque started.

By nine o'clock in the morning, Sam was back. His mother and father, John and Julie Morrison, were there, along with Christine's sister, Dana, her son, Jeremiah and daughter Karly. CLA would generally allow a child to go home for birthdays or other important events, especially if they were nearing the end of their time in one of the homes. The standard time to return home permanently was thirteen.

CLA had no authority over them and were often unfair about when and who they would allow to go home for visits. It depended on how the parents had reacted in cases where payments had not been made, and CLA contacted them. When David died, there was a woman in Karly's home who struck a true friendship with Dana. She and Dana prayed together many times after the deadly accident that had killed David.

CLA tried to teach children to think differently about what their parents described as lost freedoms. It was the main reason CLA was founded. But Karly was smart and had made a good impression on those in her home. She had not been influenced at all from what she was raised to believe. Karly always followed the rules. It made things easier, but at ten years old she already knew who she was and who she would continue to be.

At the birthday party, Dana would ask Karly to tell everyone about a conversation she overheard in the Step III home. Karly had already told her mom something that could potentially bring about the end of CLA's power.

At the moment, there was a tradition taking place in the Conder home concerning birthdays. Frank would spend an hour in the gym with the boys, no matter whose birthday it was, and the conversation would be about manhood. What they believed about it and what they wanted it to be. On Christine's birthday all three men, young and thirty-eight years old alike, would listen to things that were important to their mom or wife in Frank's case.

It was Frank's birthday, so he began the conversation. "Liam, I would like to hear from you first. From what we already know you had a big day. I want you to justify your actions from a point of being the kind of man you want to be. Do you believe that what Steve Polarano did could have been handled differently, or do you believe your way was the best way?"

"It's not like I can beat him up." Liam said, "and I'm not sure that would have been the right way. If I was able to do that and did, I would be seen as wrong by at least half of everyone on the bus. I will see how it turns out, but word has it that his girlfriend split up with him, and I could not have hoped for a better ending after what he said about you. The best part is that I am not seen anywhere in that. I didn't do this to him for thinking Mom is pretty, but because he insulted you. I wanted him to pay for that. I will admit that I don't like him and never have. He's got a big mouth and doesn't care about anyone but himself. And even makes jokes about his girlfriend when she is not around."

Jeff waited for a pause and jumped in.

"I would have hit him right in the nose," he said, "as hard as I could. I wouldn't care if he knocked me out. I would get him someday, and I mean it. It's a good thing he will be out of school when I get there."

"Well, it might not be what your mom would want me to say, but I totally agree with both of you. What he said was a direct attack on your manhood Liam; more than against your mom or me. He didn't think you would do anything about it and by that alone he had called you a coward. No one might ever know you are the one who got him, but you fought back, and you are standing by your decision. I'm proud of you."

"Jeff, I cannot come against what you said either. What a man feels in his heart is not to be given up lightly. I will probably never be in the right place to tell you when to fight and when not to, and might not if I could. The way Liam handled this does not have to be the way you would handle it, or me. There is not a one-size-fits-all here.

"It's a good thing Sam wasn't there—if Steve was a

grown man talking about your mom and me. Sam has been involved in a lot of things we probably don't know about, and I am sure he can dish it out when he needs to. I am proud of the choices both of you made. Liam, I will ask that you always think ahead to know if others could be hurt by the things you are able to do. And Jeff, I don't know about you. You are just dangerous."

Frank was smiling, "I hope you only fight when you are right, but I know things can happen fast. I love you guys. I already said it, but I am proud of you both. I would trust either of you with my life. Let's go help your mom and Sam get things ready.

"Liam, I don't know if Dana and Karly are here yet, but Dana wants to talk to you about something she says is important."

Frank's boys trusted him, and Christine admired that in Frank. He listened to his sons as if they were men, equal in every way to himself, but he still was Dad and there were chores to do and rules to follow. After agreeing that goals set during the last birthday party were being met, they headed into the house to help out.

John and Julie Morrison were already there, and Dana had just arrived. Frank's boss, Brian Redding, came with his wife, Faye, and their two daughters. Brittney had just turned seventeen and Chrissy was thirteen.

It wasn't long till a pile of beef ribs was ready, along with all the extras, and Christine asked Dana if she wanted to pray before they dived in. Dana was always outspoken about her faith and often prayed during family dinners.

This time she turned to Sam and said, "Sam, Frank is your best friend. Will you pray for the meal?"

Frank's eyes went straight to Sam's.

Sam said, "I would be honored." He prayed about his friendship with Frank and for the food that had been prepared.

Frank and Christine had always seen Dana and Fred pray, but had never thought about Sam that way. Sam had either been put on the spot, or there was another part of his life Frank didn't know about.

Near the end of Sam's prayer, he asked God to help Frank be better looking and to help him age well as he was getting old now. Frank only partially had his head bowed and could see Sam breaking into the great smile he always had.

Sam was in blue jeans again, this time with an untucked, orange and brown, half-inch checkered print shirt with a factory rolled cuff about mid-bicep and a short collar. His western boots were rough-cut, heavy leather with a stitched seam crossing over each arch. They were well-worn. He looked like a rodeo cowboy who had come to Portland for the Professional Bull Rider: *Unleash The Beast* event. And once again, parked at the side of the house close to the arboretum and pool was his perfectly restored Chevy Cheyenne truck. He parked there to be away from other vehicles but also knew his truck complimented the setting around the pool and arboretum.

Frank was still looking at Sam. He caught himself wishing Sam would be more open about his life away from work. The Sam he knew was a retired Navy Seal who in his prime had probably killed every bad guy that ever crossed his path. But now he was praying and sounded very natural doing it. Frank wasn't sure how those two things fit together.

After the meal and after Frank opening gifts, the kids changed and headed for the pool. All but Liam. He remembered that Dana wanted to talk to him about something. At the pool, Jeff and Jeremiah wasted no time pushing Brittney and Chrissy in, and they both screamed as if they had not wanted to get into the most luxurious, heated pool within miles. Back in the house, Dana asked everyone to sit down and listen to what Karly overheard in the home where she currently had to be.

Karly was bold like her mother.

"I was supposed to be in a reading class with my roommates," she said, "when I thought I heard Ashley, who has become good friends with Mom, crying. I didn't know if I should, but I started to go in her office. Then I heard someone talking to her. It was a man. I never got to see him, but he was talking about the accident at the Step I home where David and the other kids died, and whatever he said made Ashley cry. Then he got quiet, but I heard him say if she was smart she would forget about that. I didn't know anything else they said, but Ashley said to the man that Penny's husband told her those kids dying was not an accident. Then I could tell the man got mad. I didn't go in there, but I'll bet Ashley's friend knows something about what happened."

When Karly mentioned David she started to cry. That made Dana and Christine begin to cry, then Faye and Julie began to cry.

Sam's expression changed. He did not look like the same man who had been barbequing earlier and praying. Sam's dad said he wanted to talk to Sam and Frank in the kitchen and Liam got up to join them. John said that maybe he should not come right now.

Frank answered quickly and said, "Liam will want to hear anything we talk about."

John was okay with that as long as long as Frank was.

They went to the kitchen and John said, "Frank, I think you know I was Air Force and part of the Presidential Airlift Group where I flew Air Force One for several years. I only say this because I was not pure Air Force, so to speak. And neither has Sam only served as a SEAL. He is involved in a lot of things I am sure he never talks to you about."

John's outward appearance was that of a man only seventy and one in very good shape. But for the first time Frank saw something very different in him. From just a few soft words spoken by a ten-year-old girl, John's mood had escalated to where it seemed that he was ready to go to war. John was passionate and convincing. He believed Karly could be in danger.

Frank remembered saying to his boys once, "There is no character like passion. It either loves deeply or hates. There can be no in-between, or it is not passion."

John continued, "We have got to get to the bottom of this and fast. Dana must keep Karly home now, and she can do it under the pretense of illness. Julie and I know an important doctor who will write such a letter, and Julie will arrange that. She will bring Christine the letter tomorrow, sealed in an envelope. Dana can take it to Karly's home. No one will question the letter, but someone might suspect that Karly or all of those kids overheard the conversation. They could all be in danger."

"Can I say something?" Liam said. "All of the property where CLA operates must be under 24-hour surveillance. There would be parents trying to break in and take their kids. I'm going to see if I can find the cameras."

The same passion Liam saw in Sam and Sam's father was rushing through his veins. It was a feeling he liked. He had felt like a boy when he said he could not fight Steve Polarano with his hands, yet right now he would if Steve was the enemy—but he wasn't. What happened with Steve seemed like nothing after hearing what Karly said. If David's death was not an accident, someone was going to pay, and Liam vowed to himself that he would be the one to make it happen.

Sam put his hand on Liam's shoulder and said, "Please do what you can. I know you will find those cameras."

Liam headed toward his room, and the other three went back to the living room. The ladies had recovered from crying which was part of what the men ran from. They were talking now as if everything was okay. Whatever else needed to happen would, but they were at a birthday party now. For the time being they were happy again.

Liam texted his dad: "Bring Sam. I'm in."

John followed and they could hardly believe what Liam had found. He had broken into CLA's video data files and had done it in just minutes. Getting into the live cameras would have been one thing, easy for Liam, but the odds against viewing the control panel and seeing the string of keystrokes required to open additional files seemed impossible.

Liam said they could not only see through CLA's surveillance cameras now but could access all of their files, and he told them how he had done it. As with every cash register in a grocery store, he believed CLA would have a camera watching the person who operates the cameras and sends videos to files. He was right. He was able to see the person enter a password to access video storage files, and he wrote the password in a notebook next to his laptop.

It was more than he hoped for. There was a different password to unlock each level of data and Liam had them all. As the men watched, he went to file locations and found the address of the home David had been in. He then selected the date when David died. And there it was! At 3:15 AM someone was outside the west wall of the home. Liam had not seen the footage yet. They watched together as a man pulled a long hose from a reel which was mounted on a truck parked at the curb. Then they saw him push a hose into the building through a partially opened window and turn a valve on. It was high quality video and all the proof they needed. David and those other kids were murdered—apparently because they had not scored well in CLA's testing.

It was not the first time accidents in Step I homes had happened. The man in the video remained at the window for nearly ten minutes then made the one mistake they were waiting for. He looked up toward one of the outside cameras. He removed the hose and slid the window shut. They did not know the man, but Liam recorded the video as they watched. They had seen his face. All bets were that Ashley would know who he was, and he could have been the man who threatened her when Karly overheard them talking.

CLA didn't know it, but Ashley attended the same church where Dana and her family went. Had they known about that, her relationship with a church would have prohibited her from applying.

Some type of chemical had been purposely put into the Step I home. Liam pointed to numbers painted on the front fender of the truck just ahead of the side mirror. It was OR-131. With the clear video he had captured they should be able to find the truck. The tank had an orange tarp over it, tied down at the sides of the bed. It looked temporary as if they were hiding what was written on the tank.

Liam was overwhelmed with his drive to catch this man. He was a lot like his dad but something was different. His dad would work hard to get the law involved, hoping they would build a case against CLA, but Liam did not believe that would work. He could only feel hatred for the man in the video—and for CLA.

Frank and John watched as Liam closed the program, but Sam wasn't in the room. He had seen what he needed to see. They went to the living room to find Sam, but he and Christine had gone to the back porch. Sam wanted to talk with her about the lottery ticket. He wanted to know if she had told Frank. She said she had not but had received a letter concerning it. The letter said she had been accepted as a contestant in the lottery. She was told to report within three days to a place called The Induction Center, and that she would receive instructions once there as to when she would begin her first hunt—and when she would begin to be hunted. It was obvious to Sam that Christine still did not take the situation seriously. She believed she would simply give the ticket back and that would be the end of it. Sam told her he would do what he could in the next few days but that she had to tell Frank. She promised she would but said she planned to wait till his birthday party was over. She did not want to tell him in front of everyone that what began as a joke had now come to this.

***

Jeff and Jeremiah had pushed Brittney and Chrissy in several more times since they first went to the pool, but they were all having a good time. Karly joined them after telling her story about the man who made Ashley cry.

Christine and Sam went back into the house and found Liam telling the story about what he found concerning CLA.

For a man well up in years, John was pacing and angry. As far as he was concerned the party was over, and they needed to find the man in the video. Frank assured him that they would easily find the truck and the man. He told John they would turn the video over to local law enforcement the next day.

It was proof to Liam that he was right about how his dad would want to handle this, but he respected him enough not to say anything. In contrast, he could see a fire burning in John. Liam was more interested in whatever plan of action John and Sam would take.

Three

By profession Frank was a highly skilled programmer, and that is what he did for NASA. His job was to write code protecting entry into NASA's immense, electronic database, and he had been surprised to learn that every employee privileged to top-level information was watched and protected at all times. The year 2035 was a year which defined government surveillance. Governments had no trust for the people, and the people had very little trust for Government.

At sixty-one, Sam still worked but not because he needed the money. He worked mostly because he enjoyed working in a relationship with Frank where he could try to break into the programs Frank had protected.

All information that passed over Frank's desk was protected by the software he developed, and that made him the target of every in-house agency who feared a leak in information. Those whom he protected loved him. Those whom he did not work directly for feared the fact that he could enter their database. He and Sam had met under those circumstances years earlier. Frank was called to a meeting where he would meet the man who had hacked into his highest security program. But where the two could have become rivals they became lifelong friends.

When Frank called Sam earlier from the Dog Mountain Trail, he was sure Sam would know someone in the right place to put a stop to the staged Marburg scare, but he did not want to get Liam in trouble. He told Sam everything Liam admitted and said he sided with his son completely; that Steve Polarano would not suffer sufficiently shy of being dragged through the actions he could yet face. The Marburg virus was thought to be undetectable during the first few weeks. For as many as sixty days. That was going to keep Steve Polarano under guard for a long time.

***

Christine was sitting on the back porch at a desk made of wood with a four-inch slab of old-growth Western red cedar making the top. The top was 36-inches by 60-inches with a raw edge on both sides. It had been sawn from a single piece near enough the center of the tree to have light, natural edges with the classic red center. She sat facing the stream as it flowed for seventy-two feet through the arboretum to where it dropped into the massive twelve-thousand cubic foot pool. From her desk the sound of that rushing stream and the sound it made cascading into the pool was as real as if she was walking the wild, high-country trails where she regularly guided tours.

Frank had designed the creek himself. With a mixture of native shrubs, potted noble-firs and white-barked birch, the stream wound through clumps of bear grass and other native species. Boulders had been placed along its edges to give the feeling that a high-country, silver-haired marmot might be seen at any moment. It was Frank's intension to imitate a high-elevation landscape. Some of Christine's favorite memories were of local tours into Goat Rocks Wilderness. To be sure, a visit to the Goat Rocks is a fair-weather adventure, being careful not to get too high during the fall season. More than two feet of snow can fall in a single day or night. But at higher elevations her clients might hear the high pitched whistles of pikas. They might even see them in the rugged shale rock slides. Those times can be rare treats, a reward worth hiking the hard miles to see. Annual snowfall has been recorded at more than 25 feet as elevations rise in the wilderness from 3,000 feet to more than 8,000 feet. Most of her tours were along the Pacific Crest Trail #2000 which offers 120 miles of adventure near or above timberline. But her tours never included the full distance of the trail. They focused near the Goat Rocks and in the Gifford Pinchot National Forest.

Today, however, Christine was reading a letter that was about to change her life. She received it by email from a place called The Induction Center. The letter acknowledged her purchasing a winning lottery ticket to enter 'The Hunt for Money.' It stated that she was required to report immediately to The Induction Center in San Francisco. Christine could not believe what she was reading. Buying that lottery ticket had been the biggest mistake she would ever make. But now this letter was real. Was it something she really had to follow through with, or could she simply give the ticket back? Those tickets were highly prized by people hoping to make millions of dollars. Maybe she could sell it. But whoever these people were at The Induction Center, they made the matter of buying a winning ticket sound serious. The letter said Christine must report by November first, and that was in just three days.

Sitting there in the arboretum, she texted Frank and ask him to get away from the boys for a bit and come out. He was in the house talking with Liam and Jeff about all that had happened. He wanted to get Jeff caught up on Karly's story. The house was mostly cleaned up, and everyone had gone home.

There were never great sunsets over Cimarron Street, but sunrises could be spectacular when the sky was clear. On this evening, however, a photographer's dream was settling across Mt. Hood in the distance. A pink to purple hew of the softest pastel colors reached across the eastern horizon and set softly on a fresh dusting of snow on the mountain. As Christine sat by the noisy stream, she wanted Frank to just hold her. But even the majesty of this rare, alpenglow setting could not change what she needed to say to him.

Frank sat down beside her and they watched the colors

in the distance changing. The glow would only last another few minutes.

"Hey Baby," he said, "I see what you're doing out here. This sky is the prettiest I have ever seen."

"Are you okay?" he said. "Are you thinking about the conversation Karly told us about. I have never seen Sam or John so upset."

Christine didn't say anything.

"I'm sorry," Frank said. He guessed that she just wanted to be quiet and enjoy the time together. It had been a long day. He set her hand on his leg and put his arm around her. They would not have been able to say whether the purple sky had turned to red, or the red sky had turned to purple, but the busy day was behind them.

"I need to tell you something," she said, trying not to move at all. Frank's arm was still around her, and his other hand was on her hand.

"I bought a lottery ticket for 'The Hunt for Money.'

Then it was Frank who didn't say anything.

"I thought it would be funny," she said. "I knew I would not scratch it, so what could they do to me? I would have thrown it away after the party, but then a letter came from the lottery people. They say I have a winning ticket and that I have to go to San Francisco and talk to them. I'm going to call Sandra and see if she can put a tour together at Lands End. If so, I will do that on the same day when I give the ticket back. That way it will not be a wasted trip. The address where I have to go is very close to the Lands End Trail.

It was a long evening at the Conder home as Liam and Jeff looked at CLA's surveillance videos. Liam was able to go all the way back to CLA's beginning. What he was looking for was a video showing another of the Step I homes where there had been an accident several years earlier, and he did find a newspaper record of the earlier incident describing an explosion. The article said it was caused by a natural gas heating system.

Frank and Christine decided not to tell the boys about the lottery ticket until she had given it back, and then they probably wouldn't feel the need to tell them at all. But one thing was certain. She had to leave for San Francisco on the thirtieth. Frank was certain they would not want anyone in the hunt who didn't want to be there. There were people of all ages trying to win, and there were stories of people winning millions of dollars once they were in the lottery.

***

When Christine left for California, the morning was calm. It was perfect for the long drive. She would travel for more than 10 hours south on I-5 to the busy town of San Francisco. She kissed Frank goodbye and told him she would get out of the lottery ticket and come straight home after the tour at

Lands End Trail. That tour would be in the Golden Gate National Recreation Area.

Leaving at 4 AM put her on the south side of Portland before traffic was heavy and speeding would well describe her driving. Christine's job with the SunDay Travel Agency put her on the road often, and in a salaried position less time on the road meant more time at home. It had, therefore, become a necessary part of her work to use the latest technology in radar detection equipment. Her current unit was similar to Sam's surveillance subscription. From the sky it could see all radar frequencies within a distance she could preset. All police band radar showed as hot spots on her map and she could even see them moving. If an officer was closing in behind her, she knew it. There was simply no radar that could hide from the Sardac affiliate, iTinerant Inc. Their subscription packages highlighted every police radio frequency. Air patrol was seen in bright blue while ground was seen in red. Even Forest Service police could not hide from her. A USFS officer would be seen in green.

Christine felt safe and made good time on I-5. She would arrive at her room in plenty of time to carry things in, have dinner, and prepare for the next day. The normally expensive Suites by The Sea offered rooms with a view of the ocean and a 5-star lounge with exquisite dining. Discounts were offered to SunDay Travel clients.

Lands End Trail was one of the best hikes in the San

Francisco area. As the tour was located in the Sutro District of Golden Gate National Recreation Area, the tour would be very close to her room. SunDay Travel reserved the room for two nights allowing Christine time for the tour, then to spend another night relaxing before driving home the next day. Visitors would see the Golden Gate Bridge from several viewpoints, as she taught the rich history of the coastline. But what her company didn't know is that she would report to The Induction Center immediately after her tour. The duration of that appointment would determine if she drove straight home or stayed a second night in San Francisco.

The next day Christine's tour went well, but she wasn't the cheerful, lighthearted guide her clients deserved. There are miles of trails in the park and many spectacular viewpoints, but she had to be back to her car by 2:45 PM. Her clients parked at the end of Geary Avenue in the parking lot nearest the Sutro Baths. They would get a quick tour through the Visitor's Center for maps and information about the park, then hike down to the Sutro Baths. Christine did not allow much time there, and they set out on the Lands End Trail.

From Point Lobos, they stopped for pictures and from there began to climb a long flight of stairs to access the higher trail. She took them to the second set of stairs and up to where they could see the bridge. They would also see the USS San Francisco Memorial and finally Lands End Point where they would have a spectacular view of the Golden Gate Bridge. They walked past Mile Rock Beach without going down to the water and on to Eagle Point Overlook. From there they headed back. Christine shared some history of several sites they would not be able to visit, but her thoughts were increasingly taken to the lottery ticket in her pocket.

***

At 3:45 PM she was standing in front of a cold, steel door at The Induction Center, her heart beating faster than when she and Frank had pushed uphill stretches on the Dog Mountain Trail. People who bought lottery tickets to enter 'The Hunt for Money' did not know their pictures were taken as they purchased the ticket. They did not know that winning tickets were issued by choice according to who and what type of contestant Nancy Lee's staff was looking for.

Christine stood outside of a door that separated what had been a peaceful, joy-filled life, from a taste of what Hell might actually be like. Dana had talked to Christine many times about places she called Heaven and Hell, but Christine never paid much attention. Her life was too busy to think about anything she couldn't see.

The unlocking of a heavy deadbolt brought Christine back, and she walked through the door.

"Good afternoon Christine," a tall man behind the counter said. "Please follow me. We have been expecting you.

Are you carrying a weapon?"

Christine said she did not have a weapon and realized while answering him that she never had owned one. Yet here she stood, being guided to a room where she would learn that her life and death contest with a young man named Tom Hundley would begin just five miles from where she now stood.

Christine told a man named Colin Brown that she wanted to return her ticket, that she would be glad to let someone have it. She told him she only purchased the ticket as a joke for a birthday party.

Colin nearly cut her off, "I am sorry Christine, but you have put yourself, and us, in a situation where we have no choice. When a winning ticket is drawn, our computers begin matching contestants for age and likely ability. Using photo recognition, we know who you are and when you purchased the ticket. Our computers do a quick search on your background, occupation and lifestyle, and use that information to match you with another contestant.

"Things move fast in this lottery game. After a successful hunt if you are fortunate to win, you will be added to the next class and will hunt with persons more skilled. And that is where the money gets big. I have a hard time believing you purchased a chance to hunt in this lottery without knowing what it is."

"In this lottery," he continued, "eliminations happen fast.

We have very little time to coordinate hunts, and furthermore we cannot entertain those who wish to test the rules. If a contestant chooses to operate in a way that is inconsistent with our rules, we have agents who will eliminate them quickly. I hope you understand what I am saying. These men and women are professionals, and you do not want them after you. We will not allow anyone to cheat or break the rules. It is important that you have a fair opportunity. Most contestants enjoy the hunt once they settle down and begin using their instincts and skills.

"We do allow each contestant to meet their opponent. We believe it is important for you to know what he or she looks like, even the sound of their voice. But you need to be aware that some wear masterful disguises. They may not be who they appear to be. Your first opponent is in the building right now. I will bring him in, and a doctor will come within a few minutes. She will give each of you a shot similar to the vaccine children in schools are required to receive, but in your case, as a contestant, you will receive a tracking code.

"The code allows you to obtain credit when you eliminate another contestant. To receive payments, you need to put yourself within a close distance of the contestant you have eliminated. You will not have to worry about anything else. We have staff in every state and in every county who will respond quickly to remove the deceased."

Aaden Bradley came into the room accompanied by the doctor and a young man named Tom Hundley.

"Come in Tom and have a seat. My name is Colin Brown. I understand that you have talked with Mark Anderson about the rules. I can tell you—there are no exceptions."

Christine stood up and shouted, "I am not doing this, and I am not getting any tracking device, and I am giving this ticket back."

She started toward the door, but Aaden Bradley did not move, and he was nearly the size of the door.

Colin said, "Christine, I thought I made it clear that we have strict rules here. You have been matched with Tom Hundley, and it would not be fair to Mr. Hundley for us to let you walk out. Please understand that there are millions of dollars already set aside for your participation in the lottery, and for Tom's. One of you will become extremely wealthy if you are successful for a period of time.

"You should not have purchased a ticket if you did not want to be part of this. It is printed clearly on every kiosk that purchasing a ticket means you have accepted the rules. Now you will follow those rules just as Tom will. You will each receive the tracker—right now—in this room."

Christine said, "I told you I don't even have a gun, and I am not going to kill another person."

Aaden assured Christine that she had been careless to say

that in front of Tom; that according to the rules it would be Tom's choice if he would let her have time without being hunted. Aaden said he was obligated to honor Christine's first request to participate in the lottery as was indicated by her purchasing the ticket. And that meant receiving the tracker.

In a move surprisingly quick for a man Aaden's size he took Christine's right arm, turned his back to her, and pinned her arm under his powerful right arm. That put her behind his back. She frantically beat on him while the needle was put into her arm. Tom received the tracker next and asked if he could say something. As Christine cried, Tom said he would give her a head start but that according to the rules, after they were five miles from The Induction Center, he would kill her. He said he was sorry for that, but that his future in the lottery would depend on his 'no mercy' approach and quick ability to kill.

"Tom," Aaden said. "We do not use the word kill. We prefer to say eliminate. Normally a contestant is willing to hunt and to be hunted by the rules. If our monitors show that either of you eliminate the other within five miles of this building you will both be out of the game. I hope you understand what that means.

"And this will be important to the winner: No matter how far away your opponent is when they die, you must position yourself close to them, or you will not receive credit for their elimination. In that event you will not receive payment.

"For your first hunt the person who wins will receive $250,000. After that, payments grow quickly. If you make it to the top, you will be eligible to hunt with multiple hunters, and your winnings could be $100,000,000 for a single event."

For the first time, Christine wanted to call Dana and ask her to pray. Christine had never wanted to talk about prayer before, but this seemed like the right time if she was ever going to ask. Dana prayed about everything. She believed that prayer could change things. Today might certainly be a test of that, because there was no way Christine would be able to hide from a guy who probably had a machine gun in his car and a license to kill for money.

They had been warned to leave the five-mile safety zone and were told it would be a violation of the rules if they did not. Contestants could not hunt or be hunted within a certain distance of their home, on property owned by commercial airlines, in federal buildings, or on school property. But they did have to be in legal hunting areas for a minimum of twenty hours each week and eighty hours each month.

Christine and Tom Hundley left The Induction Center at the same time and the door locked behind them. Tom had the appearance of not having money, and Christine wondered if she could possibly offer him enough not to kill her. She wanted to run for her car but at the same time did not want Hundley to know which car was hers. There were more than thirty cars in the parking lot. She walked to a car that was not hers and acted like she could not find her keys, hoping Tom would go to his own car and leave. But she really knew he would never leave without following her.

Then Tom said, "Hey Christine. You can't fool me. That's not your car and if you don't get away from here like they said they will kill you, and I won't get paid."

Christine was a quick thinker but now faced an impossible situation. Tom was leaning against his car, the oldest and probably slowest car in the parking lot, and she had to leave.

She said, "Goodbye Tom. Please go home and forget about me, and we will both be okay. If you want, I could get you an amazing job where you are paid to travel. You could be happy and live an honest life."

Tom said nothing.

Christine went to her car; certain he could not catch her before she got home. Once there, Frank and Sam would figure this out. Sam knew everyone. He would make some calls.

"Christine, I said I would give you a chance. I like you, but I will have to kill you today. It's for the money. I have nothing against you."

Tom came to her car as she was getting in and said, "No one can beat me Christine."

He grabbed her door before it closed. In the same second he bent down and tried to kiss her. Christine fought to get away, but Tom had accomplished his goal and put more fear in her than she had ever felt.

"And by the way, that's a nice car," he said. "I'm going to let you have a few minutes to get ahead of me. You better make the best of it, because I am a good driver. You might never guess it, but I run drugs for a living and get away from the law every time."

He stepped away from her car and she left the parking lot. Tom was from North Dakota and knew nothing about the roads here, but Christine would not stop to look in the floorboards behind her driver's seat until it was too late. Tom Hundley walked toward his truck, unlocking it when he was half way there. His truck was quite different than the small car he had gone to first. He stepped into a 2034 F-150 Taipan. The Taipan was a descendant of the earlier Shelby Super Snake and at 885 horsepower even a person who did not know engines would have said it sounded like a fast truck.

Tom was not in a hurry as he sat for a few minutes looking at something. He held an old Garmin GPS in one hand. It was a 655T, and on its screen Tom could see a small image moving—Christine's car. In a hurried attempt to get away from him she headed straight for I-5 but then thought of heavy traffic and turned toward the winding, sometimes dangerous Highway 101 along the coast. She watched her radar and saw few patrol cars on 101, and she did not want to be pulled over.

After entering onto Highway 101 Christine tried to relax and make good time without getting stopped. But relaxing wasn't going to happen. Frank had not answered when she called. Sam was her next call and he did not answer either. They were probably in meetings—but within the next 100 miles Tom would catch Christine.

"There is nothing so likely to produce peace as to be well prepared to meet an enemy."

–George Washington

Four

Guardrail posts were going by like pickets on a picket fence. Christine had learned to watch her radar, but it was critical now. She did not want to be parked in front of a patrol car and have Hundley catch her. Legally Hundley could shoot her in front of any officer of the law, but before they knew he was a contestant in the lottery he would risk being shot himself.

Traffic was not heavy, but still there were cars, and there were small towns with speed limits. She had some relief in the thought that Hundley would be on I-5, but he was catching her as she sorted through the many mistakes she had made recently. She slowed down through towns to avoid being stopped and Tom didn't. He might not know the roads, but he could see exactly where Christine was, and he wore a logo on the rear window of his truck that made police officers quickly back away.

In the years that followed 2020, countless clashes between law officers and the trucks or cars displaying the large bullseye with a red skull in its center had ended in more than 800 officers dead. The 'Skull Runners,' as they were called, were heavily armed and would come to another's assistance at any cost. It was impossible for police to know where they were or how many might come. They were part of a well-organized, wide-ranging, deadly brotherhood that had formed following that time when police were told to step back and allow protesters free access to destruction and murder in the cities.

There were a few neighborhoods where armed citizens stood their ground during that time, and they were mostly left alone. It had been a time of unprecedented change in America. Police were not allowed to do their jobs when it mattered most. In response, citizens purchased weapons and armed themselves like never before in the history of this country. Record gun sales were recorded month after month while government tried to maintain control over the people—and that was when 'The Hunt for Money' began. It was the largest, deadliest government sponsored lottery in the world. Government capitalized on what they could not control. They allowed a society that no longer trusted them to legally do what they were already doing, and it put government in a position to make money from the sale or tickets and advertising.

***

As Tom left San Francisco, hitting speeds exceeding more than 140 miles per hour, police radios buzzed all over the city. An officer had been close enough to see the bullseye on Tom's rear window and backed off. He radioed dispatch telling other officers they would see a black truck with the bullseye logo, that it was running a North Dakota plate, and to leave it alone. In 2024 a military helicopter had been used to destroy three skull runner trucks as they headed toward a location where a roadblock stopped one of their members. Before the sun set that day, armed attacks on police officers in cities all across the nation erupted.

It seemed now that no one could stop Tom Hundley from catching Christine. Meanwhile, at the Induction Center Aaden Bradley, Mark Anderson, Colin Brown and their boss, Nancy Lee sat around Aaden's desk watching the chase unfold. Christine was in a fast stretch of road—and just minutes from Tom Hundley catching her.

"Mark," Aaden said, "if he kills her you will answer to Nancy. And I will not be at your side during that meeting. You have to end this now."

Aaden smiled at Nancy.

Colin said, "This has been fun. I would love to keep Hundley in the game, but I suppose we have no choice."

He said, "I have never seen anyone cover so many miles so fast, and Christine is pretty good herself."

Mark excused himself and within a few minutes and many miles away, Tom Hundley's truck hit the guardrail, rolled over, and left the highway to land in a field of boulders below. Mark had waited until Hundley was close enough for Christine to see him behind her.

There was a car coming from the north and it stopped at the place where Tom went over the guardrail. Christine turned around and drove back to park behind the southbound car. There was one reason she went back. As much as she did not want to be part of this there could be $250,000 added to her bank account if she got close to the truck and to Tom Hundley.

Christine told the man and his wife standing by the guardrail that she and the driver of the truck had been traveling together. That they should not go down to the truck, and that she would report the accident. The man and his wife were glad to leave.

There was no way Tom could have lived through such a violent crash. When Christine first saw him coming she did not know who it was, other than a crazy driver so she slowed down to let him or her pass. That put Tom doing only 85 when he lost control, but she had seen him clearly in the rearview mirror. By allowing Tom to get so close, Mark planned for Christine to see him. Aaden wanted her to be credited with Tom's elimination, and he wanted it to look like she killed him.

Two more cars went by while Christine stood looking down at Tom's totally destroyed truck. It was all she could do, but she stepped over the guardrail and started down through the rocks. Tom's truck was 90 feet from the road—and Christine could hear him faintly calling her name.

She knew if he was able, he could easily shoot her when

she got close to his truck. She stopped and listened. Tom was still saying something but not as loudly. Christine started to softly cry. She was a woman and a mother, but she had to get to Tom. For some reason it was more than about the money. All of the glass was broken and the truck's roof was smashed low enough that it was tight against the steering wheel. Trembling, Christine got down on her knees and looked into what remained of the truck's cab. There was blood everywhere, and it was visibly running from Tom's head. His left leg was on the top side of the steering column with the cab smashed over it.

Struggling to hide her emotion Christine said, "I am sorry Tom, but you know there is nothing I can do."

"You have to stay here till I die," Tom could barely get the words out.

"If you can find my billfold take it and call my mom. I have a lot of money. Please give it to her. And there is money hidden at her house."

He told Christine where it was. But his voice was no more than a whisper.

"Watch out for them," he said, "they did this to me."

Tom's last words were "Please tell my mom I'm sorry."

Christine drove away from the crash. The highway was running close to the ocean, and she pulled to the side of the road again. It was dark. If it had not been for the clear day and a bright moon, she might not have been able to see that it was Tom behind her. She took a leather-bound journal from the passenger seat and a small bottle of water from a cooler on the floor. Because of the speed she had been going, the time was still only 7:45. The ocean was as tranquil as she had ever seen it. The sun had settled below the horizon, and she would need the dome light to write. Tom's billfold was the only thing in his truck that wasn't covered in blood. She had tossed it behind her driver's seat, not knowing the GPS was there.

Christine began to write: "I love you Frank. I know you have never read anything in my journal, so if you are reading it now I am gone. Things did not go well for us at the Induction Center. I was forced into 'The Hunt for Money,' and I mean hands-on forced. It is possible there could be a large sum of money in our bank account now from a young man who just died, but before he died he told me they did something to him to make him not be able to move or steer his truck. There may have been something in a shot they gave us that caused him to crash. They said they were giving us a tracker in order to know where we are. But if they caused him to crash, they can do it to me too. Maybe it is how they get out of paying.

"It's a long story, Honey. I am so sorry for this. I tried to call you. I know you and Sam must have been busy trying to help me, and you might even think I am spending another night in California. My phone stopped working right after the wreck. I am sure you tried to call me. My battery is good, but I suppose they could make my phone not work if they wanted to. It is terrible to write as if I am not going to see you or the boys again, but I will drive through the night if they let me.

"His name was Tom Hundley. I have his billfold and a phone number for his mom. He has a lot of money hidden under her chicken house. He wanted me to tell her that he loves her and that he is sorry. He was carrying thousands of dollars. Please find his mom and give her the money if I can't. I don't think he was a nice guy, but that doesn't matter to his mom. Well, if anything stops me from coming home, tell the boys I love them and that I'm sorry.

"I love you, Frank. You are an amazing husband and have been the best part of my life. If I die, I will remember how you always loved me. Smile! If my phone starts working again I will call. Goodnight."

***

Christine wasn't speeding now. It would be at least six hours before she arrived home. She would leave Highway 101 and take US-199, eventually merging onto I-5 North.

Throughout the night her mind was flooded with all that might come next. If Tom was telling the truth, that they could control her ability to move or not move, then she was not safe even though Tom was dead. But why? What reason would they have to stop him from killing her? She did not know of their plans for a pay-per-view event and that they wanted her to be in it. The PPV would be the first event ever of its kind, and they hoped to cast her as the star contestant who eliminated a professional drug runner and killer on an opened, lonely stretch of highway within hours of when the hunt began. They might even up the stakes by revealing that he was a member of the Skull runners, and that she eliminated him easily. But they surely wouldn't do that until she was inside the PPV event protected by agents who would keep the skull runners out.

They might even enjoy bringing some of those gang members to an area where they were better prepared to deal with them. Members of the Skullrunners had been in the lottery before and were not as threatening alone as they were in numbers.

Being dark, it was an uneventful drive toward home. Christine wondered if Tom might have just gotten out of control and hit the guardrail. She could understand a chemical tracker in his body, and hers, but could not be certain about their ability to control a person's movements. They hadn't done anything to her. She did check her phone earlier to see if it was working and it was, but she didn't call. Frank would be sleeping and everything Christine had to say could wait. Home was not that far away.

***

It was 3:27 AM when Frank heard the garage door open.

Christine was home. He opened the door from the house into the garage just before she got there and stepped out to take her suitcase.

"Hi Baby. I'm so glad you are here."

He set the suitcase beside his leg and put his arms around Christine's neck. She laid her head against his chest and started to cry. Frank could feel her pain but didn't know anything about what she had been through. Having been in bed, Frank came to the door in just his shorts, and that alone lightened Christine's mood. She went to the bedroom and went in to take a shower. Frank went back to bed but not to sleep. He reached over and threw the blankets down on her side.

The bathroom door was opened and while she was drying he said, "I tried to call you a dozen times, but your phone must have been off."

Christine got into bed and Frank was closer to her side than his own. He was ready to hold her until she went to sleep, but she told him everything that had happened.

Frank was up early the next morning. He called in and took the day off. When he thought the time was right he appeared in the bedroom again, this time with coffee and a breakfast of sausage and eggs with a slice of toast.

"Baby, I am so sorry," he said. "but we know Sam will deal with this. He will know someone who can get you out of the lottery, and you are safe here for now."

When Christine got up she checked her mail. There were already two notices from the Induction Center. The first recognized her elimination of Tom Hundley and reassured her of a thirty-day period before the opening day of her second hunt. The letter came from Colin Brown. He wrote that as quickly as Tom Hundley had been eliminated, her fame was beginning to be known among fans and that another match was scheduled to begin on Saturday, December first.

If she was successful, he said, it could get her into the big money fast. He told her about the PPV that was coming. It would be held as soon as snow allowed in the Ochoco National Forest and a web address was given where she could view the profile of the contestant she would hunt next—the same person who would hunt her in just thirty days.

The second letter was about money and a web address where Christine could watch for a payment of $250,000 to be posted to her account.

***

Frank went to the door, "Hey Sam. I knew you would come this morning. Have you found anyone who can get Christine out of this?"

"I haven't. I have never had a reason to tell you, but another job I do includes keeping track of certain things related to government. The Hunt for Money has been a non-issue for me until now, but I am able to monitor that lottery. Can we sit down and talk? I know Liam has some skill at breaking into surveillance cameras. Like I said, I've never cared before, but what I cannot do is get inside of this program. I tried last night. I think it is more complex than what we see at work."

After a brief pause Frank said, "I can. I wrote it. I have never cared about it either but wrote it by request from a separate department of government than NASA. I would be in jail for the rest of my life if they knew that, but when I write programs I create a window that I can go through. It is so complicated no one would ever see it. My ability to enter remains on this side of whatever passwords they create. When I first show them a program I advise them to erase my temporary password and create their own, but mine never really goes away. It only disappears until I enter a special password."

Jeff was up and walked into the room, "Hey Sam. Are we going to shoot some bad guys today?"

He was on his way to the gym. He and Liam had been up early looking at more of CLA's videos.

"You guys have got to see some stuff Liam found," Jeff said. "He's got enough to put CLA away forever, except that the government probably protects their own. That's the stupid part of all of this."

"Good morning Sam." Liam was right behind Jeff.

"I really hate CLA," Liam said. "They have cameras

inside all of their step homes as well as around the outside. And it's obvious they never thought anyone could get into their video vault. You would think they would have destroyed some of the videos I found and copied. They've got some sick people working in there."

Christine heard them talking and came from the kitchen into the living room, "Liam, Jeff, we need to talk. I know there is hardly anything more important than going after CLA, but there is something you both need to know. I bought a lottery ticket when Sam and I went to the mall shopping for your dad's birthday. It was only meant to be a joke, but I bought a ticket to enter 'The Hunt for Money' lottery. I was going to tease your dad, telling him we would be able to get Karly out as soon as I killed a few people. That's what I need to tell you. I have already been credited with killing someone. I didn't, but they say I did.

"When I went to California I went there to get out of this lottery, but they wouldn't let me. Now there is a man dead, and another person will be hunting me in thirty days."

"You have got to be kidding me," Jeff said.

"I wish I was, but if we can sit down for a minute, I will tell you what happened on my way home yesterday."

Christine told them about Tom Hundley. She showed them the needle mark in her arm and told them she would be hunted again and again if they could not figure out how to get out of it.

Frank said, "Well, let's look at what we have. I do not know what good it will do, but I can enter the program for the lottery and see everything they can see. That means we will know the location of any person who is hunting your mom."

He looked at Jeff and said, "We will know who they are. Whatever the Induction Center knows about a contestant we will know."

"Getting into just a little of what I do," Sam said, "aside from working with Frank, I watch several different agencies. This is private stuff, and you boys cannot talk about it—ever. When anyone comes close to the president, I can see them through the government's private security systems. Because of the dangerous nature of the lottery, I see numbers on my monitors representing people who are hunting. Contestants are not allowed close to the president or any of his administration. It is my job, along with some others, to make sure they do not come close to him. But that is all those numbers have ever meant to me."

"But now," he said to Frank, "you will be able to go deeper into the program. I haven't been able to access any additional information."

Liam added that in the lottery it would be impossible for them to have cameras everywhere, but that by knowing where each contestant is, he might be able to access privately owned cameras, along with county and state cameras.

Christine said, "Well, on the first of next month someone will kill me if we can't figure this out. Maybe I should go someplace where I can't be found. But the people at the Induction Center can always find me, and it might be against the rules for me to leave. I will find out? I am scheduled to take a trip to Italy soon. I will be taking a group to Mount Etna. My boss might let me go now if she can get clients lined up in time. She planned for me to wait till the season slowed, and my contact in Catania says it has, partly because there is the possibility of an eruption soon.

Frank said, "I like that idea. You need to see how it works when your work takes you overseas."

Jeff was getting more and more upset. "Like that idea," he said. "How about we just blow up the whole lottery thing. That's what you do isn't it Sam? Take me with you. That's how to get Mom out. You just show me what to do, and I blow everything up."

Liam hadn't been saying much but said, "And if we can't do that I have an idea. Mom, if you believe the guy wrecked because of something they did to him then it's possible Dad can find out how they were able to do that. If so, maybe we could do it. There would have to be a satellite involved. Something had to cause a neurological response in the Tom Hundley guy. I'm thinking of an article I read where Sardac was able to locate and kill poachers in Africa using one of their satellites. Four men were found dead along the northern edge of the Black Rhino Game Reserve in Pilanesberg National Park in south Africa. In the article, it was believed those guys were eaten alive by wild dogs without a shot being fired.

"That would imply a neurological attack that was able to stop all four of them from moving. I know satellites have the ability to do that, and it might be what they did to the guy who was chasing Mom. At school we can input environmental boundaries of a location, on land or water, into a program and a Sardac satellite will cast the coolest color you have ever seen onto the exact location of the plot. It increases accuracy and saves the time of laying out each plot. There is just one thing, the school has a contract with Sardac."

"That would be the problem," Frank said. "They are not going to allow us to buy a hit on every contestant who gets close to your mom, and if they would, the cost would be unbelievable. It's a good idea though."

"Well, I have an idea that's better for today," Sam said.

He could see that Jeff needed a break from thinking about his mom being killed.

"Why don't we get my boat?" he said. "Let's get Jeff on the water where he can show off, and we can work on these ideas later. Frank, what do you think?"

"It sounds good."

Frank told Sam that if he needed to go home first, they could all meet at the boat.

"The wake boards and skis are on the boat," Sam said, "and I have everything I need with me. I almost called before I left home to see if you guys wanted to go out today. We were not ready for what Karly told us, but with the videos Liam copied it will be easy to catch them now. I will not be surprised if we put CLA out of business forever, and you can bet there will be threats of violence when this gets out."

He smiled at Jeff and said, "And we might not have to blow anybody up. Do you want to call Jeremiah and see if he wants to come?"

"Okay, but they mentioned going someplace since Karly is home. That was a perfect idea John had about getting her out of there. I'm still for blowing the place up and getting all of those other kids out, but Liam's videos will probably do that."

Liam and Christine had already left the room to get ready for the day. It was early and forecast to be warm.

"I'll get the truck," Frank said.

He had just bought a new F-350. They liked to camp and had an expensive travel trailer but had never purchased a boat. With Sam's boat always available, they didn't need one. Sam was generous and usually wanted to go out if the weather was good.

When Jeff confirmed that Jeremiah would not be coming they loaded their things and left for the moorage. Christine was in the middle, and Sam was by the door. The boys were in the back seat with a pile of gear between them to cover everything they might want to do on the water. Karly wanted to go, but her mom had made plans with friends to celebrate her being home. It would have saved a lot of stress in Dana's life if she had known a year ago that Karly would never again be in one of the Step Homes. When the abuse that happened in some of those homes was proven by CLA's own security videos what had been named 'Children's Learning and Advancement' would be completely dismantled, seeing a few workers get prison time and three receive the death penalty for what they had done.

As it turned out, the man who was seen pushing a gas hose into the Step I home where David died was never found for trial. There was speculation that he left the country, which would have meant he left his family behind. There were several in the Conder home; however, who never asked but believed the guy may have seen his last day in the presence of a man named Sam.

Law suits would be filed for years against various branches of government as children told of things they had been afraid to talk about while in the homes. Threats had been held over them. They were told they would not be allowed to visit their families if they caused trouble.

***

Sam's boat was moored at Marshal's Marina just seven-tenths of a mile west of the Interstate Bridge. As well as a card lock entry and exit and over one-hundred covered slips, Marshal's offered fast access to Washington's famed reservoirs along the North Fork Lewis River. After loading the boat, they would arrive at Speelyai Boat Ramp within one hour and launch into Merwin Reservoir. Lined by mountains along both sides, Lake Merwin as it is called, is a paradise of privacy, tranquility, and open water.

Liam and Jeff did not mind disturbing that tranquility as they taunted populations of wildlife nearest the reservoir. They cut through the water heading west, then east, and then west again. Jeff was a natural on skies and riding wakeboards. He boisterously challenged his brother to abandon caution and get crazy. Sam was not too bad himself but had suffered a couple of injuries during his life and rode the skis more calmly now than either of the boys. His boat was a fifteen-year-old Malibu Wakesetter 20 VTX. It had always been under cover and looked like new. And the black/pink color combo held its own with any boat colors.

Sam had never been married but bought the boat for a woman he was in love with once. When it became evident that she could not marry a man who was on call twenty-four hours a day, risking his life protecting others, they decided it would be better not to continue the relationship. Both heartbroken, they moved on. Chrystal went back to Wisconsin where her family lived, and Sam although no longer the commander of a SEAL team, continued to work as a bodyguard for the president and many of his staff. Rather than being at their side, Sam was the one who stopped incidents from happening before they got there. He justified his work by understanding that there will always be people who kill for money or power, and when those people threaten our nation, or the values we believe in, he was in the right to stop them. He was protected by government and would only answer to God on his last day.

They all took turns on the water. Jeff and his dad both barefooted a few times with Christine running the boat, and Sam dared to try barefooting with Jeff behind the wheel. Jeff was the wild one but a regularly patrolled reservoir with a 40 mile per hour speed limit kept him in check. Jeff had recently passed the test for his Boater Education Card but had operated Sam's boat many times before being legally old enough.

"The most effective way to do it, is to do it."

–Amelia Earhart

Five

It seemed like very little time had passed, and Christine was planning for her tour to Mount Etna in Sicily. She made calls, and the weather was great. Karly had been home since Frank's birthday, and CLA was shut down nationwide. Lawsuits overwhelmed the courts. Children were back with their families, and people would not pay any debt which had been owed to CLA. They were suing for past payments to be returned. Liam had been able to access and copy videos within CLA's most secure electronic vaults, and an attorney named Alexander Darius was hired to represent thousands of families after Dana arranged for him to talk with Liam.

Across the nation attorneys were busy with the number of families asking for help. Liam legally owned the videos he had discovered and copied, but could not find it in himself to charge families for their use. He knew firsthand the pain this government agency has caused in the lives of so many people.

Courts were asking every day for Liam to provide additional evidence. He had become a household name associated with the return of children to their homes. There was a website developed in his name and people were sending money for the commitment he had made to destroying CLA.

Fighting government was an expensive battle but the people were winning. Alexander Darius never questioned that they would. Governments from city to federal were afraid to fight back. In light of the videos, they knew it would be useless. The federal government had allowed CLA to operate unchecked and uncontrolled. Mayors of cities were being sued for their part in not governing CLA within their jurisdictions.

Finally, it was November 29th at 3:49 AM and Christine's flight rose into the air from Portland International Airport. She was leaving for the Italian tour on Sicily's world famous, smoking Mount Etna. There was talk of an eruption which could happen at any time, but most eruptions on the mountain were not life-threatening. People she would encounter there would be mostly news reporters and professional writers. If there was a significant eruption, she would be alongside her longtime friend, Chiara D'Angeli. Chiara was the head of the Catania operation centre of Italy's volcanology institute. Although they believed that a major eruption was coming, few reports had been let out during the tourist season. But now the season was winding down and the subject of an eruption was being covered on every news channel.

Christine's employer, the well-known SunDay Travel Agency, had an office in Catania and through their ability to sponsor her Christine held a license to guide tours on the mountain. She was allowed to drive the rough Jeep roads as well as being allowed to access the higher elevations where tourists could not go without a guide. She had been there many times yet had never been lucky enough to be on the mountain during a significant event—if one would call that lucky. But two things were about to happen. Christine and her group would experience the most powerful eruption in seventeen years, the last being on Christmas Eve in 2018, and she would encounter on that mountain a contestant in 'The Hunt for Money.' He would be the person she thought she had left behind in the United States. There was a questionable mystery in the fact that this contestant, Brian Cooper, known to be in Catania and was signed on as one of Christine's clients for the Mount Etna tour.

Not many people would want to be on the mountain when warnings were broadcast every thirty minutes to stay clear if at all possible. Maybe those who live and breathe volcano science or report on life threatening events might want to be. If Christine had not arranged for Chiara D'Angeli to accompany her on the trip, she would never have been allowed to guide tourists during the likelihood of a powerful eruption.

Ten of Christine's thirteen-person group had declined to make the trip, choosing rather to stay at the lodge in Rifugio Sapienza. But others not originally on the ticket had signed up. Two members of the Italian TV network, RAI, asked Chiara if they could accompany her. One of them was her brother

Lorenzo. Chiara talked with Christine, and they were invited to come. The third person was Sam Morrison. It was not until Christine's flight left PDX that Frank had seen a contestant's number in Sicily. He had not thought to look for a contestant along Christine's stopovers in Atlanta, Rome, or in Italy, but now he saw the number of Brian Cooper already in Sicily.

Italy was one of several countries which had not allowed contestants from the lottery to compete in their country, but it was well known that the Induction Center did not care where the hunts happened. If a contestant could hunt and be successful in another country, without getting caught and charged for murder, it was within the rules to do so and added to the challenge.

Sam had called a friend with a private jet and arrived in Atlanta shortly before Christine landed. On the way to Rome and then to Catania, they talked about every possibility Cooper might use to kill her without being caught. Sam knew he was there but did not know he was one of the thirteen persons signed onto the tour. Brian was smart enough to use a different name. But if he got caught killing Christine in Italy, he would be held for his crime in their country. In times past, he might have been extradited to the U.S., but things had changed since 'The Hunt for Money' became popular in America. Italy would deal with any illegal actions in their country, and that would mean murder in the case of what Brian Cooper planned. It was a serious matter, and Sam could be held the same way if he killed Cooper in Sicily.

There was a good chance with his impressive credentials that Italy would let him go but maybe not. Another matter of great importance was the fact that only a few close friends knew Christine would be in Catania, yet prior to her leaving for Mount Etna someone told Brian Cooper where she was going. It could not have been a coincidence.

On November 16th Christine had been invited to the Induction Center to meet Cooper. She declined to attend that meeting, remembering all too well that if it was within the hunt dates competitors were allowed to engage as soon as they were five miles from the building. Christine had seen a picture of Brian Cooper on the website and felt she would recognize him from that, but he did not appear to be in her group today. Then she received a call from Frank. He told her that Cooper was in Sicily and as near as he could tell was very close to her. He told her that Cooper might be wearing a disguise and from what he had learned could very possibly look like a woman.

It was time to leave for the journey onto Mount Etna. They were at the Sapienza Refuge in Nicolosi ready to get into the cable cars when Sam received a text from Frank. It was a picture of Brian Cooper. Cooper was posing for a photograph after eliminating a contestant, and he had a smile on his face. The picture appeared to be one of a stocky, short woman.

When Sam saw it he was certain the woman standing by Chiara was Brian Cooper disguised as a woman again.

Chiara was getting into one of the cable cars. Lorenzo followed her, then the stocky, short woman and then Sam. Christine got in another of the cars with the man and his wife who were in their forty's, die-hards from the original booking. Lorenzo's team mate for the TV news channel got in with them. There would be eight people arriving at 2504 meters when the cable cars stopped. From there they would take a 4x4 Bus up to 2,900 meters, or 9,514 feet, and if the mountain was calm they would hike for an hour and a half to the summit. That would put them at 10,958.01 feet.

It was an unusual opportunity for Christine, as all tours on the mountain had been canceled due to volcanic activity. Seismic readings from the volcanic institute were predicting an eruption at least as powerful as the one in 2018, and Christine was only allowed to go because Chiara would be with her. After discussing the predictions with her office, Chiara believed the route they were taking would be safe. Readings pointed to an eruption near the top on the west side. They would be on the south side.

Everything was dependent on the mountain, and the mountain was about to show its natural, untamed, unpredictable personality. Small eruptions occurred all through the night, but Chiara felt it was safe if they stayed on the road.

They would drive slow and turn back if they needed to. Chiara was in constant contact with her office. The wind was right, but there was a dark cloud covering the top of the mountain. Chiara believed the cloud could be hiding lava explosions, but there should be time to turn back if conditions became worse.

Christine drove. Normally paid drivers would have taken them to the end of the road, but when tourist activities were cancelled that day the crews went home. Therefore, even with Chiara and the news team as guests, Christine was required to drive. SunDay Travel sponsored the tour and wanted her to turn back at the first sign of trouble.

The stalky woman, or Brian Cooper if Sam was right, did not seem to watch Christine like Sam thought he would if he was looking for an opportunity to kill her. All Sam could do was watch for something unusual that might give away whatever Cooper was planning.

Sam still could not imagine how anyone would think they could kill a member of the group without being caught. But because of the picture from Frank, Sam was certain it was Brian. There was the younger couple, and that woman was a woman for sure. Sam wasn't wrong about that. He had to consider, however, that Brian Cooper could be the man with her. Maybe she was there to distract people and help him kill Christine. It wasn't likely, but Sam would not let his guard down.

They were nearing the end of the desolate, dustbowl road. It ended just shy of a small parking area at 9,514 feet. They were ready to park and begin hiking when a deafening eruption shook the slope so badly that their bus was turned sideways on the road.

Chiara shouted, "Do not open the windows! Stay in the bus and put your seatbelt on if it isn't!"

Outside the day had gone in less than a second from a sunny, bright morning to darker than midnight. Sam moved quickly to stand between Christine's seat and the rest of the bus.

Chiara shouted over the sound of the erupting mountain, "Do not touch the glass or the sides of the bus! We could experience extreme heat. If you have a coat with a hood or a hat, put them on, but do not stand up!"

Chiara knew the mountain well, and within seconds it was over 50 Celsius inside the bus, 120 degrees. Lorenzo asked if everyone was okay, and Christine turned the dome lights on. The bus was slowly being pushed down the slope by a boiling wind coming at more than 125 mph. Normally that wind speed might not have moved the heavy bus, but on the rocky, pebble-covered road traction was questionable to begin with.

Christine remembered that the bus had air conditioning and turned it on. The temperature inside began to drop and just in time. It was difficult to breathe the hot air, and being at an altitude of more than 9,000 feet didn't help. Sam was still standing against the back of the driver's seat looking directly at Brian Cooper. Brian didn't know it, but as the bus turned into a furnace he had wiped his forehead and face with the sleeve of his jacket, and now there was as much makeup on his sleeve as there was on his face. Christine saw him too. It was definitely Brian Cooper.

Sam was smart and did not let on that he knew anything about Brian or Christine. He quickly took his eyes from Brian, or at least his direct stare, and Lorenzo began taking pictures. He was a news reporter and a photographer, and the photos he took that day would be seen around the world.

As swiftly as darkness had covered the mountain, their part of the mountain anyway, it was a bright, sunny day again. Chiara was on a portable radio talking to her operations centre, and there was already an airplane flying a short distance from the top of the mountain close to the bus. Chiara told her office that everyone was okay. She understood them to say it had been a small eruption, but very close to their location. It had not been at the top as expected. She told them she would attempt to get some readings and a few pictures before turning back and told them the bus had been turned half-around and pushed down the mountain an unknown distance during the blast.

Chiara talked about the wind and heat as if giving others

a chance to record it in case something happened and her reports might never be found. It was making Sam a little uneasy. He had been in dangerous places but had never willingly decided to get out of a bus and try to find a torn, bleeding hole in the earth's crust where molten lava might be flowing down the road.

Christine asked how everyone felt in light of the report from the airplane. She told them it was a relatively small eruption and that her people did not believe it was going to blow again. The general feeling was that everyone felt good about getting out of the bus. They wanted to see what it looked like out there.

Brian was a sight with a quarter inch of makeup sliding down his face. But in reality he was an expert with special effects makeup and had eliminated two contestants at close quarters without them ever knowing who he was. He could not see how he looked now, but others on the bus were trying not to stare at him.

"Okay, listen up," Christine said. The company I work for is in charge of what we do now, and I have permission to go out exploring, but only to a certain point. Chiara and her brother Lorenzo have a lot of experience on this mountain. It looks safe now, and we have confirmation from the air that it should be safe. But at any time, if Chiara or Lorenzo say to go back, that means we get back to this bus fast. I don't hear the rumbling any more, but that doesn't mean this mountain has gone to sleep. Lorenzo and Nick will be taking pictures. If any of you do not want your picture aired all over the world tell them now and they can try to film around you. We are literally having the experience of a lifetime. We are the only visitors on this mountain, at this altitude anyway. Imagine the stories you will be able to tell, and please remember that the SunDay Travel Agency made this possible. But if anyone does not want to go out, tell me now. I feel like it should be all or none. We will turn back right now if that is what you think we should do."

Everyone agreed that they would like to be part of the history of Mount Etna, having the bus they were in pushed more than seventy feet down the mountain then going outside for pictures.

"That was quite a wind that hit us," Chiara said. "We might be out of the bus for more than three or four hours, but if it starts to look dangerous we will come back, and I mean that. No arguing or trying to get one more picture. Are you all good with that? You might not think so, but it will be very cold outside. Bring your coat."

Christine added, "At all times keep thinking about where the bus is. Look back in order to know every bend in the road. Could you run back to the bus in poor visibility if you had to? There is still a dark cloud moving to the northwest. We should be okay, but winds can change fast up here. Be sensitive to temperature. If it starts to feel warm, we will go back to the bus. It is not naturally warm at this altitude in November."

Chiara said, "The smoke you see coming out of the ground up ahead, that is called a fumarole. It means there is a mixture of gasses coming out of the ground. Let's be really careful. I do not remember seeing a fumarole in this location before. What you see is carbon dioxide-rich air, and if you get too close to it, for too long, it could kill you. Animals have been found dead by vents just like these. What we are seeing is probably related to the blast—and we may be closer to a new crater than we think. This is really exciting. The airplane will be overhead until we are safely out of here."

Sam remained calm but walked close to Christine. Brian Cooper had seen himself in a mirror before they left the bus and wiped as much of the makeup off as he could. He must have thought Christine had not viewed his profile on the Induction Center's website. If she had, she would surely have known who he was. Christine had spoken directly to him with no sign that she recognized who he was. That was hard for her to do. She knew very well that her life was in Sam's hands.

As they walked up the road Sam spoke to Brian. He said, "I don't know how to ask this, but what did you have on you face back there?

"I didn't think it would matter up here," Brian said, "but

I am to be in a play, very soon actually, and needed to know if this amount of makeup would stay in place. I still don't know. The heat we just experienced made a mess of it. The roles I play are serious, and I need to not be recognized."

Sam was surprised how easily Brian turned the situation into a simple matter. The caricature of an actor, and he was good at it. He also could not help noticing that although Brian was not tall, what had made the stocky appearance on the old woman was muscle. Sam couldn't believe he hadn't seen that in Brian's hands. His hands looked like the hardened, wide hands of a heavy weight lifter. Sam had seen men like that in the gym.

Every step they took up the ascending, rock covered road was truthfully balanced on the edge of eternity. Sam knew he could not let Brian leave the mountain alive. If Brian could not find the right moment to kill Christine today, he would vanish into another disguise and another time. And undetected, he would kill her.

Sam thought about the things every person thinks about when they willingly put their life on the line for another. He had done it successfully many times and had watched a close friend, a Navy SEAL like himself, do it unsuccessfully for him. He knew that in a worst case scenario if he had to lock his arms around Brian and take him into a new crater, glowing with molten lava, in order to save Christine, he would do it. But there had to be a better way. If he lost in a fair fight with Brian, Christine wouldn't have a chance. That simply could not be an option. Sam would have to be smart. As he first didn't know how Brian could kill someone in such a public setting, now it was him who had to do it.

Sam noticed that Brian was breathing hard. It is a well-known fact that muscle burns energy, and the thinning atmosphere as they hiked wasn't helping Brian. Sam picked up the pace a little. He had noticed Brian falling behind from the beginning and chose to stay with him. The others were about 250 meters ahead. Christine had not talked with Sam about anything since they got out of the bus, but she was leading the group at a fast pace. She was certain Sam would win in a fight with Brian, but she didn't fully recognize the strength in Brian's frame.

Sam saw them stop at the place where the fumarole was, but they left without spending much time there. The road turned just beyond that, and smoke from the fumarole partially covered the road. If Sam was correct, there would be a short time when one group could not see the other—either through smoke or because of the corner. His phone was set to vibrate only and Christine sent a text. He did not stop to read it but kept up the pace.

The message read: "Chiara tested that steam beside the road and it's really dangerous. Don't breathe it. Carbon dioxide and sulfur dioxide are high."

Sam knew something about carbon dioxide but did not know that Sulfur dioxide affects one's ability to breathe, and quickly. It can cause bronchoconstriction, affecting the airways in the lungs.

Remembering what Chiara said earlier, Sam said to Brian, "The end of the road must be up there around that corner. We were getting close when the blast hit us. Let's pick it up a little. They want to go separate directions from there, and I want to go with Chiara and whoever goes with her. You can go with Christine and the other two from your tour—that is if we get there before they go. It's not far. Let's go. If we split up from there, Chiara thinks we might find the new crater. Imagine the news coverage if we do."

Sam was playing to a man that loved camera's and probably loved killing as much. It was only another 60 meters to where they could see steam rising out of the ground and Sam did not mention the poisonous gasses. All he could think about was what Chiara had said about animals found dead by volcanic vents.

It must take them down pretty fast," he thought, "or they would get away."

Brian was a man who pushed himself hard towards goals. He owned the same mentality that has injured many bodybuilders. He cared more about building muscle fast than he did about his health.

A struggle for life and death was about to begin, and only one man could walk away from it. Sam didn't know if it was right to pray for Brian to lose, but that's what he was doing as they neared the corner. He knew war was an act of saving other people, and that is what he had to do right now. If it was the right war, he thought, and he fought for the right motives. But how could he ask God to help him kill Brian. It was a question he might never know the answer to. He was an excellent swimmer, and as a SEAL had been able to stay under water for 5.1 minutes. But not while fighting a 240-pound man.

As they came into the steam at the corner in the road, they were on one of the steeper inclines. Brian was bent forward with his hands pushing on his legs just to keep going, blowing air as if he was about to explode. His only goal was to arrive at the end of the road in time to go with Christine and from there find a way to kill her. He hoped to make it look like an accident, but if he had to he might kill the other two as well. He would earn close to five-million dollars when Christine was dead, and that thought was what kept him going.

Sam asked how Brian was doing and Brian stopped just inches before entering the steam cloud. His chest was heaving, and he did not have enough voice to answer. The promise of so much money had driven him hard. Sam took a deep breath, fixed his eyes on Brian, and pushed him as hard as he could in the direction of the steaming vent. It was surprisingly close to the road's edge.

Brian turned to break his fall, and that gave Sam his back. Sam lit squarely on top of him, hard, forcing him to the ground. But Brian threw him off and stood up. At that moment, Brian looked like a giant, dark shadow standing against the whitish colored steam. Before he could turn fully around Sam lunged into him again locking his arms around his chest. Sam pinned him face-down almost perfectly over the smoking vent. Brian struggled and gasped for the air that would quickly kill him. He was in the same state of uncontrolled panic a drowning person experiences. Sam held Brian's face over the vent. It was not long and Brian stopped breathing. The cold, toxic mixture of carbon dioxide and sulfur dioxide had circulated through his lungs until finally he was dead.

Sam was nearing the point where he would either pass out or have to breathe. He got off of Brian and walked back down the road till he was out of the smoke. Then he sucked in the cold, fresh air surrounding the mountain. He was not in a hurry but after a full minute went back to check Brian's pulse. Brian was dead.

Sam sent a text to Christine.

Knowing his text could be found by law enforcement if they wanted to look. He simply typed, "Catch up with me."

Christine told Chiara she wanted to run back and see how

the others were doing, that she would be back in a few minutes if they were okay.

Sam moved Brian into a position in the center of the road and back down out of the steam, as if he had been administering CPR. There was still enough of the plume from the fumarole above the corner that the airplane had not been able to see them.

Christine was sad but very grateful for what Sam had done. And those inside the Induction Center would believe Christine had eliminated Brian Cooper.

"Why would anyone want to do this," she thought.

There was still something missing that Sam could not figure out. At the Induction Center, Mark had caused Tom Hundley to crash over the guardrail, but now they had done nothing to prevent the possible death of Christine.

After Christine messaged Chiara, the others came to where Christine and Sam were, to the steaming tombstone which would forever mark Brian Coopers death.

Sam offered to go get the bus, and Christine went with him. She said she had to be the driver, and the two of them left.

"Sam, that was a good message. I knew when you sent it that Brian was dead. I'm sorry I've gotten you into this. I don't know how I would live if something happened to you. My family would never forgive me. You are the big brother I never had and I love you."

Her tears began to flow. She walked with her hand gripped tightly onto the back of Sam's shirt sleeve. He told her that he had asked God to help him kill Brian so that her life would be spared and that he wondered what Dana would think about that.

She said, "I don't know about any of that. Dana has always told me I should pray, but I never have. I just don't know. Maybe if there is a god, he made this mountain that wore Brian out, so you could save me."

"I do believe," Sam said, "and I will tell you something. Your sister is the reason why. I watched her have so much peace when Fred died, and then again when David died, and then when Karly was taken away. I have never had peace like that.

"Today when I looked at the fumarole I knew I had to do something and told myself it had to be by the time I got there. I've never been so afraid of what would happen if I failed. When Brian and I got to the steam column, my biggest fear was that I would be laying in the road with that goon bashing my head in with me wanting to tell Frank and the boys I'm sorry I couldn't protect you but them never hearing me."

"I need to tell you something Big-Brother. I haven't told Frank yet, because what if I didn't come home. But today you saved two of us. I'm pregnant."

Sam put his arm around her. His hand was on her shoulder, and as they walked she never turned loose of the back of his sleeve. On the way up to get the others—and Brian Cooper—Sam drove.

Chiara called ahead, and there was an ambulance waiting at the bottom to take Brian. With no way of knowing that she was protecting Sam and Christine, Chiara told the police about Brian overexerting himself and falling nearly on top of the fumarole. She told them how he had cut his face and arms on the sharp volcanic rocks. She said the wind had been favorable for the others, but as Sam and Brian came close it changed.

Sam had described to Chiara how he fought to hold his own breath as he moved Brian away from the vent. And he was telling the truth.

During the flight home, Sam wanted to do everything for Christine, and she had to assure him that being pregnant didn't mean she couldn't do anything. She added that fighting with Brian Cooper might have been more than she could do.

Christine arranged for Frank to pick her up at PDX, and Sam took a cab to his car at another airport not far from there. That airport catered to private jets, and Sam had been lucky enough to reach a friend who owned a charter service when he needed the fast flight to Atlanta.

Six

Christine was glad to be home again. She had already received $250,000 from the elimination of Tom Hundley and now would receive $1,754,597.00 for the elimination of Brian Cooper. The Induction Center never offered set prices per hunt and few contestants made it past the third hunt anyway. But a third hunt could earn as much as $5,000,000 if both contestants were popular.

Online betting odds had been heavily against Christine in the contest with Brian, and those who took the long chance made large amounts of money. Brian had been previously interviewed on national television for his ability to defeat all opponents and now with Christine the Induction Center owned a contestant they would promote as the most mysterious ever to compete in the lottery. They would make millions if she continued to win, and they would deny any knowledge of where she killed Brian Cooper, but would say she had eliminated him easily in hand-to-hand combat. They would truthfully say that no weapon was used.

People who followed the lottery had known that Brian Cooper was very successful and very unlikely to be eliminated easily. In only a few years 'The Hunt for Money' had become the highest paying lottery in the world. Christine had already earned more than $2,000,000.00 and would not be hunted again for thirty days. But on that hunt she would be matched with another contestant who again had been extremely successful and who's cunning was estimated as the most frightening in all of the lottery.

***

The next morning after Frank left for work, both boys talked with their mom.

"Mom, I can't believe this is still going on," Liam said. "You know what's going to happen. Sam is going to get killed protecting us. He might be good, but they are already sending more dangerous people after you now."

"Do you think I don't know that Son? I just don't know what to do. You did an amazing thing with CLA, so now I need you to help get me out of this. I don't even know when Sam worked last. He worries every day about keeping me safe. I doubt if I can just tell him to go home and not get involved anymore. He wouldn't listen, and I wouldn't make it past the first of next month if he did."

"I don't know, Mom, but something has to happen," Liam said. "I can see the location of every contestant now. Dad showed me how to get into his program and said if I get caught, he will be out of a job and that agents from the Induction Center will all come after him.

"I feel like quitting school and going after every person who gets matched with you. And you need to talk to Jeff. Just between you and me, his grades are going down. All he talks about is how easy he could kill people if he wanted to. He said that to Jeremiah yesterday and Jeremiah told me, so you can't say anything."

They heard Jeff's bathroom door open and stopped talking.

"Kind of quiet out here," he said, "you must be talking about me."

"We were," Liam said. "I told Mom we need to find the records in the Induction Center and destroy them. The problem is that they might be kept on too may computers, and we couldn't find them all."

"Well, you just watch." Jeff said. "I will do something. You notice Dad hasn't given me the passwords to find out who's hunting Mom and where they are, and I know you have them."

"Boys, it seems silly for me to say this, but I don't want to think about this now. I have other things on my mind. I haven't told your dad yet, but can you keep a secret till I talk to him?"

"Sure. Not one thing about this lottery can be a secret though," Jeff said.

"I'm pregnant."

"You are kidding me," Liam said. "It's poor timing don't you think? You buy a lottery ticket to kill people then get pregnant. And why doesn't Dad know this?"

"I was going to tell him when I got home from Italy, but I will tell him today. He has a meeting this morning and will be home early."

Jeff said, "I think I will skip school today to see the look on Dad's face when you tell him his killer wife is going to have a baby."

The phone rang, and it was Christine's boss with SunDay Travel, "Christine, I heard that a man died from overexertion on the Mount Etna tour. I am sure sorry. He booked online, and I was never able to meet him. Was he badly out of shape or what happened?"

"Good morning Sandra. No, he was just the opposite. He was a bodybuilder, in incredible shape, but he and another man were walking a couple of hundred yards behind us, and we think he had a heart attack."

"I'm sure you saw his name in your folder," Sandra said. "His name was Spencer Williams, and we don't know anyone to call. When they saw his I.D, they must have found someone to notify. I guess it's not our problem but sad to lose someone on a tour."

"Yes, one of the men with us worked on him for quite a while, but he was probably dead when he fell."

"There is one other thing, Christine. My husband told me that he saw a picture of you on TV. He said you were pictured in an ad for that lottery game where they hunt people. The woman's name on the ad was Diana Austen, but Jim said it was you for sure. He gave you quite a compliment. He said no one in the world looks like you, in a good way."

"Tell him thank you for that. And your call is quite timely. I was planning to call you today and let you know that I will need some time off before long, maybe in a couple of months. I am pregnant again."

"That is a surprise. Isn't your youngest in his teens now?"

"That's Jeff. He is twelve going on twenty-something," Christine said with a laugh. "He works out in our gym and holds a record on his swim team. I guess I am bragging, but he is at the top of his class at NSWC here in Portland and will attend Wesley Jackson Academy with his older brother next year."

***

Frank called to tell Christine he was on his way home and asked if she wanted to meet him in town for lunch. He said he had something important to talk about. She said she would love to and they met at O'Connell's Bar in Hillsboro. Frank ordered a Murphy's Irish Red for himself and the O'Connell's Irish Coffee for Christine.

Christine turned to Caelan and said, "I just want a

caramel macchiato like you made before."

She turned back to Frank and said, "I want to go first, and no matter what you tell me, what I tell you will be more exciting."

Frank said, "Well, I can't wait to hear this. Tell me that Sam pulled some strings and got you out of the lottery?"

"No, that's not it. It's bigger than that." She took a sip of her coffee.

"Nothing could be bigger than that. Tell me."

"We are going to have another baby."

There was silence on Frank's end.

"Say something please—I'm not joking."

She wasn't sure what Frank was thinking, as he lifted the glass of Irish beer to his lips. Finishing it, he held the glass at arm's length above his head, the signal at O'Connell's for another one. Caelan had overheard what Christine said and came promptly with another glass for Frank.

That gesture broke the silence, and after thanking Caelan Frank said, "Baby, I was just remembering the first time you said those words to me. I had always wanted to be a father, and now I want just as much to do it again. We will figure things out."

Caelan brought their sandwiches, and Frank spoke in a softer voice, "You were right about what would be the most exciting, but I do have some good news. John told me today that Julie knows a man who is an engineer. He owns a company where he builds complex instruments. Julie was thinking about a way to help you, and asked this guy if it was possible to build a device that could detect the scent of another person, if it had been close to them before. He said it was and that he could do it. Julie was a little surprised, because this man introduced himself to her and then talked about the lottery we are in. He said he knew a lot about the Induction Center; that he used to work there but didn't have a cold enough heart to be involved in that. Julie shared what we are going through. I wish she wouldn't have done that but too late now. I told her he could be a contestant for all we know. His name is Daniel and she wants us to meet him."

Frank and Christine thanked Caelan for their lunch and left. Frank called Julie on his way home and said he would meet with Daniel to see who he was and what he could do to help them. Maybe as a former employee he would have some pull and could get Christine out of the lottery.

Julie said she had talked with Daniel again and that he had an idea for a unique type of glove that would easily hide the olfactory sensor he had talked about. He said if he were to build it, he would need an accurate hand size for Christine, as the glove would be built to fit the contours of her hand.

John and Julie agreed to have the meeting at their home. It would be John and Julie, Frank and Christine, and Sam.

Frank told Sam that he did not trust Daniel. He didn't believe Daniel should have known they were involved in the lottery.

***

When Jeff got home, he was excited about a visit his class had made to the Portland Center for Science and Technology. He was particularly interested in the relation of living organisms to one another and to their physical surroundings when linked to invasive species populations. He had been writing a paper on ecological changes in terrestrial and aquatic environments as ecosystems are linked to the influence of receding habitat, and he was intrigued by how much natural systems change over very short periods of times.

Frank didn't know Christine had told Liam and Jeff about the baby and he said, "Hey Jeff, what would you think about having a baby come and live with us?"

Jeff played it well and said, "If you have that much energy and want to take care of someone's baby, I guess it's okay with me. Whose baby is it and for how long?"

"It's ours."

"Seriously Dad? You've had a baby with someone, and we didn't know about it. I guess we wouldn't, though, or Mom would have already killed you. She has that in her you know."

"Okay, it's mine," Christine said, winking at Jeff, "and he or she will be here in about eight months. I hope it is a girl to help me keep you guys in line."

Liam also came home excited about what he had done during the day. "Guess what, Dad. I am into the cameras inside and outside of the Induction Center, and wouldn't you know it; they are high-end audio recording cameras. I'll bet the people who work there don't even know they are being recorded. Who can get them in trouble? No one.

"I went to the library today, put my earbuds in, and listened to a few videos. And I was able to watch Tom Hundley put a tracking device in Mom's car."

He turned to Christine and said, "That's how he knew which way you went when you left down there. He could see you on his receiver. When he grabbed you in the car the cameras recorded him dropping something behind your seat—along with every word he said to you."

"Well," Frank said, "let's think about how this can help us. Blackmail comes to mind. There is no way in California they can legally record conversations without a person's consent, but what court would take that case against an organization who employs professional killers? Your mom was told they have agents who will kill anyone who breaks their rules."

"The obvious," Liam said, "would be to know if they talk about doing anything to Mom like they did to Tom Hundley. But how can we monitor every minute of their videos and conversations?"

"Your mom and I are going to meet with a man who used to work for the Induction Center. I am sure he knows a lot. Probably not the incriminating things they do or he would be dead, but Sam's mom met him and thinks he might be able to help us. I talked with Sam today, and he doesn't like the idea, but says he wants to be there when we meet the man. Sam doesn't trust anyone till he knows them. Julie on the other hand trusts everyone until she knows them. The meeting is set for next Friday at John and Julie's house. I would love to take both of you but not this time. Jeff would probably punch the guy in the nose, and you Liam would probably steal his billfold while he was on the ground and run a background check on him. That actually sounds good as I say it."

"I would punch him for sure," Jeff said, "or Sam could knock him out and we could photograph his I.D. We could put everything back before he woke up, and he would never know it."

Christine said, "Okay you guys. I am lucky you are all willing to risk your lives to save me, but somehow we will survive this and get back to being a normal family. Liam, it is amazing how you can break into everyone's security cameras. And you, Jeff, are just plain dangerous. Courage is respected at any age. And you, Honey, are the best husband in the world. Maybe after a certain number of hunts, they will agree to let me retire. I will look at the rules and see if I can find that.

"I haven't told you boys, but your dad and I have put over $2,000,000.00 in the bank from this lottery. We want you to give us some ideas about Christmas presents—and don't get crazy. Our best gift this year was keeping Karly home. Get us an idea of what you want and help us with gifts for Jeremiah and Karly. I already know what I am getting Dana. Someone to take her on a date. She needs that."

When Frank and Christine arrived at John and Julie's home Daniel was already there, and Sam had been there most of the day. John reminded Sam that if things did not resolve with getting Christine away from the lottery that they both had friends who could place a pinpoint strike on the Induction Center. They would only need to have the right people involved. People at the top who could explain what happened after the fact. With the right connections, investigations could be controlled if it came to that. He told Sam that certain people could even seize bank accounts held by the lottery.

Sam listened intently to his father. John had served with men and women at the highest levels in government. He knew many people with influence and a few of them had children working near the same levels now.

***

The time of Christine's next hunt was approaching fast, and Sam's instinct was proving right. He did not like Daniel from the first minutes of meeting him. But a more dramatic event had been Christine's expression when she met Daniel. The way she had grasped the back of Sam's shirt sleeve on Mount Etna must have been a means of safety for her, because now she had the back of Frank's shirt sleeve the same way. Only this time there was a bit of his arm in her grasp. Frank looked at her for only a moment and then directly at Daniel. Something about Daniel had scared her and Frank knew it. Daniel would be a formidable opponent, but the feeling of protecting his wife was building in Frank's chest. He would charge into Daniel without hesitation if he ever had to. Maybe his deep, buried instincts were more like Sam's than he would admit.

Daniel also did not miss Christine's reaction when she saw him.

He said, "Christine, I know what you are thinking. I have already told John and Julie that I worked for the Induction Center a number of years ago. But I didn't tell them that I am Aaden Bradley's brother and that we look a lot alike. My name is Daniel Bradley. I can assure you that a phone call will prove to you that Aaden is in the San Francisco office.

"He and I are not close. I shouldn't discuss that, but we parted ways after a disagreement we knew would never be resolved. I hope you believe that I am willing to help you, and I know how to do that better than anyone else."

Daniel wanted to prove that he was there to help Christine. He showed them a model of the glove he and Julie talked about. It had not been made to fit, and Christine did not understand how it could work, but Daniel said there was a tiny transmitter in the glove that would cause a temporary neurological attack if she touched someone with it. It would not kill them or even hurt them, but they would be unable to move for a few minutes. Frank caught himself wishing Liam would have been there to ask questions. Then Daniel asked if anyone would be willing to test the glove. He said for the price he was asking, he could not expect them to put money down without knowing it worked. He offered to let Christine use it on him but pointed out that he could probably fake its affect, and they wouldn't know it.

John said, "Do it to me. I am still pretty strong, and it's hard to believe this device will do much to me."

Sam could have said his dad was not going to do it, but he was certain Daniel would not do anything to put his own life in danger.

Playing that card, Sam said, "Dad, hand me your gun before you do this."

Sam had his own, but the statement offered Daniel a chance to change his mind if he did not trust the glove with his life. Now there was a loaded .45 in Sam's hand. Daniel reached out and touched John's leg with the glove, and John collapsed instantly. When he could move again he sat up in his recliner, his pants noticeably wet, and asked to be excused.

John said, "You might have suggested that I visit the restroom first. Please excuse me. I will be right back."

The effect of the glove had lasted almost six minutes, but John could see and hear during that time as if nothing had happened. He left the room to change clothes and Frank told Daniel about the incident where a satellite transmission was used to immobilize four poachers. They were unable to move for a long enough period of time, he said, that wild dogs killed them without a shot being fired.

Daniel agreed, saying that if you had enough money you could buy that service. He assured Frank that the glove was not capable of that strength, telling him it was, however, possible for those satellites to destroy airplanes; that their electrical systems could be shut down, leaving them as no more than pieces of metal on the ground or in the air.

Frank was not willing to give away information about where he worked but knew more about that system than Daniel would have guessed.

Christine's bank account more than allowed them to buy the glove, and Daniel agreed to make one to fit her hand. He said the glove could do just what they saw it do but to remember it would only be of use when she was close enough to touch someone.

He told them it would also be possible to build a needle into the glove that would inject an incredibly deadly poison but said he was afraid that could be dangerous for Christine. He continued to say the needle would be covered and only penetrate through the glove under deliberate impact.

Daniel believed most contestants would never allow Christine to get close enough to use it, but he was sure there would be times when she could. And he wanted to make the sale.

"What if you were wounded," he said, "and your opponent was right there beside you? The needle could save your life."

A price was set on $100,000 and Daniel said he would have the glove completed within a week.

Sam had a question about the poison, and Daniel said he knew of only one that could stop a person instantly. He told Sam that in cases where an opponent's identity wasn't certain the neurological attack would stop them. It would give Christine time. If identity was certain, she would be able to use the poison while they were still paralyzed. He said the toxin had been discovered accidently by a research team looking for the deadliest poison in the world. They found that by mixing nerve toxin from a golden poison dart frog with venom from a reef stonefish the resulting formulation was nearly too dangerous to handle. It would cause instant paralyses and death in humans within seconds.

Frank asked about the cost of the toxin and availability in the event that she used it. Daniel assured them that people could provide it before the next hunt would begin. He told Frank he would need $25,000 to reload the needle each time she used it.

The meeting ended with a check being given to Daniel for the glove and the toxin. They would have the finished glove within one week.

***

The next morning began as a quiet day in the Conder home. It was Saturday. The boys and Frank were home with Christine, and the subject over breakfast focused on several international exhibits which were to be presented at the Portland Center for Science and Technology. The exhibits would focus on environmental changes in terrestrial and aquatic environments as those environments are linked to human activity. Jeff hoped to see a live demonstration of a satellites ability to recognize and preserve native species while at the same time destroy non-native species. It had been proven to work. The hope was to preserve and protect natural ecosystems worldwide. The boys wanted to go.

As peaceful as it sounded, the same technology could be used during a future time to recognize and quarantine different people groups. If used in that way, people with different genetic codes could be restricted to assigned areas and suffer severe consequences, including death, if they moved outside of those areas. It was claimed that the satellites used for these studies could detect DNA differences in all species, allowing regulators to rid certain species and preserve others.

There was particular notoriety given to one exhibit. It would show a satellite transmission able to penetrate the roof of the Science Center effectively destroying invasive insects found in forests in the United States. In a seven-hundred square foot display of native forest trees there were a counted number of insects, both native and non-native, released into the forest. After the release, a call was made to Sardac Global Technologies, and the invisible beam from their satellite entered through the roof to exactly cover the designated area. It killed the entire population of non-native species. Among those killed were the emerald ash borer, gypsy moth, and hemlock woolly adelgid. Nothing like it had ever been shown to the public. It was accomplished by the detection of genetic differences.

It was not likely that countries would successfully destroy every pest, but the technology was there. The downside was cost.

They found an unexpected exhibit sponsored by Sardac. There was a glass aquarium fifteen feet wide and thirty feet long filled to a depth of six feet. In the tank were several species of sharks. A pink cast covered one half of the tank. It was accomplished with lighting and visually separated a portion of the tank where Sardac's beam would prohibit the sharks from swimming. The beam's efficiency was obvious. There was a piece of raw fish in one end of the tank, and the sharks would repeatedly bump into the line where the invisible coverage loomed. Then immediately, as if touched by an electric shock, the sharks would swim away from that end of the tank. There was a large video screen in front of the tank showing live footage of sharks along California's coast moving wildly away from a swimming beach as the satellite sent a proportionately shaped beam onto the water. The most amazing thing was that the beam penetrated into the water rather than reflect off of it.

In 2030 a commercial fishing company had hired the satellite giant to surround and herd salmon into an estuary where they would all be caught for market. But shortly after that laws were established prohibiting satellites from offering that service. A few more exhibits and a few more wonders of modern technology and they were headed for a late lunch at Dana's house.

"A strict observance of the written laws is doubtless one of the high duties of a good citizen, but it is not the highest. The laws of necessity, of self-preservation, of saving our country when in danger, are of a higher obligation. ... To lose our country by a scrupulous adherence to written law would be to lose the law itself, with life, liberty, property and all those who are enjoying them with us; thus absurdly sacrificing the ends to the means."

--Thomas Jefferson

Seven

To see Karly standing in the front yard when they arrived was more exciting than anything they had seen in the exhibits. She ran to Christine for a hug and from there to Frank. Even though she had been home for several weeks, each day was like the first day after John told them she would not ever go back to the Step home. Had Dana known that CLA would be gone forever they would not have needed a medical excuse to keep her home.

Dana was four years older than Christine and now three years without her husband. She had joined Frank and Christine many times for outings after losing Fred but had never dated since his death. At times Christine felt she was putting Sam in a tough place but would almost always ask him to come when they went out. She wanted Dana to have someone with her, and Sam was always glad to do it. Not so much because Dana looked a lot like her sister and shared her wonderful personality but because he was older and believed he would not present any pressure to Dana like a real date would.

Frank and Christine's family had become Sam's family. On one occasion when they were out to dinner Christine told Dana she really needed to meet someone. She used the usual line, that Fred would want her to marry again and not be alone, to give the kids a second dad.

With a pretty smile Dana had put her hand on Sam's, looked directly into his eyes, and said, "I think I will marry you."

Sam took that for how he believed it was intended. He had only been in love once but his job came between them. And for all of the years after that, the same job had kept him from finding love again.

Dana did not move her hand that evening as quickly as Sam might have wished. Her hand on his not only sent a shockwave through his whole body, but it caused him to realize how lonely he was. He was twenty-one years older than Dana.

An oldie by Aerosmith came on the radio, "I Don't Want to Miss a Thing," and Dana asked Sam to dance with her. As they danced she started to cry. She hid her face on his shoulder. It was her and Fred's favorite song. Sam happened to look at Christine and she was looking right at him with tears forming in her own eyes. She loved her sister more than anything and couldn't help but wonder how Sam was handling Dana's emotion. Sam turned his back quickly to Christine and that was her answer. He was not as tough as he thought he was. Maybe with men and with guns, but not here. Not with Dana.

Christine and Frank came out and caught the last half of the song, as Stephen Tyler sang, "Cause even when I dream of you, the sweetest dream will never do. I'd still miss you, Babe, and I don't want to miss a thing—Lying close to you, feeling your heart beating, and I'm wondering what you are dreaming, wondering if it's me you're seeing—and I don't want to miss a thing."

The song ended and Sam was glad to have been there for Dana. He thought of something his mom said to him after he and the woman he loved each went their way.

She had said, "Son, our lives are reflections of how we have lived, how we love, and how we have helped others accomplish their dreams."

She told him that he was kind and loving for being honest with Amy at that time, for not entering into a marriage that might have broken her heart. She said that living with his dad through all the years when he worked was very hard. She told him that his dad would never tell her when he was going into danger.

"But wives know those things," she said.

***

The sun was shining when Sam drove into his parking space in the old Chevy Cheyenne. He had been invited to lunch with Frank and Christine. This time he was in a white tee-shirt and blue jeans with the same western boots.

It had been hard for Dana to keep the house after Fred died, but Frank and Christine had recently paid the house off for her. Sam was lucky he wasn't there when they did that. Dana and Christine both cried. Frank was used to it and had talked to Jeremiah and Karly about school while Dana and Christine shared their emotions.

Today Dana, Jeremiah and Karly would be at Frank and Christine's for lunch.

Frank knew Karly had settled into the new school as if she had never been anyplace else, but Jeremiah was not doing as well. Frank found some time with him before lunch. They talked about whatever Frank could get Jeremiah to talk about. Jeremiah felt like Liam and Jeff didn't talk to him much anymore. Frank guessed what was happening and asked Jeremiah if he knew any of what was going on with Christine. Jeremiah said he knew nothing about it, and Frank shared everything. Then he told Jeremiah that all of them, including Liam and Jeff, were so deep into the problem that they were apparently neglecting family. He apologized for everyone and encouraged Jeremiah to let the boys know what he had shared with him.

"Then," he said, "they will be talking to you nonstop because that's all we can think about."

Jeremiah said his mom would not tell him and Karly the details of what they were praying about, but that they had been praying every day for Christine for a long time. He said he understood now why his mom did not go into detail. She hoped their aunt would get out of the lottery and never have to tell them.

Frank could not help thinking, as he talked with Jeremiah how much like his dad he was. He remembered that when Fred prayed it was always about important things, and it was always from his heart. Frank believed Fred probably prayed the same way when no one was around to hear him as he did when they were, and he could see that in Jeremiah.

"Guys," Dana hollered from the kitchen, "lunch is ready."

When they were all at the table, Jeremiah said, "Mom, I will pray."

They all held hands, and Jeremiah thanked God for everything. Frank was again impressed by how natural it was for Jeremiah to pray.

After asking blessing for the food, Jeremiah said, "Lord, I particularly thank you for our family. I ask You to protect all of us from the dangers we bring on ourselves and from the ones that come to us for other reasons, and thank you again for my little sister being home. In Jesus name, Amen."

When dinner was over Sam suggested that Dana and Christine visit, while he and Frank cleaned up the kitchen.

Sam said to Frank, "It's clear that Jeremiah knows about Christine and the lottery ticket."

"Yeah, he does now. Dana had not told him or Karly, but

I filled Jeremiah in just today. I asked him to share everything with Karly."

With the kitchen cleaned and dishes in the dishwasher everyone began to talk about Christmas. Christine told Jeremiah and Karly that she and Frank had come into some extra money.

They shared what they had told Liam and Jeff, "Don't get crazy, but tell us what you really want for Christmas."

Karly looked dead serious, and said, "How much money are we talking about? I want a horse and I want to keep it at Uncle Sam's house, and I will have to have food for it."

Sam said, "Well, I'm willing to keep the horse if anyone is willing to buy it, but good horses cost a lot of money."

"I know," Karly said, "I was just being honest. The next thing I want if I can't have a horse is a dog. Abraham got old and died while I was gone, and I didn't even get to say goodbye to him. He was so black you couldn't even see him at night, and I want another dog just like him."

Dana said, "Your dad did a lot of bird hunting with Abe. He was a good dog, and he sure loved you."

Jeremiah said, "I have to ask the same question. It's hard to work and save money with school and all, but in a few months I will be old enough to get my driver's license."

Frank interrupted, "We will tell you if it is too much, but for now tell us what you really want and don't be embarrassed."

Mom said I could have Dad's truck but it's pretty nice and doesn't get good mileage. I would drive it for some things, but a car would be more practical till I get some money saved up. It's probably too much to ask, but I don't need an expensive car. I could work on one if it needed some fixing up, and I would pay you back when I could."

"Do we get a turn?" Jeff said.

The mention of a truck was exactly what he had in mind, and Jeremiah had broken ground.

"I want a truck just like Sam's," Jeff said, "and I know where it is. I have a friend whose grandfather has one in his barn. It doesn't have tires or wheels, but he says there is also no rust. It looks pretty good for being old, and he told me I could get it for a good price. He said his grandpa would like to see it back on the road."

Frank said, "Let Christine and me discuss these ideas."

Liam had not been saying much all through dinner, but said, "I don't know what I want. I think having Karly home is the best present I will ever have. It wouldn't matter if I never got another Christmas present."

At that Karly went to where he and Jeremiah were sitting and fell backwards onto the couch so close beside Liam that there was no room between them.

He put his arm around her and said, "I'm using you to get more out of Mom and Dad. Just wait till I figure out what

I want."

Christmas was on a Tuesday just two weeks away. With the situation Christine was in she and Frank had not had time to plan for it, but Christmas this year would be a great time for the kids. Every one of them would get what they wanted.

Sam said he would be honored to have Christmas at his house, and it was agreed that he would. At eleven years old, Karly might have wanted a pony for Christmas, but that isn't what she got. In Sam's barn there would be the prettiest quarter horse any of them had ever seen. It was an eight-year-old AQHA gelding. He had been a winning barrel racing horse belonging to a family whose daughter road him in the Molalla high school rodeo for three consecutive years.

She told Sam she was leaving for college and agreed to sell the horse for $2,500.00—as long as he went to a young girl. She showed Sam where to touch the horses' front leg and when Sam touched him he bowed down. The young woman told him Dusty would stay in that position while Karly got in the saddle. Sam gladly paid extra and bought all of the tack Dusty's owner was willing to sell, and he refused to let Frank and Christine pay him back for the gift.

Jeff got the truck from his friend's granddad for $2,000. Sam had told Frank and Christine the truck was a steal for that price and offered to help with the restoration project.

Jeremiah got a clean, but old, 2020 Honda Civic Type R.

It was Rallye Red and had a 306 horse power engine. It still got 28 mpg highway and looked great. There were better mileage cars, but Jeremiah could not have been happier with this one.

Liam thought he had seen everything in Sam's barn, and he had, but he had not been behind the barn until his dad said, "Follow me, Son."

Behind the barn was a 1979 Ford F-350 long-box with a first generation Cummins conversion under the hood. The truck needed some work but for the price Frank and Christine paid they would owe Jeff a lot of help in the restoration of his truck.

Jeff and Liam both promised they would work as long as it took to see their trucks look as nice as Sam's. Liam's was close already.

***

Christine checked the email on her phone. It was a letter from the Induction Center reminding her that the thirty-first of December would be her last chance to meet the opponent who would hunt her beginning Thursday, January second. She was told her opponent would not be able to meet after the thirty-first or engage in the hunt for a short time following that date. It was good news in one sense. She would be able to return home from San Francisco without being hunted. Frank and Sam still planned to go with her.

They already knew her opponent's name, or stage name,

but Paul Elijah Thomas had used his real name.

They landed in San Francisco for the meeting with enough time for lunch. When they arrived at the Induction Center, they were shocked to see the resemblance between Daniel Bradly and his brother Aaden. Frank and Sam were not allowed to go into the room where Christine would meet Paul Thomas, but they would meet later outside in the parking lot.

Paul was in the room when Christine walked in. He was a handsome man about her age. Christine was self-conscious wearing the gloves Daniel had made. Only the one on her right hand carried the devices Daniel had built, but he had made a matching glove for her left hand. No one would have known by looking that they were not normal gloves.

Paul was different than Tom Hundley. He was a businessman and did not appear disguised as Brian Cooper had been. Christine offered him her hand and he gladly accepted. The glove would remember his smell. During the introduction Paul told Christine he had business plans and would not be able to begin the contest on the second.

He said, "Please do not trust me on this. You should expect at all times that I will hunt you—and I will come for you soon. But not until my business is finished. That will be on the twelfth of January. You are, of course, legal to hunt me at any time, but I will be hard to find. You should enjoy your time with family while you can. Have your things in order, Christine.

This is not personal for me. It is only business."

Paul was very articulate, and if his goal was to scare Christine he had done it well. He was confident and seemed to be a man who reached his goals regardless of what they were.

When the meeting was over, Christine and Paul walked back into the front office at the same time. It was easy for Paul to tell that Frank and Sam were waiting for Christine, and he first offered Sam his hand.

"My name is Paul," he said. "It is sad but exciting that we will share this contest together. And you, are you Christine's husband?" He reached for Frank's hand.

Outside in the parking lot Paul was again the first to speak. He said, "Goodbye Christine. Frank, Sam, I am sure you will both try to protect Christine, but you will not win. I have done very well in this lottery. Christine would have done well to contest this match and try for a less experienced hunter."

Sam lived by a strict rule of not giving away the danger he would become to anyone on the other side of an imaginary line he might draw. In this case Paul Thomas was on the other side of that line, and Sam did not say anything.

There was not a lot said on their way back to the airport. They had just met the most confident man they might ever meet. Sam was certain Paul was lying, that he would come after Christine on the second of January. Frank had no experience in this type of intimidation and was noticeably shaken.

"Sam," he said, "we need to kill this man—soon. I'm sure the rules say nothing about him sending men to kidnap Christine and hold her till the second. I know we can find out who he really is, and I will go with you to kill him. I will even be glad to do it."

"That is not a good idea Frank. You need to be armed at all times and stay with Christine. When we find out who this guy is I will kill him before the hunt begins. Christine cannot be close to him when that happens, and that means no payday, but that is fine. Killing him early will be murder, and I will have to be careful."

Sam made a phone call and asked the person on the other end to check all flights into San Francisco within the last week and look for a man named Paul Thomas. Sam knew that would not be his name, unless he was so confident he had used his real name just to raise the stakes. But everyone has a weakness and Paul just met his.

If Christine was not employed to hike trails in nearly every country for the SunDay Travel Agency, she might well have been a famous artist. Part way through the flight, she had a near photograph image drawn of the man they had just met. She asked Frank and Sam if she had missed anything, and they could not offer a single suggestion.

Frank took a picture of the drawing and said he knew exactly who to send it to. He smiled and sent it to Sam's dad.

Sam tipped his phone toward Frank, "I have him on the phone right now."

John promised to not sleep until he knew who the man was.

***

"I'm sorry Susan, did you say what I think you said."

"I did John. I am certain this man is Paul Elijah Thomas. He is an internal affairs investigator currently working for the Department of Justice. He is a private contractor with several irons in the fire. Do you want the full list?"

"Please send that to me. I have to locate Paul immediately."

"I will send it within a few minutes."

"Sam, I've got him, but this is a hard one to believe."

John explained what Susan had told him.

"Thanks Dad. I cannot imagine why a man in his position would buy a lottery ticket that could get him killed. Maybe his job is not interesting anymore, or maybe he is sick and hides behind this lottery to kidnap women and get away with it. I suppose he could hold an opponent for an indefinite period of time and kill them when it is legal to collect the money. This thing they call a lottery has some serious holes in it."

John said, "Doesn't matter Son. If you know for sure he is a contestant in this lottery you have to kill him, or he will do what he promised. You know he will have men hired. From what you say, he made no attempt to hide and apparently doesn't believe we can hide Christine from him."

January first: "Vance, go find the woman whose picture I sent you and call me. Do not hurt her, and I mean it. You do not touch her, only bring her to me."

***

"Good morning. My name is Vance. I'm with the census bureau. I am following up with families who have not returned the forms that were mailed to them. I only have a few questions. How many live in your house? What are their ages? Do you have any firearms in the house? I need both you and your husband to sign this. Is he here?"

Christine was not an actress and Vance could see that. He had found her alone and would have no fear of being beat to death by a jealous husband or shot. But quicker than he was able to think, Christine slammed the front door and ran out through the back door. His face was burned into her memory. He went after her but seeing how fast she ran caused him to quickly stop. He guessed she would have a phone in her back pocket and would be calling the police while she ran. Normally, he would have robbed the house. That is the kind of a person he was but not getting caught now was of greater importance. He ran back through the house and to his car.

He was right. Christine was on her phone with Frank. "Paul Thomas lied about waiting. He sent a man to get me. I don't know where he is, and I'm not going to the house till you get home.

Frank was in a meeting that truly tested his boss's patience when he said he had to leave. During the last few weeks Frank and Christine had each purchased a handgun and Christine had learned a good lesson about having hers with her. These were not ordinary times when she might choose to carry her gun or leave it in a drawer. She would not be caught without it again as long as she was a contestant in the lottery.

Christine hid in a small wooded area waiting for Frank to get home. Then a terrifying thought swept through her. Jeff always got home from school before Liam, and he would be there now. Christine took off for the house as fast as she could run. She circled to see the front of the house, and there was no vehicle parked there. She rang the doorbell, then moved to the end of the house and watched the door and the curtains. There was no answer, and the curtains didn't move. Not that this man would answer the door, but with no car in the driveway Christine was sure he must have left.

Jeff would be home any minute, and Liam not long after that. She would feel safe when either of them got home.

Christine ventured into the house. Once inside she began to sketch Vance's face. Then she heard Frank pull into the driveway. Not sure what he would find, Frank came in through the back door with a Glock 40 in his hand. He had chosen that model when he and Christine both purchased handguns. The 10mm cartridge could serve as protection against bears and Cougars when they were hiking and would be an intimidating weapon against any attacker.

"Are you okay?" he said. "This is really getting crazy. I called Sam when I left work but no answer."

"I am okay. I was hiding, but thought of Jeff coming home and came back. I'm glad he was late today. He might have gone to Jeremiah's house. He was talking before he left this morning about them doing something."

"Please call Dana and see if Jeff is there. I am going to go through the house and make sure no one is here. Did you say the guy was parked in front of the house and gone when you came back?"

"Yes, but he could have parked somewhere else in case a sheriff came and then came back again. I have his picture finished."

Christine looked up from her drawing and Frank was already gone. He crept through the house opening doors to the different rooms and even going into the attic. He wished Sam would have answered his phone.

"Honey, Dana says Jeff is not there and Jeremiah hasn't heard from him. He should have gotten home while I was down in the trees, and I'm just about to lose it. Let's go. We have to find him."

Frank didn't answer. Although Frank lacked the skills Sam would use, he did not want to give away his location in the house. Christine called him again. If he didn't answer within another minute she would go looking. She had a 9mm Glock 43 in her hand and had spent some time with Frank and Sam shooting at Sam's property. The pen and ink sketch would be sent to John as soon as she found Frank.

Frank met her in the hall as she was coming to find him, but the longest night of their lives was about to begin. Liam arrived home and they called every friend they thought Jeff knew—but he was nowhere to be found.

Eight

In an uptown house in Walnut Creek, California Jeff sat in a nicely kept room. Its furnishings were that of a family or person with money who had a taste for the better things in life.

Vance had been running through the house to get his car exactly when Jeff reached the front porch from the school bus. A fight, as much as Jeff was capable of against a forty-six- year-old man followed, and Jeff was taken away in Vance's car. Headed for Walnut Creek, California. When Vance was close to needing gas, he pulled to the side of the road and taped Jeff's mouth. Then put him in the trunk of the car. After filling the tank and buying some drinks and food he pulled over again and brought Jeff back into the seat beside him. It was difficult along I-5 to stop where other cars couldn't see what he was doing.

Vance didn't know Jeff's name but said, "Boy, I have a gun right here and will kill you if I have to. I will just throw your body out beside the road, and no one will ever know who did it. So let's work this out. I am taking you to a man who will pay me a lot of money. You can sit up here and talk to me, or you can ride in the trunk like a dog all the way to my friend's house. What do you want to do? I would just as soon kill you as not. It's your choice."

Jeff made the trip to California under those conditions. He was hurt from being punched in the stomach, and his pride was hurt. He had been taken so easily, but other than that he was okay when they arrived at Paul Thomas' home.

***

"Jeff, I have done my homework and know who you are. You have surely guessed why you are here?" It was Paul Thomas talking to Jeff.

"I want you to listen to me." Paul spoke calmly, "Weigh your odds. There is nothing you can do to get away from me. I have already killed several people in the lottery game your mom is involved in and you could be next. Your mom has made some pretty nice kills herself, so I am not going to let my guard down.

"I have been following her enough to know she is smart. Not many moms can kill like she does. Either that or she has experienced men to help her, but you are the one who will bring her to me. I can put you in a hole and let you soil yourself, or you can face this like a man. Who knows, maybe when your mom comes she will kill me. You can enjoy your stay until she comes, or Vance will tie you up and throw into an old hand-dug well a few miles from here."

"When you put it that way," Jeff said, "I will play the game, but not while you are killing my mom. You must know that. I will go crazy on you then, and you will have to kill me too. And that will make you guilty of murder."

"Of course I know that. You are a smart young man Jeff. I have a number of persons employed, and they are all like the man who brought you here. If you do anything, and I mean anything other than what I tell you to do, I will send those men to kill your mom, your dad, and your brother. I obviously know where you live. I even know where your brother goes to school. Jeff, I am a good man. This is only about money, the same as it is for your mom.

"Although, I think it was foolish for a pretty woman like her to think she could go up against every contestant the lottery would send after her. I have made millions doing this but enough of that. This is where the game really begins for me—and I have already won—I have you. Your mom will trade herself for you without question. It is a weakness mom's have. Mine would do the same for me."

Jeff knew better than to argue with Paul. He knew the ultimate contest would be between Sam and this well-spoken, cunning man who was trying to scare him. He had more faith in Sam than he did fear of Paul, and he had a backup plan.

"Okay, what are you going to do? Am I supposed to call my mom now; tell her where I am and to come and give herself up. If that's what you think I will do, why are you putting it off."

"This is fun. You are smart for your age. Do you think I would have you call your mom from my house and have the call traced? We will do that tomorrow. Do you play chess? We have a long night ahead of us, but I will have Vance watch you while I get some sleep. After we play the game maybe."

"Sure, I have played enough to know how to move on the board. Well enough to beat a jerk like you."

They played one game that evening. Vance was awake, watching Jeff after the game while Paul got some sleep, and Jeff was asleep on the couch where he had been sitting when he lost in the chess match.

Fifteen miles away, blue smoke trailed behind the tires of a private jet landing at the Oakland Airport. The plane stopped at a building away from commercial airline traffic. Frank, Liam, Christine, and Sam Morrison walked away from the airplane after a long, meaningful handshake between Sam and a pilot who had fought many battles beside him. Dan now called his private charter service retirement.

It was four o'clock in the morning and dark as they walked toward a black Chevy SUV that had been parked nearby. Frank looked at his phone again before getting into the passenger seat. Sam got into the driver's seat and waited for directions. The phone in Jeff's back pocket was the one thing Vance had overlooked and Jeff was much too smart to give that away.

Four people with a desire to kill anyone who would take Jeff knew exactly where he was.

Before getting into the SUV Sam and Frank placed several pieces of high-tech, life-ending equipment into the back seat with Christine and Liam.

Only on a private jet could Sam have brought the weapons they would carry into battle in just minutes. Knowing they would arrive in the night, they were all wearing dark clothes. To Sam it was second nature to wear a helmet with night vision attached. His night vision attached side by side with a thermal vision monocular on the same harness. He wore them, now, tipped up out of his line of vision.

Frank held a Barrett MRAD .338 Lapua Magnum topped with a Czech radar rifle scope. Only a few years earlier Czech radar was too bulky to be rifle mounted. This type of radar could see efficiently through walls up to ten inches in thickness. The rifle was loaded with a 10 round magazine and one in the chamber with the safety on. Frank had never seen such a rifle, let alone one that could see through walls.

When they moved from the vehicle toward Paul Thomas' house Sam carried the Barrett. Frank carried an AA-12 fully automatic 12-gauge shotgun with a rotary magazine. Frank could take care of any up-close work with that gun, and Sam would be able to shoot through most walls if it came to that.

They decided not to allow Christine and Liam close to

the house. They would stay with the vehicle and be ready to take them out of there when the job was finished. If police arrived when shots were fired, the black SUV with government plates would look like FBI or BATFE. If the police came past that, Sam's identification would diffuse the matter.

Christine had a full-auto AR-10 variant with a loaded magazine inserted and one in the chamber with the safety on. She would wait behind the wheel.

Sam told her, "Do not shoot this unless things go bad, and we are down. It can shoot through walls and into other houses. Keep your headphones on."

Liam had just shut down all cameras within 1000 feet of Paul Thomas' house. Frank's phone was on to monitor the location of Jeff's phone, and Jeff's phone wasn't moving. With the cameras down, there was no way Paul Thomas could know they were coming. If he had found Jeff's phone, he would have disabled it, but it was the one thing he overlooked.

Frank was nervous. He had never been involved in something like this, but his son was inside the house, and he was ready for anything he might have to do.

Frank had never thought about dying for his family, but he was ready to do just that if he had to. Sam scanned the surroundings as they moved toward the house. He used thermal vision first then switched to night vision. He saw a cat with the thermal vision. It glowed white. He would easily see anything that created a heat signature.

They were twenty yards from the house when Sam began to use the Czech radar. Looking through the first wall he saw the slumped body of a man sitting in a chair. He scanned the same room and saw the image of a person laying down. They continued around the house. Sam saw one more person laying on a bed. There were only three people in the house, and they all appeared to be still. Probably sleeping.

Sam was as calm as he would have been at a business meeting. This was normal duty for a person who had been a Navy sniper and a SEAL Commander.

Sam leaned close to Frank's ear and said, "It's good inside. I'm going to unlock the back door. You talk as quiet as possible to Christine and have her meet us at the back of the house. Tell Liam to stay with the vehicle. Tell Christine to bring the glove."

Christine left the AR-10 with Liam and moved quickly to the back of the house. Sam unlocked the door easily enough that Frank knew he had done it before. In the red glow of a headlamp Sam brought out a small tablet. He diagramed rooms inside the house and wrote Jeff on the location where he was sure Jeff was sleeping. There was one thing Sam didn't know. He could not be sure if the glove would work in his hand. If he knew that, he might have left Christine with Liam.

Daniel had told them that Christine's hand needed to be

in it. Sam pointed to the mark where a person was slumped in the chair. He told Christine to use the glove forcibly, but quietly, and they moved slowly toward that room. The house was lit more brightly than they would have liked. It was obvious that Vance wanted to be able to see Jeff, even though Jeff was handcuffed to a heavy table which had been moved close to the couch.

Frank soundlessly laid his automatic shotgun on the table and clamped his hand over Jeff's mouth. It was a risky move. He knew his son would be ready to fight. But Jeff's eyes opened without the slightest struggle. Frank put his finger to his lips as if Jeff would have made a sound. He picked up the shotgun again. When that was done Christine pushed her gloved hand against Vance's face. He didn't move. Frank carefully took him out of the chair and laid him on the floor.

Next they entered Paul's bedroom. It was dark in there, but a small amount of light entered through a partially opened bathroom door. Frank moved ahead of Christine to the edge of the bed. He must have been hoping she would not grab the back of his arm with her gloved hand. When Christine was close enough she slapped Paul's face with more hatred than she realized. He was no longer just a contestant. He had taken her son. Paul, of course, could not sit up in the bed. He was paralyzed as John had been and as Vance still was.

Sam stepped past Christine and sat down on the edge of

the bed. Paul's eyes were partially opened, and Sam opened them the rest of the way.

He said, "Paul Thomas, I know who you are, and I don't like men like you. You took a woman's child. Doesn't something in you call for better than that? It's a stupid lottery Paul. You know you are going to die now without being able to fight me. I'm sorry about that, but you would not be worth my time in a fair fight.

"Christine is going to make $5,000,000.00 right now—and you thought you were smarter than her. I know you can hear me. You were not even smart enough to take Jeff's phone. Goodbye Paul. The world doesn't need men like you."

More easily than she thought she could, Christine reached out and pressed the tips of her fingers against Paul's neck. It was a fast death for Paul Thomas. The fear in his eyes lasted for less than two seconds. Paul's number on the monitors changed to the signal of death and Christine earned 5M dollars. The way she killed would remain a mystery to those following her in the lottery.

Frank went back to Jeff, and after retrieving the key from Vance's pocket unlocked the handcuffs.

Vance was conscious but still could not move. The glove worked as Daniel said it would.

Sam said, "Jeff, was this man good to you or did he hurt you."

Jeff said, “He slugged me in the stomach at the house, and on the way here said he would gladly kill me if I did anything wrong.”

“He said he would be happy to kill you?” Sam said.

Then he said, “Would you guys take our gear back to the vehicle. I want to talk to this man alone for a minute.”

***

It was 5:45 AM when Sam called Dan again. He was in the lounge at the airport drinking coffee. Sam also called another person and told them the black SUV would be exactly where they left it for him with the key in the same place.

On the flight back to Portland, Jeff said, “I knew you guys would find me, so I didn’t even fight.”

He said he couldn’t believe Paul and Vance were so stupid as to not check him for a phone. Then he asked Sam what he had said to the guy in the house.

Sam said, “I told him I didn’t like him. I told him I couldn’t like a man who would steal a mother’s child for a few bucks. That was all I said to him.”

Jeff said, “I can’t believe a man like Paul didn’t have alarms and cameras everywhere.”

Then he looked at his brother sitting on the other side of Christine.

“You killed them all didn’t you? I don’t know how you do that so easily, but you have to show me. I’m sure you could change my grades if you wanted to. I know you could."

"Why would I do that," Liam said. "You let yourself get caught and beat up and made us come all the way down here to save you."

When they landed in Portland, Sam told everyone that the guy who took Jeff had a lot of money in an envelope in his shirt pocket and that he wanted it to go to a good cause. Sam suggested they have a big breakfast and asked his friend, Dan if he had time to join them. Dan said he did have time and would be glad to. He was smiling about the story of the man giving his money to Sam.

Dan and Sam were the last to get off of the airplane and there was another sincere handshake as Sam handed Dan the money in the envelope. Dan knew it would be too much but didn't want to count it. He and Sam remembered many exciting and tough things they had been through together.

Dan said, "Thank you Brother. I will give you as many trips as you need to make."

***

Christine called Dana, "We just got back, and Jeff is fine. I'm sorry I didn't call sooner. Are you okay? I didn't want to call too early."

"I'm okay, but we were worried sick about Jeff. Have you asked the lottery people if you can retire now? This lottery surely cannot be for the rest of your life. There has to be a time when it is over."

"Let's have lunch today," Christine said.

"Okay, call me. If we can do it early, the kids won't be home yet."

Over lunch, Christine told Dana everything. She told her she had killed someone now. She had done it, not Sam.

She said, "Dana, you have to know there is not much chance of me surviving this for too long. So far they have not known Sam is protecting me, but he might not always be there when someone finds me. I've been wanting to talk to you about something. If I get killed, you should pool the kids and marry Frank."

Tears began filling Dana's eyes. "Something will happen," she said. "Sam has experience in things like this, and I am not going to marry your husband. He is Jeremiah and Karly's uncle, but thank you for the offer. He is great guy."

Dana tried to change the subject and Christine said, "Do you love Sam? Is that why you will not go out on a date—and not marry Frank if I am gone?"

"Yes, I love him. So do you."

There was a pause and she said, "I suppose it is different for me, because I am not married. But Sam doesn't think of me like that. You and I are sisters to him, and Frank is like his brother."

"Are you sure that's how he feels? Did you ever ask him?

"Christine," she emphasized her name, "What are you saying? Sam has been there for me every day since Fred was killed, as a friend, but he is twenty-one years older than me."

"Okay, so you have thought about this and done the math. You surely don't think men never fall in love with a younger woman?"

"Nothing is going to happen to you," Dana said. "Look what Liam was able to do to CLA. What a blessing that was and now we have Karly home again. And you told me in private that Frank got into the computer program the lottery uses."

They both looked around to make sure no one could hear them.

Dana asked, "You will be hunted again in February won't you?"

"I have already talked to the woman in charge of the lottery. It was hard for me to get past the goons that work there, but I told her I was pregnant, and she didn't even care. She is not nice at all, but there is one instance that will get a contestant time off. She told me if I was badly wounded during a contest I would get an appropriate amount of time off to heal.

"She says she has been watching my hunts more than any of the men who are competing against other men. And I learned there could be as much as $100,000,000.00 available for the winner of a coming pay per view event."

Dana said, "You are not thinking about money are you? I know you would not put Sam's life in danger for money."

"Dana! surly you are not saying I would stay in this lottery for the money."

"You know I don't mean that, and I do know you realize how serious taking a life is."

"What have I not done to get out of this? I have tried everything? The way it is, if I were to stop and just say no more killing, I would be dead in thirty days. This is my fault, you are right, but I do not know how to get away. Tell me how if there is a way."

"I know you are right Christine. And I'm not just worried that you will live for another year or two years or five. You know where I am going with this. There is a God and The Bible talks about a time when there will be a new heaven and a new earth. Sis, I have to have you there with me. Dana was fighting not to cry. Did you read the book I bought for you after Fred died? It was "Heaven," by Randy Alcorn and I'll bet you didn't read it."

"You are right—as usual. I didn't make time to read it. It is a thick book, but maybe with the baby coming I will have time."

"Do you know there are fifty-five-million people who die every year in America, and that is not counting abortion. None of them had a tomorrow."

"Okay, it's not that I am disagreeing with you. I just need to think about it more. Let me ask you this, when Sam prayed before we ate, does that mean he is a Christian like you?"

"No, a lot of people pray who are not Christians but Sam is. I would say that prayer is not the defining mark of what a person believes. Prayer and faith are different."

Christine said, "I don't mind you praying for me, and I hope you pray for Sam too."

"Oh I will," was Dana's answer.

Christine was relieved to move away from their conversation about Heaven and God. The subject went back to whether or not Dana loved Sam.

Nine

With the next hunt scheduled for the first week in February, Frank and Christine wanted to take a vacation. Liam and Jeff would be able to keep their classes up online. Christine had guided tours in Yellowstone National Park, but they had never been there as a family, and she had never been there during the off season. It was decided. They would take a winter trip to Yellowstone.

Jeff was excited about doing the Snowcoach Tour. He liked big tires and trucks but had only been off-road a few times. As plans were made they asked Sam if he wanted to come, and he said he would. Christine didn't know if Dana could get time off, but everyone thought it would be fun if she and Jeremiah and Karly came along, so Christine called her.

"Hi Karly. Is your mom home?"

Dana came to the phone.

"Hi Dana, we are thinking about a trip to Yellowstone. Sam is coming too. Is there any chance you could take off work and bring the kids?"

"I will have to ask about getting time off. How long do you think it would be?"

"We would like to plan a full week. Frank said if you guys

can come he will rent one of those twelve seat vans and we can all go in the same vehicle."

Dana's boss gave her the time off and Frank rented the vehicle. With seventeen days until Christine's next hunt they set out on the 845 mile, fourteen hours long, Yellowstone journey. They promised not to think about anything but the trip.

Frank rented the new 12 passenger Ford Transit Van with a diesel motor and bucket seats in the front. He was driving and Sam was in the opposite seat. They left early and were just going through Boardman, Oregon when Sam's phone rang.

"Hey Phil, how are you doing? The last I knew you had been shot. Are you okay?"

"I'm good Sam. But there is a situation, and I was asked to call you. Are you in a good place to talk?"

"I am, but I am on vacation and on the road."

Phillip was a short, stalky man, black also, with a shaved head and muscular build. If you were a bad guy, you would not want him to find you. He had worked side by side with Sam where they intercepted threats to the President and his team.

"You know what?" Phillip said. "I am not going to tell you why I called. Have you ever taken a vacation before? I mean one the government didn't pay for?"

"I don't remember, but thanks Phil. If you are sure this

can happen without me I am going to hang up and stay on vacation. I'm not going to tell you where I am. Maybe I will turn my phone off."

Phillip hung up. Sam held his phone out where everyone could see it and turned it off.

Frank smiled and said, "There is no way you are going to leave that phone off. If they need you, we will find ourselves letting you off at the nearest airport."

"No you won't. It's off. I'm on vacation." He handed the phone behind him to Dana.

He said to her, "Please hide this from me. If Mom or Dad needs me they know where I am."

There were the usual coffee and bathroom stops, but at 7 PM mountain time, they were parked in front of a magnificent, privately owned lodge Christine had been able to reserve near the west entrance to Yellowstone. The 6,200 square foot log home had been made available to her on short notice, because she knew the owners and it was during the slow season.

Knowing approximately what time they would be there, the owners catered dinner. It was a great time as they enjoyed roasted quail served with garlic mashed potatoes, asparagus, and homemade cornbread. The dessert was a coconut-lime cheesecake with mango coulis, and there was a variety of drinks in one of the two refrigerators. There was also an espresso machine on the same wall in the kitchen. Beside the espresso machine was a full bag of Hawaiian 100% Kona beans, grown on the volcanic slopes of Manua Loa on Hawaii's Big Island. And next to the coffee sat three Stanley Classic vacuum bottles.

They needed to be in the park no later than 6:30 in the morning and would be out for twelve hours on the first day. Dana worried about having enough winter clothes, but they would have the warm 4-Wheeled drive snowcoach to relax in after periods of picture taking and wildlife viewing. There were also bathroom facilities along the way.

Dana suggested the kids get to bed by 9 or 9:30, the adults would not be far behind. They would all be up by 5 in the morning getting ready.

There was a fire burning in the wide, stone fireplace when they arrived and a supply of logs in a box not far from it. After dinner they sat in fireside room and talked about the next day. There were stories told of past camping trips, and when it was near bedtime Karly asked Sam if he would come in and tell her a bedtime story. She was very close to her Uncle Frank, but Sam was a better storyteller, and he was like another uncle to her. Liam, Jeremiah, and Jeff were busy making plans. Frank and Christine were sitting close together on a loveseat by the fireplace, and Sam promised to come in and tell Karly the bedtime story after she was in bed.

When Sam went in, Dana was leaning against the heavy,

blue-stained, plank headboard of the bed. She was on top of the blankets, and Karly was leaning against her but under the blankets.

She said, "Okay Uncle Sam. I want this to be a fun story."

Sam sat down on a chair beside Karly's bed and said, "Once upon a time there was a little girl like you, and she had a horse—not as pretty as your horse but nonetheless a very pretty horse. She went out to get on his back one day, and the horse said to her, 'I cannot go on our ride today.' I am going to see my mother and father.

The little girl pleaded with the horse, that if she could go she would be quiet and not be any trouble at all. She asked where the horse's mother and father lived. The horse loved the little girl and said she could go, so she got on his back and he walked behind the barn where no one could see them.

Then he said, 'you are supposed to kick me in the ribs now, and then we will go.' So the little girl gently kicked him in the ribs, and he took off running so fast she almost fell off. When she looked down, the barn was just a speck in the field below and she said, 'Where are we going?'

He told her, 'We are going to see my mother and my father.'

Soon in the sky she could see the prettiest colors she had ever seen and the horse was slowing down. She asked, 'Aren't you afraid we will fall if you slow down?'

He said, 'No, it is different here. We are in a different pasture now. We are as close as we can get to the King's barn until a time when He opens the gate for us, but my mother and father are already there. Fields are bigger here than where we came from, but the King will tell them we are here.'

Almost as soon as he said that, a magnificent stallion and a beautiful mare appeared, and the colors the little girl had seen began to change. She could now see a brilliant, glowing emerald pasture beneath their hooves. The colors of their bodies were of a depth and brilliance like the little girl had never seen before.

She asked the horse, 'Can they see us?'

He said, 'I am not sure.'

'Whenever I am here,' he said, 'they come and dance and kick and buck as if they know I came to see them. And when they leave I know it is time for me to go back.'

The little girl said, 'I am glad I came with you. I can see that they are happy. Everything is so pretty, and I think they know we are here.'

The little girl had not noticed, but when she finished talking to the horse they were back at her home behind the barn again. She asked more questions, but the horse said, 'Not now. I have to eat some hay and it is time for you to go to bed.'"

Sam kissed her on the forehead and said, "Morning will

come early. Sleep well. I love you."

He said goodnight to Dana and went to his own room.

***

The next morning was clear and a chilling five degrees, but the snowcoach was pleasantly warm inside. The temperature would raise to twenty-five degrees in the afternoon. They would see Old Faithful, Lower Geyser Basin, Firehole Canyon, the Grand Canyon of Yellowstone, Hayden Valley, and Madison Junction, among other sites. During the trip they would see river otters, coyotes, bighorn sheep, one mountain lion, fox, elk, bison, and a pack of wolves on an elk carcass. Their guide said it was the most wildlife they had seen on one trip for a long time.

At one point Jeff asked the driver if he could sit behind the wheel of the big 4x4 and have his picture taken. The driver was glad to accommodate.

Throughout the day, everyone returned to the same seats, as if there was assigned seating. Frank and Christine sat together nearest the driver, the kids were in two seats near the back, and Sam and Dana sat together in one seat in the middle of the coach.

On the second day of their vacation, they all went on a snowshoe walk led by one of the park rangers on the Riverside Trail. Then in the afternoon they visited the Grizzly and Wolf Discovery Center where they were part of a scheduled program which explored natural and cultural resource topics.

On the third day the guys left to ride snowmobiles in the park. Dana and Christine planned to take Karly on a sleigh ride but to do that they would have to travel more than an hour to a large elk feeding area. When morning came, they decided to stay inside and visit by the fireplace. Dana said life was too busy, that she and Karly had not had enough time to visit with Christine after Karly came home.

Christine and Dana each had coffee and Karly a cup of hot chocolate as they walked from the kitchen into the fireside room. Frank had built a fire that morning before he left, pulled the screen closed in front of it. The setting was warm and nice as temperatures outside plunged to three degrees below zero. Christine opened the fireplace screen, and the three of them sat snugly, nearly touching each other on a vintage, Chesterfield leather sofa facing the fire. The mood was perfect for anything they would talk about. The firewood logs were split Tamarac, seasoned perfectly to give the famous snap-crackle-pop common to a country fireplace, and Christine began the conversation.

She said, "Karly, it is so nice to have you with us. Guess what I know that I haven't told you yet."

"Okay." Karly's big, pretty smile gave away her excitement about surprises, "you are going to buy me another horse so I can have friends come over to Uncle Sam's and ride with me."

Karly had gotten red hair from her dad's side of the family. Fred had reddish-brown hair, but his mom Elva was a fiery red-haired woman. She was now red and gray, which the family said was the prettiest hair they had ever seen. But the temperament so well-known among true redheads was not gray at all. At Christmas when Karly had received Dusty, Elva told everyone in the family that Karly was not to be unattended with that horse. Fortunately, Karly's granddad had been married for 51 years to his red-haired wife. He convinced her that everyone would see to it that Karly was safe. Elva and Karly were the only two redheads left in the family.

"Well," Christine said, "that is not what I was thinking about."

"Okay, tell me."

"Uncle Frank and I have decided on the name Hannah for our daughter. Her name will be Hannah Karly Conder. Do you like it. I wanted to name her Isabella Karly, but Uncle Frank liked Hannah and Hannah was my second favorite."

"Wow, I love that name."

Dana said, "When she is naughty I will call her Karly.

"I'm not hardly ever naughty. I did tell Jeremiah if he wouldn't drive me to school in his new car, I wouldn't talk to him anymore, but I said I was sorry after I said it."

Christine said, "I really believe that is the naughtiest

thing you have ever done," and put her arm around Karly pulling her closer.

"Put your hand right here," she said. "I think Hannah is enjoying the fire."

Dana said, "I am sure she is. I am sitting here praying for Hannah and her mom," she smiled at Christine, "and for you Karly. We have such a wonderful family."

"There is one boy," Karly said, "who was in the home with me, and I always prayed for him. His name is Jacob, and his dad got killed. In a different way than mine. He was a policemen and got shot. Jacob wanted to go home then and take care of his mom. He is the same age I am, but they wouldn't let him go home. He told me he was going to run away, but the doors were always locked. He even told me some bad things he wanted to do to people who wouldn't let him go home, and I just prayed for him more. I'm sure glad Liam got that place in trouble, because Jacob is home with his mom now."

"I think Karly kind of likes him," Dana said to Christine.

Christine smiled at Karly and said, "Well, you didn't ever tell me about Jacob. Does he and his mother live close to us?"

"Yes, and he calls me sometimes. He is nice and wants to ride Dusty. I asked him already if he could come over to Uncle Sam's with us."

Dana said, "I haven't met Jacob, but Karly thinks he is

kind of cute."

"Mommm," Karly said.

Christine said, "If Jacob is able to come and ride Dusty, I would like to come over and meet him."

"Mom, can you ask Uncle Sam as soon as he gets back?"

"Yes Mommm," Christine said to Dana. "The last thing I remember you asking Uncle Sam was if he would dance with you. I suppose you asked him to remodel your kitchen too—or he just offered. He is good at things like that for a single guy."

"I did not ask him to help. He was at the house, and Jeremiah was sketching how I wanted to change some things, and he just offered."

"I see," Christine said. Smiling at Karly.

Then she said, "Sit here in front of me Karly, and I will braid your hair."

Karly got up and sat down between Christine's legs, and Christine began to pull her hair back, brushing through it with her fingers. Dana left the room and came back with Karly's hairbrush. Then she went to the kitchen to make some breakfast.

When Dana left the room, Christine said, "Karly, maybe I shouldn't ask this, but do you ever think about your mom getting married again. Your opinion is very important to her, and Jeremiah's too. If she went on a real date with Sam do you think it would be like she was dating your uncle."

"It wouldn't be like that for me. Did Mom put you up to asking me?"

"No"

"I do see the way Mom looks at Uncle Sam sometimes, even when he was telling me a bedtime story last night. I think she loves him. I love him too. He is one of the nicest people ever. I just don't know if Mom is going to ever get over Dad being gone."

"You are right. I can tell you that she will never forget your dad."

Christine looked over her shoulder and saw Dana standing in the doorway.

The doorway coming into the fireside room was framed with twisted juniper pillars each side and opened above. It was opened to the expanse of a high, vaulted ceiling. Dana was either on the edge of tears or smiling, and being her sister, Christine knew it was tears. Dana had lived with so much pain since Fred died, and now uncertainty about what the rest of her life might be like without him, without a husband. She was not upset with the questions her sister was asking.

"Are you ladies ready to come into the kitchen for breakfast."

"Yes Mom. We have been talking about you."

"I know you have," Dana said, "and maybe it is

something that needs to be talked about."

Over breakfast Dana said, "None of us know how Sam feels. He is twenty-one years older than me and might not feel the way you guys think. He has never once offered to kiss me. The closest he has gotten to me is to hold my hand sometimes when I needed him to, and that is mostly if I am crying."

There was a short pause as they ate and Christine said, "Believe me Dana, Sam has feelings for you. We have spent a lot of time together since I'm part of this hunting thing, and when he looks at me it is not like when he looks at you. Don't try to tell me you have never looked into his eyes. I don't think he is ever not thinking about you. It's hard for a man. You cry on him when you're dancing and he is supposed to ask you out—or ask if he can kiss you?"

"I agree with Aunt Christine. I've been away for a long time and don't know Uncle Sam as well as you do, but I think he loves you Mom. I'll bet he doesn't think you could ever love him because of Dad."

At that, Dana burst into tears and went back into the fireside room. Karly got out of her chair and Christine took her by the hand. Karly was starting to cry, and Christine only held her for a few seconds. With her other hand on Karly's back, Christine gently pushed her in the direction of the fireside room.

In a barely audible voice she said, "Go hug your mom. I

will clean up in here."

On the way home from Yellowstone, the guys talked endlessly about the snowmobile trip they had experienced the day before. They had used maps to find areas in the park they had not seen from the snowcoach, and they had a few close encounters with wildlife, trusting the powerful machines to get away fast.

The three women did not talk about the conversation they had in the lodge, but the subject was still on their minds. Sam was in the driver's seat as they pulled onto HWY 20 and Jeremiah in the opposite seat. It seemed that those two never ran out of things to talk about. Liam was looking at his laptop.

"Hey Dad. Have you logged into anything since we got to the park?"

"No, I haven't. Remember the deal, Son? There will be time when we get home to catch up on that."

"What are you talking about, Liam?" Christine knew it had something to do with the lottery.

"I found some new information in a file named PPV1NF. I am assuming it means the lottery's first Pay Per View in the National Forest. I might not have seen the site if it wasn't about cameras. Near Prineville in the Ochoco National Forest there are hundreds of cameras out. It appears that they are powered by Sardac, and I learned that the Induction Center has had a contract with Sardac since 2027. I was able to download coordinates for the cameras.

"And guess what else? Just like everyone does, their security cameras are watching the person who accesses the files. Once I was into their security cameras I looked through the video vault and watched a man enter the password for a Sardac file. When he got there he entered another password and up came a file named 'Sardac Neurologic.'

"It seems that the Induction Center regularly influences the outcome of hunts by hiring Sardac to disable one of the opponents. Those at the top must be betting on contests and making millions when they can be sure who wins. I even found a file with names of contestants Sardac has hit. They could do that to you Mom and there is nothing we could do to stop them."

Frank said, "Liam, we agreed not to talk about this till we get home, and I am serious about that."

Ten

With the Yellowstone vacation behind them Sam's anxiety concerning the next hunt settled over him like a heavy layer of fog. Surrounding. The kind you cannot see through—and Sam had been in that situation before. He parked the rental van in Frank and Christine's driveway and was hit with the reality of what was coming again and again and again if they could not get Christine out of the lottery. The next hunt would be in two weeks.

The family began to carry things from the van to the house, but Sam sat there with the driver's door opened. He remembered standing in a hopelessly heavy fog many years ago. It had robbed him of being able to see his men. He nearly lost his life that day and believed he should have.

Standing in a fog so thick, he had less than ten-foot visibility; he had been able to hear gunfire everywhere. The memories were like yesterday. He knew he had to get to the men who were with him. They were straight in the direction of the gunfire—and they were fighting for their lives. Sam had been separated from them for only minutes as he held the hand of a friend he knew would not live for long, but Sam could not let him die alone. They were ambushed in an area with no cover. They knew the area. They knew where they were, but they had never seen such a blinding fog as it was on that morning.

Sam's men were shooting at a hidden enemy, trying to drive them away from their fallen brother. In that fog Sam knew they would be in arms reach of each other, touching each other, shooting outward into where they couldn't see. Their enemies faced the same problem, so both sides emptied their rifles toward the sounds of gunfire and the dim color of muzzle flash when a rifle fired directly at them. The battle had taken place with no more than thirty yards between themselves and their enemies.

Sam thought about the fact that to us they are the enemy, but to them we are the enemy. Thinking back, he wished they could have called a truce and started over again in some different place. Like it was on Christmas Eve in 1914 in Belgium, in a place called Bois de Ploegsteert. Men met half way on the battlefield in a bitter cold winter. They shook hands, shared what few supplies they had, helped their enemies collect their fallen brothers, and they deeply respected each other.

A British soldier named John Ferguson told it this way: "Here we were laughing and chatting to men whom only a few hours before we were trying to kill."

It was an incredible moment in the history of wars.

The young man Sam knelt by died. His hand fell from

Sam's, and Sam ran as straight and fast toward the gunfire as he could. He knew his own brothers might hear him running and shoot that way. In those moments, in the middle of a close range firefight, men are desperate and sometimes make mistakes.

Before Sam found them they were gone, every one of them. An equal number of the enemy lay so close that Sam knew it was nearly hand to hand combat at the last. Without knowing it, the two groups of soldiers had come face to face in the fog. The number of men who survived, Sam could not know, but he counted his and he was alone.

He could hardly believe, now, how quickly he had remembered the fear of losing someone. A few good days on vacation and then the kind of hell he remembered all too well. Who would Christine's next opponent be? Would he or she be young and foolish, someone a man would hate to kill, or would he find his equal in skill, in experience, in stealth, in confidence?

Christine's life depended on how well he could see into this fog, into the days that were coming. What if he was not able to save her?

In truth, it was a gorgeous, clear winter day at Frank and Christine's home. But Sam relived the fear of not being there at the right time—this time for Christine and for Hannah—and all of their family.

***

"Sam, are you okay? I will drive to my house if you want, and you can spend the night. We can take the van back tomorrow."

Dana's voice was more of a comfort to Sam than she knew. He wanted to take her in his arms and protect her from whatever was out there.

He said, "I'm okay but maybe I will stay over. I've got my own couch, and I might know another bedtime story." Sam knew if he went home there would be no sleep. He would only think about the next hunt.

It was strange to think that a warrior like Sam might only sleep soundly at Dana's house.

It would not be that many days until Christine would be allowed to meet her next opponent, and then on February 1st the next hunt would begin. Everyone had carried things into the house except Karly. She was standing beside her mom looking at Sam. He had not even seen her there.

"Uncle Sam," she said, "I want to go to your house and see my horse. Can we go there in the morning?"

"I'm going to stay at your house tonight, but in the morning, yes, we will go see Dusty."

When Karly first saw her horse on Christmas day, she decided to keep the name he already had. His registered name was Dusty of Green Mountain Farms, III. Sam had asked while buying Dusty if he could bring Karly to see the stallion and the mare. And he learned his first bit of horse trivia that day. They were invited to come again and visit the sire and the dam. Not that what he called them was wrong.

Dana, Jeremiah, and Karly went with Sam just two days after Christmas to see Dusty's family. They saw his grandfather also. He was a powerful, proud stallion, as Dusty II was. Sam was sure Dusty III had only been gilded for their daughter's safety while competing in rodeos.

***

The family talked briefly about being home from Yellowstone, then Sam and Dana left with Jeremiah and Karly for Dana's house.

Frank was trying not to think about what Liam said, about the lottery having an account with Sardac to stop contestants when someone in an office chose that. He was sure they had killed Tom Hundley, and even though Frank was able to work in the program, they didn't know how to control the lottery's relationship with Sardac Global Technologies. It might be that the Induction Center would hire Sardac's service whenever a contestant was owed too much, and for the next match Christine stood to make over $9,000,000.

***

At Dana's house, dinner was over and it was time for the bedtime story Sam promised. On their way home, Dana had ordered dinner from Victor's Barbeque Basin, and it was an impressive looking feast after the trail of fast-food they had eaten on the way home from Yellowstone.

Jeremiah opted out of dinner for visiting a friend's house. First he washed his car, then took a shower. And Karly said, "Tell Charlotte hi for me."

Jeremiah hadn't mentioned where he was going, but Karly knew and so did Dana.

With Karly in her bed, it was time for the bedtime story.

Sam began: "Once upon a time, there was a man who never knew where he was going. He would ask his dog sometimes, 'Do you know where we are going,' and the dog would say, 'If you turn me lose, I will take you where you want to go, but if you keep me on this leash I will not take you.'

One day the old man said to the dog, 'I will not put you on the leash today, if you promise not to run away, or chase the neighbor's cat, or bite the neighbor's dog.'

The dog said he would not do those things, and they left for their walk together. The neighbor's cat walked right in front of them like she always did, and the dog didn't chase her. Then another neighbor's dog came out and started barking. He said some mean things, in the language of dogs, but the man's dog didn't bite him. But when the dog knew they were almost home, he ran away. The old man decided he should go home but didn't remember how to get there. He could not remember anything.

The old man didn't know how long he had been sitting down, but he saw a policeman running after a dog—and it was his dog. Just as they came close the old man laid down. When the policeman saw that the dog had brought him to the old man the policeman called for help and soon there were two doctors kneeling beside the old man.

One doctor said, 'I believe we are too late. The old man has died,' but the dog licked the old man's face and laid down on him. The doctors didn't tell the dog to move and pretty soon the old man sat up and put his hand on the dog. One of the doctors told the old man that his dog had saved his life. The old man asked the doctor how his dog did that, and the doctor said he did it by running away and finding the police officer who then brought us, but they said they had done nothing to help. It was only the dog.

When the old man was up again he told the policeman and the doctors that he was okay and would walk back home. Then when he thought they were not listening, he asked the dog, 'Which way is home?'

The dog quietly said, 'I will tell you if you promise not to put the leash on me again.'

The old man leaned close to the dog and said, 'You didn't chase the neighbor's cat, and you didn't bite the other neighbor's dog, but you ran away and caused me to fall when I tried to find you.'

The dog said, 'No I didn't. I knew before you fell that you were going to fall down, and I ran away to get help. Then when I got back you looked like you were sleeping, so I licked your face till you made me stop.'}

Sam put his hand on Karly's and said, "Some dogs really do talk. I am sure they do."

"Yes," she said, "I think they do."

Dana was standing in the doorway to Karly's room and said, "I agree with both of you. I believe dogs talk, and I miss having one."

Sam kissed Karly's hand and said goodnight. He told her that the story about the old man and the dog was really true. But he said it was only possible for people who understand and love dogs like the old man loved his dog and like the dog loved the old man.

***

Dana apologized for not ordering dessert on the way home, and she and Sam went to the living room where Sam would spend the night.

"That was a great story, Sam. Thank you for loving my kids like you do. When Fred died, you were the only one who could have kept Jeremiah on track. I don't know if I have ever thanked you enough for that. You were always there for us, and I know Frank and Christine feel the same way."

"Well, I am borrowing your kids because I don't have any of my own."

"If you asked them, I am not sure they would say you don't have any."

"Sam, there are things that are different for me now. I've been looking for a time when we can talk, but I have been afraid to."

"You can tell me anything. I hope you know that, but I might not be sensitive enough to give you the right answers. I live a hard life in some ways, my work mostly, but I struggle with not knowing what to say sometimes. And too many years alone have not helped me learn how to talk to a woman. Especially one… who makes me nervous like you do sometimes. Like you are doing right now."

"That's what I am talking about, Sam. I feel like. Well, like you are afraid of me."

"Dana, this is exactly what I'm talking about. What if I say the wrong thing, and it's not what you want me to say?"

"Try it. Say something."

"Okay, remember when we were having dinner with Frank and Christine, and Christine said you needed to go out on a real date. I understood that that wasn't me and that she didn't mean it in any way against me. Then later we danced and you cried. Then you put your hand on mine and said, 'I think I will just marry you.' I remember every word you said that night. I remember that I had never looked into your eyes so deeply."

"I remember all of that too, and you looked like you were going to run."

"I didn't want to run, Dana. I don't remember anything in the room that night other than you. It was July 3rd, and we were coming home from the St. Paul Rodeo. You were wearing white dress pants and a tangerine colored, delicate top, with light brown leather sandals that didn't have anything on the top except three thin leather straps over your feet and around your ankles. And please don't take this the wrong way, but you do remember that I was and still am twenty-one years older than you. You were and still are the prettiest woman who has ever been at the St. Paul Rodeo or on the dance floor that night. And Dana, you had only a couple of years earlier lost your husband. Have I missed anything? I would have given my life for you that night; just for you not to cry."

Sam had not looked away from Dana, and Tears were filling her eyes. In her room Karly was sobbing, holding her hands over her mouth, trying to be quiet. Sam had either thought she was asleep or forgot that the house was so small. But now he could hear her.

"Sam, don't leave and I mean it. I will be right back. We

still have things to talk about."

"Oh Karly, she said. "I love you so much. Are you crying because you are happy?"

"Yes. I love Uncle Sam so much. I don't know why you can't just tell him you love him? I know he loves you. I would have to be blind not to see that and so would you."

Dana was sitting on the bed, whispering as best she could, "So you want me to go out and tell Sam that I love him? What if he doesn't…"

Karly's eyes moved just then from her mom to Sam. He was standing in her doorway. He moved to the edge of her bed and extended his left hand to Dana and his right to Karly.

"Karly, there is something I have to ask you. How would you feel if I asked your mom to marry me? Would you ever be able to love me in that way?"

In true fashion like her mom, Karly wiped away her tears and said, "Go ahead and do it and see what happens."

Sam slid down off the bed onto one knee. He said, "Dana, before you answer me consider Jeremiah. Do you know how he would feel?"

"I do know."

"I know how Al will feel about it. What would we do about that?"

"Dad will be okay. He doesn't think differently from Mom. He has always loved her like that. Christine will be the worst. She wants me to marry Frank if someone kills her in the lottery."

"Well that is not going to happen!" Sam said.

"Dana, God knows how much I love you, and He knows how afraid I have been to ask you this question: But will you marry me? You know all of the dangers that I live in and around, particularly with Christine and my work for the government. I have saved quite a bit of money and promise to quit working for the government. And I want you to promise that you will not work anymore. There is not enough time in the next forty years for me to be away from you—for even one day. I will be about a hundred then."

"Sam, I will marry you. And If you would have waited another ten minutes I would have asked you to marry me. There is a reason Jeremiah is not home yet. Karly, will you call Charlotte and tell her Jeremiah can come home now?"

"Sam, this question had to be answered for me today, not one day longer. I have been afraid that you didn't feel about me like I have you… for so long, and I have been afraid to find out the answer."

Dana and Sam both said goodnight to Karly and closed her door this time. In the kitchen Dana turned squarely to Sam and said, "What are you going to do with me now?"

"Well, I am going to stand here and look at you for as long as I can because I have always tried not to. Then I am going to hold you in my arms in a way that I have disciplined myself not to, and I am going to kiss you in a way like I have only imagined. Then I am going to ask you how quickly you can arrange the wedding because there are other things I have had to be very careful not to think about when I am with you.

"Then I'm going to marry you. And between now and then I am going to sleep a long way away from you."

"Sam, I want you to go back to the part about kissing me in a way like you have only imagined," and she moved closer to him.

***

At the Conder's home things were very different from what was going on at Dana's.

Liam and Jeff were making up for lost time thinking and talking about the next contestant who would hunt their mom. Their mom who was now four months into her pregnancy. And it wasn't like the guys needed to protect her from this conversation. It was all she could think about. There were the normal things, of course, that come with pregnancy, but Christine could not find peace away from thoughts of her next hunt. For one thing, there was something different now. She had never killed anyone before Paul Thomas, and she couldn't get it out of her mind. She couldn't stop seeing his face, the fear in his eyes while he couldn't move. Her only consolation was knowing that if she and the others had not gone there Jeff would be dead. It was either her or Frank or Sam who had to kill Paul, and why should it have been one of them. She was probably more fit for it than Frank.

Frank went to Christine and said, "I found the picture of your next opponent. Do you want to talk about it or sleep on it?"

"Well, we might as well talk about it!"

With the baby, Christine's moods were changing. She didn't mean to but she had snapped at Frank, the love of her life and the most patient man she had ever known.

"I am sorry Honey. I didn't mean to sound like that. I just don't know what to do. Physically, I am not going to be able to do this much longer, and I have Hannah to worry about now. If it was only me, I would just go out with a sign on my back that said Diana Austen and get it over with before anyone else gets hurt. I have already asked Dana to marry you and bring the kids into one family."

Frank said, "Baby, you stop that. None of that is going to happen. I will quit work or take as long a leave as we need, and I am not going to marry your sister."

"I hate to say so," Christine replied, "but you are no better than me at hunting people and killing them. And if this is a numbers game, what number do you think Sam is on? Maybe one left. What can we do about that? I saw him sitting in the van when we got home. He looked like he was afraid, and I have never seen him look that way. I've done this to him—and I can't take it anymore."

At that she burst into tears and went to their bedroom while Frank was still trying to answer her.

After she left, Liam said, "Dad, stop. You can't let yourself go there with her. She is not going to get better any time soon, and I need you in this—in a different way than she does. You cannot let this take you down. I can see this guy right now, and we know where he is. With you and me and Sam hunting him, what chance does he have?"

"Son, you listen to me, and I mean it. I will crush your computer and take away everything electronic you have if I hear one more word about you hunting anyone. Jeff! Get your butt out here right now."

"You think I can't hear you and you have to holler? Well I've got you just fine, Dad. Don't you start on me like you do Liam. You will play hell keeping track of me and you better believe that. You better get it down that we are in this together. There is not going to be any telling me to sit down and shut up while Mom has some killer after her. If I find this guy, he's dead, and you better believe that. And no one will know I did it. We don't need the money, and we shouldn't wait any longer.

"The hunt has not started yet, but thanks to your program, we can start patterning this idiot. And I'm going back to my room. He can't hunt Mom for two more weeks, and we are all tense right now. This is kind of past child-raising, don't you think? So don't push me."

Jeff went to his room and Liam motioned to his dad that he needed to back off.

Frank cracked Jeff's door just a few inches, "I'm sorry, Son. I didn't mean to go off like that. You are every bit as important as I am in this. Please. Let me just ask you. Please don't go kill anyone without us all coming together and looking over our odds."

"Yeah, that's cool, Dad, and I'm sorry too. Come in and look at this. They call him 'The Man with Two Faces.' He could be a makeup artist like Brian Cooper, but this time there wouldn't be an eruption to expose him. He is an Asian guy, or made up to look like one, but I've got a bad feeling about him. I think he is the most dangerous opponent we have seen. It's just the look on his face. Look at him. He isn't afraid of anything."

"Hey guys," Liam said. "Glad you're not swinging blows in here. I just texted Sam to see if he has started looking at any of this. He said he is sorry but hasn't. He did say he wants to talk to us about something important. He wants you to stay home tomorrow Dad, and Jeff and I do not go back to school till Wednesday next week. Sam's mom and dad are coming tomorrow too, and I think Grampa Al and Gramma are coming. He must really have a line on something to drag everyone over. I don't think Grampa Al and Gramma even know what Mom has gotten herself into. Since Grampa's heart attack they live pretty quiet.

"And by the way Dad," Liam said, "Mom's over the edge. She's talking to Aunt Dana right now and crying and laughing at the same time. She has been at it ever since you went into Jeff's room. Laughing one minute, crying the next. If I was you I wouldn't even go in there."

"It's getting late, Boys. I need to go in and see if Mom is okay. Thanks for everything. It will take all of us to get out of this. Liam, see if you can find out what Sam has on his mind in case I need to prepare anything."

"No, he was done. Said he would see us tomorrow."

The boys were still in Jeff's room when they heard Frank's exclamation, "What! You are kidding me! No way!"

Liam and Jeff looked at each other but didn't want to even guess at that one.

Liam did say, "Maybe Mom is having twins."

Morning came and Christine was happy again. Everyone was glad for that. Frank fixed breakfast and joined her with it in bed. She said the boys were not to know about Sam and Dana until they were at the house but that Jeremiah and Karly knew. Frank was sure they would know but worried about how Jeremiah would deal with it. He and Frank were close. Frank had been there for him every day for a long time after his dad died.

There was talk between Dana and Christine about a wedding in less than two weeks. Dana wanted to get married before Christine's next hunt which would begin on the first of February.

***

It was a fast-paced morning at Dana's house. She told Christine they couldn't meet till 11 o'clock and reminded her that their dad didn't get in a hurry anymore. She said she and Karly were going with Sam to see Dusty, drop the van off, and would still be early for the meeting. Jeremiah said he was only coming because he had to see the looks on Liam and Jeff's faces when they heard the news.

After dropping the van off, they took Dana's car to Sam's house. They fed Dusty and traded the car for Sam's truck. He brought the truck out of the Barn looking as clean as if it had just been washed. He always kept it clean and kept a cover over it.

Sam came around and opened the door for Dana, and she motioned Karly toward the chrome step.

"Really Mom. I thought I would be sitting by the door."

"I don't know when that will happen, but right now you are in the middle. You look safer that way."

The truck did have a bench seat with three seatbelts, but it was clearly Dana's call to have Karly between them. And truthfully, with Karly being twelve years old, Sam would have put her in the same place.

"Okay," Karly said. "Just before we get to Uncle Frank's I want Mom to sit in the middle, and I get to sit by the door."

The classic 'Super K20 Cheyenne' stopped at the corner just before turning onto Cimarron Street, and Karly slid over Dana's legs to be by the door. Dana had a smile she could not contain as she slid across the seat to sit by Sam.

Sam turned and then turned again to park behind Grampa and Gramma Martin's car. The big Chevy stood tall above Al and Irene's small car, and Karly wasn't in a hurry to jump out. She hoped everyone in the house would see her mom sitting in the middle. It had been a long time since a visit but Frank's parents, Richard and Barbara, were in the house. They lived on the east coast and seldom made the trip out.

"Hi Dear. You look like a teen-ager on your way to a school dance sitting in that big truck by Sam." Irene was the first one to greet them inside the house.

"Mom, I feel that way."

Any one might have guessed Irene was Dana and Christine's mother. She was sixty-four and starting to let her hair turn from its natural blonde color, but she was very pretty. And you could tell by her smile that the seating arrangement had not gone unnoticed.

She hugged Dana and said, "A picture is worth a

thousand words."

Irene quickly went to give Sam a hug. He had been close to them for the past several years and had helped with a lot of things around the house when Al had his heart attack. The look in Irene's bright blue eyes as she looked up at Sam would have stopped him in his tracks if he had not already been standing still. The one look told him that she already knew.

"Hi Sam." Al extended his hand. "I have never seen you sitting so close to a woman—and such a pretty one. When you pulled in, it reminded me of when I used to date Irene. Her father was a tough guy and didn't think much of me. He owned a big dairy and thought anyone who would date his daughter should be interested in walking around in cow poop."

"Al, let them come in and sit down," Irene said.

Dana took Sam by the hand and said to her dad, "Dad, I would like you to meet Sam in in a very different way from how you have known him. He brought Jeremiah and Karly and me here this morning to ask you if he can marry me."

With that, she looked up at Sam. He would have given his old truck for just a fraction of her outgoing personality.

Everyone was still standing. John was in his normal position. He had one arm around Julie and was holding one of her hands with his other. As long as Sam could remember they had been inseparable like that.

Liam and Jeff were nearly frozen in place. And for some

reason, among everyone in the house, Sam could feel Jeff staring at him. Jeff was thinking, "Let's see you pull this one off!"

Sam said, "Al, Irene, I don't know what you think of me right now, but I have invited you here to ask you for Dana's hand in marriage—and I am just about to pass out. I love you, Irene, and I love you Al. We certainly have had some good times together, but I want to marry your daughter more than I have ever wanted anything. I know there is an age difference, but I want to love her and take care of her and Jeremiah and Karly for the rest of my life."

"Sam, I could not have done this better," Al said, "and as a matter of fact I didn't. Irene and I eloped because her father was going to break my legs—at least that's what he said. But in time he accepted me. This hasn't really been fair for you this morning. Irene told me before we came, but I wanted you to earn the right to marry my beautiful daughter.

"I will be very honest with you. My first thought was that you work for the government and kill people, and I don't believe God wants you to do that. I know there are different ways of thinking about that, but Dana told me you were going to stop killing people, maybe even get a job in a florist shop or something." Al smiled.

"But this is all I want to say to you," he continued. "I love my daughters and my wife more than anything in the world. If you will always love Dana that way, then you are one of the sons Irene and I never had. You and Frank will both be our sons. I'm not sure I have given you the right answer or you wouldn't have a tear on your cheek."

"Pointing that out is kind of like breaking my legs," Sam said. "And Jeff, keep it to yourself. These are man tears. Someday you will know when it's okay to do this."

"Yeah, like I'm not going to tell all of my friends that you cry like a girl."

"Hey, this is not like a girl."

Jeff came back, "There is not a girl in the house who is not crying—and then there's you."

With that, the bantering between Jeff and Sam was over. Frank said the barbeque would be ready soon and asked Sam if he would help bring it in. It had been one of the few times when no one thought about the lottery.

Eleven

Jeremiah drove himself and Karly home. Sam took Dana back to the ranch to get her car and thanked her for the night on the couch, for allowing him to know that she loved him, and for helping him talk to her father. He commented about how Karly had been calling the property a ranch since Dusty came, then asked what she thought about them keeping her house for Jeremiah. Dana liked the idea and Sam suggested they rent it to a friend of his until Jeremiah was on his own and could take it.

Dana said, "Your friend doesn't kill people does he?"

Sam said, "Not anymore, but he has fought some serious battles beside me and saved my life more than once. I suppose I saved his a few times, but he didn't do so well with all of that when we got home. He makes money and is dependable, and he would be a good renter.

"He and I served together from a few years before 9/11 all the way through Iraq and part of Afghanistan. Hard times. He came home on a disability, and I came home to keep doing what I had been doing, only at home this time. Mostly at home. I was not supposed to go after bad guys in other countries, but my job was to go wherever they needed me.

"That's in the past now. It would be good if we never talk about those things. I have given my notice to the President and will only work occasionally now for NASA. Frank and I are a good team there. I will draw a healthy pension from so many years serving different parts of government, but I am really looking forward to retirement now. To be honest, I never felt that I had anything better to do. But that has sure changed now.

"Dad and I have been talking. We are going to do something to end this lottery. Between Frank and Liam's computer skills and my experience protecting people your sister will be okay. There are actions Dad is considering, but they could cost a lot of lives. That is what makes it difficult. But I promise you, the lottery will either let Christine out within the next couple of months or something will happen to them.

"They have professional agents on staff, very capable people I would guess, and we do not know who they are right now. That is the reason I have to do this with Christine. If the Induction Center thought we were after them, they might know to come after me, and that would take them straight to Christine. I can hardly think they haven't seen me and know I protect her. They just don't care as long as they make money."

"Okay, for now I'm not going to go crazy. I know something will happen. Do you think you can get the friend you were talking about to help us?"

"He is in a wheelchair. I didn't tell you that. And he spends a lot of time reliving the past, so I don't know where we could use him, but there are other friends who are almost too dangerous to call. One whose name is Dan. He flew me to catch the airline Christine was on when she went to Italy, and he recently flew us to California to get Jeff. I have another friend whose name is Ben. He is more dangerous than Dan. I talked to him recently, and he said if he could help us to call him. I am ready to do that. I have a lot to live for. You have changed everything in my life."

Sam and Dana were sitting in Sam's truck inside the barn. Dusty was watching them, waiting for some attention, but he would just have to wait.

Dana said, "There is something I want you to do."

"Anything. There is nothing in the world I won't do for you."

Dana said, "Okay, I am going to hold you to that. Hold me for a while, and kiss me like you always imagined, like last night, and then I have to go home to the kids—and pray. I am going to be strong, and this will be over."

Dana was already tight against Sam in the truck. If he would have been magic, the steering wheel would have disappeared, but he wasn't, and it didn't. He held Dana and kissed her until he knew she needed to go. Probably Sam's greatest asset was integrity, and both of them knew it was time for her to go. He stepped down out of the truck first, going to her side to lift her to the ground. She could do it easily, but it was a high truck. Her taillights faded out of sight in the long distance of Camelot Drive.

***

Dana and Christine had decided on a Saturday wedding. It would be January 26th in the barn. Sam kept a tidy barn. He and Dana had more than enough help decorating, and it would be perfect for the indoor event. There were green colored timothy bales from east of the mountains to make seating and tables. Dusty's stall was close enough that he would be right there when it was his turn to kneel on one knee and give the ring to Dana. Karly would be glowing.

All of the family came, including those from Fred's side. There was a total of seventy. Some were close friends; others from work. For Sam and Dana, the wedding would double as his retirement party. Not as important as the two of them getting married but still a life-changing moment to celebrate. It would be a wedding no one would forget.

Shortly before people were asked to find their seats an Mh-60 Seahawk landed in Sam's field next to the barn. It was loud and everyone left the barn to see what was happening. Sam was in on the planning and had instructed Karly to stay by Dusty and talk to him when she heard the helicopter coming in.

By special permission from the President, and in honor of Sam's official retirement, Seven Navy SEAL's deployed from the Seahawk and walked toward the barn. They were dressed in gray suits with crisp collared white shirts opened at the top without ties.

The suits appeared two sizes small on each of the combat warriors, and the shirts would not button around their necks. The SEAL's walked straight to Sam, formed a line and saluted him. Sam did not do a good job of hiding his emotions even though he knew this was scheduled. He could only stand at attention and honor these men who would go from where he stood and possibly give their lives in the protection of others.

Ben Bonoski was the first to break and offer Sam his hand, then the others in turn. Ben was not a SEAL anymore but worked with Sam as a guard under the Presidential staff.

These men looked like bodyguards rather than SEALs in their tight fitting suits and rock-hard builds—and that is what they were.

Sam's longtime friend Dan was there. As well as being a pilot, he was also an unconquerable looking man. Sam had spent his career around men like that.

Dana was dressed in a light blue, full-length sundress. She wore riding boots that were much prettier than Sam's and her blonde hair was braided.

Sam wore his Dan Post boots with Levi's and a light blue dress shirt with a western cut, gray sport coat. He looked very much like he did when he and Christine had gone shopping for Frank's birthday. The dress code had not gone outside the family, but all of the women in Dana's family, and Sam's, wore full-length sun dresses with boots, and all of them had their hair braided. The barn was heated in the beginning because Sam's truck lived there. Today it was like summer inside. Sam's friend Dan was the photographer. He offered to do it, telling Sam it was nearly his only hobby, that along with going to the range to shoot. He and Sam were alike in that. They kept their firearms in perfect condition and shot together often.

Before the night was over, Dusty had bowed several times by request and had his nose petted as many times as there were people there. Along with the number of kisses he received, he was set for a long time to come with love from strangers. Sam wondered if horses liked that or just put up with it. Maybe it was just part of having a soft, furry nose.

Dana's pastor performed the ceremony and by his insistence Sam and Dana had written their own marriage vows.

When everyone was in place, the pastor said, "If there is any reason why these two should not be married speak now or forever hold your peace."

At that, the men who landed in the Seahawk stood up, came to the front and stood in a half circle with their backs to

Dana and Sam. It was a show of loyalty civilians sometimes never see.

Without a single word they had said, "We will die to protect Sam and Dana."

When the pastor secretly signaled them they returned to their positions. They stood at all sides of the room, guarding the perimeter of those who were seated. It was not done as part of a plan. I was their nature to protect.

Sam went first, "Dana, I love you more than I ever thought I could love anyone. When I look into your eyes I only want to come closer to you. I will always want you to tell me how I am doing as your husband and your protector and your friend. I promise to never allow those feelings to become normal.

"When I feel your hands in mine I know what my dad feels when he touches my mom. I have watched him hold her and kiss her and love her for as long as I have been alive, and that is how I promise to hold you and kiss you and love you. He turned to his dad and said, 'Thank you, Dad.'

"Finally, I want to be there to accomplish whatever you need from me every day. I will be faithful to you. I have too many weak points to mention now, but I will never stop working on them. I promise you that today.

"Dana, will you marry me?"

***

"Yes, Sam. I will marry you. As you have learned from your father, I promise to hold you like my mom has held my dad throughout 45 years of marriage. She has loved him and laughed with him and cried with him. She has served him with a joyful heart every day that I can remember, and never once can I remember anger in our house, only love.

She turned to her mother and said, "Mom, please never stop teaching me how to love and how to care and how to cherish."

"Sam, as I become your wife now I promise that I will always think about your needs before my own. I will be faithful to you. I will love you forever.

***

The pastor said, "Do you both understand that God loves you? Whenever there is doubt, His ways are always the right ways.

"Do you believe with me today that the union between a man and a woman in marriage is a lasting covenant before man and God? Until death do you part. Those are strong words and they have meaning.

"Sam, do you take Dana in this way? In sickness and in health? During times of trouble and during times of joy? Do you promise to love her when she is old?"

Sam smiled at that. He said, "Even when she is old. I will

love her then."

"Dana, do you take Sam in this same way? In sickness and in health? During times of trouble and during times of joy? Do you promise to love him every day of his life?"

Dana answered and Karly brought Dusty to where her mom and Sam were standing. With bright blue ribbons the two rings where braided into his mane. Karly touched his left front leg and he bowed, his left leg tucked back under his body with his right leg extended.

Dana untied and took the first ring. Sam untied and took the second ring. Karly brought Dusty to a full stand, backed him up a few feet and then asked him to bow again. When he had finished, she returned him to his stall. One of the SEALs held the gate for her and closed it when she was ready.

Sam and Dana exchanged the rings. She looked up into Sam's eyes, and he met her lips with the same kiss that was so much more than he had ever imagined.

The pastor did not want to miss his chance and pronounced man and wife.

Some who did not know about the lottery asked where their honeymoon would be. Those who did know, knew that Sam would stay close to Christine until some other time when the lottery would end.

Frank and Christine took Jerimiah and Karly to their home. They continued to celebrate the wedding and told stories long into the night. Jeremiah even talked about Charlotte, saying they were pretty serious. He said she was the nicest girl he had ever met.

To that, Karly said, "Well, excuse me. I'm a girl."

***

It was Tuesday, January 29th. Sam and Dana were married and living on the ranch, and the time had come for Christine to meet her next opponent. Frank and Sam went with her, and they caught United out of PDX at 7:58 am for San Francisco. They were in a rental car in San Francisco at 10:12 am. The one-hour and 43-minute flight was much faster than driving.

The hunt this time could begin on the 29th of January if both contestants agreed, but that was not going to happen. Sam had asked Christine to agree to the earliest date and he would have killed her opponent within five miles from the Induction Center. He did not have a weapon and would not have used one. He knew that was part of the deal when Dan was not able to fly him. They had the advantage of being able to see the contestant's location, and that would have been enough. But Tanoak Yoshida would only agree to the regular date of February 1st on a Friday.

Tanoak was a solid framed young man, five-foot-ten and twenty-two years old. He was very well spoken and had been a foreign exchange student in Houston, Texas. While there, he studied at The Cornerstone School of Martial Arts, earning a

Black Belt in Karate when he was sixteen. He was very polite. One would have thought the nicest kid on the block, but there was something else about him. His demeanor was not swayed by conversation. He was focused on Christine.

Inside the Induction Center she had been close enough for her glove to smell him, and the smell was recorded. That could mean more to her this time than she knew. There was nothing Frank or Sam could do to further identify this contestant, so they had decided on their way to rent the car not to allow Tanoak to see them associated with Christine. He had stated on the website that he would not hunt until February first. Once he signed that, it would be a violation he would be eliminated for if he eliminated her before Friday. Christine said she needed to use the restroom and Tanoak left the building before she came out.

Inside Colin Brown's office, Tanoak had told all of them that he had a twin brother who often shared a room with him and even drove his car. He requested justice if Christine would mistakenly kill his brother. Aaden Bradley and the others had not encountered a situation like this before and told him he could be the one eliminated, or his brother if they broke any rule. Aaden didn't say so, but he already knew they would not allow Tanoak to kill Christine. It was too near the planned PPV event. They would have Sardac stop Tanoak before he could hurt Christine. In a worst case, they would have one of their agents kill him. Either way, it did not look good for the young Japanese contestant. His chances of living for another thirty days were not good.

It was certain that he believed he would scare Christine enough by mentioning his twin brother that she might hesitate at the wrong moment. When that happened, he or his brother would apprehend her or kill her. The practice of kidnapping female contestants was not uncommon and not illegal. It was a huge price a woman paid to compete in the lottery.

After Tanoak left the parking lot, Christine called Frank and said she would meet them at the coffee shop around the corner where they were waiting. They returned the car at the airport and caught their flight back to Portland. Frank could see Tanoak driving on I-5 toward Portland. And then instantly his marker disappeared.

"Okay, we have a problem," Frank said with more volume than he had hoped to use. "This guy's code just disappeared."

They were sitting together just ahead of the engines in Row eight. Frank by the window, Christine in the middle, and Sam by the aisle.

"You still can't see him?" Sam said.

"His marker is gone—No. There it is. He is in Portland."

"That is not possible," Christine said. "He could not have gotten a flight out any faster than we did. He is not in

Portland."

"There has to be a problem," Sam said. "Only the Induction Center would be able to turn his marker on and off or show him to be someplace he isn't. Can they do that?"

***

"Tanoak, I have successfully shut your marker off and brought your brother in. No one, even if they saw the move, could tell he isn't you. The people at the Induction Center would not know if they watched it on their monitor's. I know those idiots. All they care about are the bets they make and the drinks they are having."

"Okay," Tanoak said. "Will they not be able to see me whenever we decide?"

"That's right, and right now you and I have a situation. I told you that when this works you owe me $2,000,000. Your brother just left my office, and it works perfectly. But he only had the down payment. I will see you tomorrow with the rest of the money, right?"

"Sure, I pay my debts. And you should remember that I have done well without you. I have made a lot of money, and I know how to find people. I would not advise again for you to sound like you are threatening me."

"Okay, I'm sorry. I didn't mean it that way. I just want you to understand that you cannot see this system work till you are here in my office, and you cannot control it. Only I can. I am going to deactivate your brother now and activate you again. With this technology you will be able to kill Diana Austen any place and any time, or your brother can. But you will receive the credit. His code is identical to yours. Two against one is good odds.

Your win this time is about $9,000,000 if I remember correctly. What I have done for you is worth more than I charged. I also know who hunts for the woman you met today. One mistake in this lottery, and you are dead by an opponent or by agents. And you would have to kid yourself to believe the pretty woman you met has killed some of the top hunters in the lottery. There is a man doing that for her, and she pays him a lot of money. But if you and I could settle on an additional amount I could help you eliminate professional men like that one. As long as you and I have a good relationship."

***

"Sam," Christine said, "I would give anything if you didn't have to be in this position risking your life for me, especially now that you and Dana are married. And from the looks of what Frank just saw, we may have lost our edge. What will we do if we cannot see Tanoak?"

"Now that you say that," Frank said, "his marker is live again. North on I-5, just like it was."

"We will figure this out," Sam said. "Frank and Liam will find something. If not, I will go like I normally do. I will go on what we know and on instinct."

They decided to stop talking about the lottery. A woman directly across the aisle from Sam was obviously listening, not that she could know anything.

The United flight returning touched down at 3:19 pm at PDX. They were not concerned at the moment about Tanoak Yoshida. He would be another several hours getting to Portland.

The next day Tanoak would personally meet Daniel Bradley and hand him a check for $1,750,000. His brother Hinoki had delivered a payment of $250,000 and received an identical injection of the serum Tanoak was given when he signed in. This was a first for Daniel. He was the only person who had successfully copied the serum.

The twin brothers had both been named after trees, mighty trees when growing in the right climates and soil conditions. Hinoki was named after Japan's tall Hinoki cypress. The tree can grow to a height of 130 feet and the Tanoak tree can reach heights of 150 feet.

They landed at PDX and left in Frank's truck. When they arrived home, Sam left Frank and Christine's without more discussion and went to find Dana. She was all he could think about. She and Jeremiah and Karly were his life now. Them and the lottery until Christine was free from it.

Sam would go after Tanoak on Thursday night. If he

could find him sleeping, he would kill him on Friday morning and would have Christine nearby. Sam was not doing it for the money, but he had to kill Tanoak to keep him from hunting Christine, and $9,000,000 was a good amount of money.

***

In bed that night Christine said to Frank, "Honey, I am tired of this. I can't go at the pace it takes to keep up with you guys, and I don't see how you can even go to work. I think you should quit."

She said, "I want Sam to stop putting his life in danger, but I would be dead if he did."

"I know how you feel, Baby, and you are right. I would not last five minutes trying to kill a contestant who has risen to the place Tanoak is. That doesn't mean I shouldn't die in Sam's place, but I wouldn't keep you alive that way."

The next morning Frank said, "Boys, we have a different situation this time with Mom's opponent."

Frank described what had happened and asked Liam and Jeff to log in and watch Tanoak's marker. He told them there was no hunt until Friday morning, but they had not forgotten how Paul Thomas had taken Jeff. It remained a possibility that someone with no marker could come at any time, and they would not see them coming.

"I have to know where your mom's opponent goes when he arrives in Portland," Frank said.

He told them Tanoak would arrive in the early hours of the morning. He said he would take the morning shift if they would watch till 11 or 12 PM. Then he called Sam to let him know what they were doing. He asked Sam to take some time off, at least until the last couple of hours before Friday morning.

Liam and Jeff were in Liam's bedroom. Frank asked them to slip in and wake him up when they were ready to get some sleep. He said goodnight and left them to watch Tanoak's location. His marker didn't disappear again, and the boys went to bed a little after midnight. Frank was up and saw Tanoak stop traveling at 1:30 AM.

***

"Honey, did you ever come to bed?"

"Yes, but I got up early to check Tanoak's location. As near as I can tell he is at 1400 Pearl Street and is probably sleeping in. I wish we could go get him. I would like to tie him up till Friday morning, but he is a lot younger than me and supposed to be a black belt in Karate. I would probably lose in a fight with him. I'm thinking about it though. I could use your glove to knock him down while I tie him up, and that idea doesn't sound too bad."

"What if his brother is there? It is likely that he went to where his brother lives. And if his brother looks like him, he is probably just as tough."

"I know you are right Honey. You are outthinking me. There is a part of me that just wants to be tough like Sam. Those brothers could be together, but neither of them knows what I look like. I think I will do a drive-by before the boys get up and want to go with me."

Pearl street was a long drive from Frank's, but he had his laptop running and Tanoak was still there. At 8:55 AM Frank was parked looking at the house. He was in an upscale neighborhood in North Portland near Antione Lake. Using his binoculars, he was able to write the license plate numbers of two sports cars in front of the house, and at 9:30 Tanoak got into one of the cars and left. Frank wanted to follow but didn't feel like he would be good at that. Then he thought about breaking into the house but thought better of that too. That was Sam's type of work, and what if the brother was in there? The sports cars were pretty; they had good taste in cars. Frank didn't know what they were but the one sounded powerful when it left. He took pictures of the house and the cars. Then he headed for home. He would let the boys know what he had done.

He could not wait to tell Sam either but wanted to respect his family time. Trying to be straight-faced, he told both boys how he could have taken Tanoak out but spared him. He told them that in a fair fight Tanoak would not have had a chance. Christine accused him of taking things a little too lightly.

She said, "Honey, those kinds of men are killers. He and his brother have made millions together if it's true that his brother helps him. You really pulled it off this morning though, but now stay away from them. I need you alive to love me and protect me."

Jeff put his laptop on the Island in the kitchen and said, "Have you stopped watching him, Dad? Right now he is on the south shore of North Portland Harbor by Hayden Island. It looks like there are some businesses there. Liam and Frank both came to Jeff's laptop.

"Very nice. Can you get me an address?"

"I don't know but we can see the building pretty well. Kind of a square building with a black roof. We could drive right to the building."

It had been a great morning. Frank said he was going to investigate and see what type of business Tanoak had visited. Maybe he would even get a good look at Tanoak without appearing to be tailing him.

He turned to go to his truck and Jeff said, "Whoa! Liam and I are going."

Frank felt nothing could happen in an accidental sighting. He agreed, and they went to the truck.

Part way there Liam said, "Did they see your truck this morning?"

Frank didn't think they had. It was early, and he had

parked on the curb in front of another house. Rich house. New truck. He looked like he belonged there.

After leaving the freeway and driving around for a few minutes, they were sure they had found the right building. Frank asked the boys to stay in the truck. He said he was going in.

Liam said, "No, I'm probably better at this recon stuff than you, and the car you saw is not here anyway. The Asian guys won't be here.

Jeff said, "They are where Dad went this morning. They are right there," and he handed his laptop to his dad.

"I'm going in with Liam. No one will suspect us."

"Okay, don't do anything in there that will get you remembered. Jeff! No punching or kicking anyone."

Both boys had their phones, and Liam turned his to silent mode and let Jeff see him do it.

Just before they walked in, Liam said, "Don't get seen, but take a few pictures. We know those brothers were here for a reason, at least one of them."

Jeff silenced his phone, and they entered the building. There was a glass door on the right that was labeled JetTec and two glass doors on the left. One was Harbor Hydraulics, and the other was Tempered Glass, Inc. There was a steel staircase and a small office door at the top. It was labeled Bradley Research & Engineering. They had just reached the top of the stairs and met a man coming out of the door.

"What can I do for you," he said to Liam.

Jeff answered before Liam could and said," We are looking for a Drone shop that is supposed to be here. Downstairs I think, but it isn't there."

"I'm sorry. I have been here for several years but no drone shop."

"Liam stuck his hand out, "Thanks, Liam Benton. My brother and I fly photography drones."

"Daniel Bradley. I am a development engineer."

Then he said, "I forgot something," and opened the door again.

Jeff yelled, "Thanks," and they bolted for the door.

While running for the truck, which hardly seemed out of line for a couple of energetic boys, Liam pointed his finger repeatedly at his dad—let's go—let's go. Frank started the truck and quickly turned away from the building, so he couldn't be seen. It also made the doors open the right way, and the boys were in.

"Wow, my blood is pumping now. What happened in there?" Frank was already heading for the freeway. At the time of purchasing the neurologic—slash—poison glove for Christine, Frank had used the name Daniel Bradley several times around the house.

"You are not going to believe this," Jeff said. "We just

met Daniel Bradley. A big guy like you said."

Liam was so excited he was talking fast, and that was unusual for him.

"His office door said Bradley Research and Engineering, and I introduced myself as Liam Benton. He went for it. This is exciting stuff. We have to get Sam caught up."

Twelve

Frank stopped at the edge of the road in front of a closed metal gate.

"What are you doing?" Liam said.

"Should we follow him, and see if he goes to the house where I was this morning?"

"Absolutely not," was Liam's answer.

Jeff spoke up too, "What, are you crazy Dad. So we follow him right to his house, he sees us, and both of them torture us to death for following him."

Frank had his answer, and they headed toward home.

Jeff said, "Dad, let me call Sam. I want to tell him about this."

"Sure, Son. Put it on speaker. When you tell him you saw Daniel Bradley I have to hear what he says."

"Sam? Have you got a minute? Jeff here."

"Sure. What's going on?"

"Liam and I just saved Dad's life. He was going to run Daniel Bradley down and kick his ass and we stopped him."

"Okay, you have my attention, and Jeff, we have talked about the language. I know your dad has too, so don't do it, okay? Most of us in this type of work, plain clothes at least, keep our language clean. We don't want to look tough or threatening to a potential enemy. The man who is the most threatening is the first to be shot when a fight starts. They find out who we are when we are ready to bring it. Not that ass is so bad, but you are plain clothes now. Keep it professional."

"Yeah, I'm sorry. Thanks for the heads-up."

Jeff told Sam everything about his dad finding the house where the two Japanese brothers were staying and about them going to see Daniel.

"Frank, you on here? It sounds like I'm on speaker."

"Yeah, I wanted to hear the plans if you had anything. And thanks for taking my wild son to the woodshed. I don't do it often enough."

"No problem. Do you guys have a plan? Daniel knows a lot about us, and it sounds like he is working against Christine if he is meeting with Tanoak."

"We are on the way home, but it wouldn't take long to come to your place."

"No, we are at Dana's loading some things. We are going to rent the house for a while. Go home, and we will come there when we finish. We are ready to leave now Dana says."

At Frank and Christine's house, Liam sat with his laptop and took notes of plans they were thinking of. He wanted every detail and was really put out that his dad didn't get close enough to see what kind of cars the brothers drove.

Christine spoke up, "I've always liked fast cars and have looked at a lot of them on the road. Can you show me the pictures on your phone?"

Frank sent the photos to his laptop.

"Wow, you guys need to get up on your cars. The blue one is a Porsche Spyder and the gray one is a… Porsche Spyder also. Those are extremely rare cars for brothers to own two of them."

A minute later Jeff said, "I've got some pictures here. They are 918 Spyders, and that is because only 918 were ever made. This page shows the original price at $845,000, with options going higher. So you think these boys have money? 608 HP and 398 foot pounds of torque. Yeah, you will outrun one of those. Never!"

Sam said, "We know only one reason they would go to see Daniel. Tanoak is in the lottery, and Daniel is helping him."

Dana was talking to Christine in the living room. Jeremiah and Karly had gone back to the ranch.

Frank said, "It is almost certain he is selling something as he did to us. We have to go after him. We have to know what he is equipping Tanoak with."

Sam said, "I can get information out of Daniel—easily. And as for the brothers, I may have to kill both of them. I would hate to do that, but they must be hunting Christine together. We have already seen something happen with

Tanoak's code. It can move to a location different from where he is. Daniel, or someone at the Induction Center, has to be doing that. Is anyone watching Tanoak now?"

Liam went from the note taking page to the program. "He is at the house where Dad went this morning. Jeff, would you bring this up and watch the house till we finish here?"

"Sure."

"Do we know where Daniel lives?" Sam asked

"No," Frank said, "just where his office is."

"I have a friend who is a police officer, Sam said. "I will step into the other room and call him. He was at the wedding.

"When we know where Daniel is," He said, "I will ask one of the men you met at the wedding to go get him. I am not ready to let Daniel know I'm protecting Christine. I don't know what he is capable of, or if he has a friendship with any of the field agents at the Induction Center."

Sam received a text message. It was the address at Daniel's residence and his license plate number. He copied it to Ben.

He said, "I know you remember the SEALs at the wedding. One of them is not a SEAL anymore. His name is Ben Bonoski and he no longer serves in that capacity. He is not far from here. He and two of his team just went through a harrowing ordeal with a handful of would-be terrorists attempting to gain access to the President, and he has some time off. I am lucky I wasn't called to that one."

At six-foot-four and 276 pounds Ben was the strongest, most threatening man Sam had ever met in person. He held several titles in combat fighting and was intimidating to say the least. He had been trained in intimidation while part of a SEAL team and hated bad guys as much as Sam did.

"They don't last long with him," Sam said, "no matter who they are. He stayed over after the wedding hoping to help us, and he is on his way to Daniel's house right now. I hope he doesn't have to kill him before getting the information we need, but if he has to he will."

***

Parked at a condo along the Willamette River Daniel's car alarm went off. A porch light came on and with a handgun in his hand Daniel Bradley began to walk from a second story condo toward his black BMW. It was parked near a large tree between the curb and sidewalk. As he looked into the car and turned the alarm off Ben Benoski caught him squarely in the spine with a knee. One hand was on Daniel's gun so quickly you could not see Ben's hand move. With the other he choked Daniel out in just a few seconds. Ben held him pinned against the car.

"Daniel, I have business with you. When you can, we will go to your house."

Daniel, knowing he could do nothing to Ben said, "I will

try. You hurt my back pretty bad. He turned toward the condo, and Ben did not feel the need to hang on to him. Daniel was clearly in pain, but he and Ben ascended the staircase and entered the house. A conversation that determined if Daniel would live or die began.

"I will talk first. I only know you, because you are involved in a government lottery you should not be involved in, and tonight that either ends, or I will kill you. I hope you will cooperate and not doubt me. The people I work for prefer that I don't kill you, but how will you convince me that I can trust you?"

"I am a businessman—and not stupid. You found me easily and could have killed me with just your hands. I have no loyalty to anyone I do business with. I will tell you anything you want to know. And I promise you, with my life, that I will not do anything your employer does not want me to do. I should not be proud of it, but I will take the side of any man who can take my life so easily. What do you want from me?"

"Do you have a Coke or anything cold?"

"Yes, in the fridge, and if you would, get me one too."

"You are bold Daniel. I like that."

Setting four cold drinks on the table, Ben asked Daniel where his laptop was and for any other communication devises he owned, including any that might be at his office. Daniel pointed to a desk in another room, in sight of where they sat, and handed Ben his phone. He said he had another computer in his bedroom. It was also a laptop. Ben asked for paper and a pen and for the passwords which he tested for each devise.

"You had one or two Japanese men come to your office today. Was it one or two?"

"One. There are two brothers, and one is helping the other to hunt a contestant in the lottery."

"What did you do for those brothers?"

"I can show you. I have programs and information on both computers. There are no computers or phones in my office. I have successfully duplicated the serum and codes they use in the lottery. I have given Tanoak Yoshida's brother an identical serum as Tanoak received when he began. I can turn Tanoak off and turn his brother on. The effect of that is that Tanoak can become invisible while his marker can still be seen wherever his brother is. As a result, Tanoak can kill his opponent without being seen in what could be an illegal area. He could take a child from a schoolyard and not be seen doing it. Not that I would condone that. Then all he needs to do is move his victim to a legal area and call me. I would turn his chip back on.

"I hope I am convincing you that I will hide nothing. I will stop helping any contestant you do not want me to help. Honestly, I have charged Tanoak over $2,000,000, and he or his brother will kill me if they suspect I stopped helping them.

But I could take a much needed vacation and hide from them till this is over. I am being honest. Can I ask who you are protecting—no, I didn't mean to ask that. I do not want to know."

With this information Ben felt he should kill Daniel to be safe, but he knew Daniel could not find him, and he knew Daniel understood he would be killed if he did. He also believed Daniel was the kind of scum who would take money from anyone then run and hide. He left with all of Daniel's computers, phones, and passwords. He took them to Sam. Sam and Frank would be able to locate both of the brothers at any time. Ben told Daniel to go on a long vacation with all of his money and not to come back or he would kill him. It seemed certain that Daniel would not do anything to bring Ben after him again. Sam now had Daniel's phone and the cell numbers for Tanoak and Hinoki.

At forty years old Ben was younger than Sam but knew him well from jobs they had done together.

Dana's house was not rented to Sam's friend yet. It was suggested that Ben stay there until they could see better to the end of Christine being out of the lottery, but Ben thanked them and said no. He offered to make a bed in the barn or put a bed up at Frank and Christine's house, so he could be there if anything happened. Sam had a lot of things to talk about with Ben and offered the barn—as long as it could be made comfortable. When Christine and Frank were told of Ben's need for a place to stay, they offered however much money it would take to build a nice room onto the barn and plumb it as needed. It was decided, and Dusty would have a fulltime companion, at least for a while.

***

"Sam, I know I shouldn't put this on you," Dana said, "but if there is a way you can save Christine and not kill Tanoak and his brother, I would like it. I cannot help thinking of a time when this is over and someone could have lived that didn't. I wish I could tell these young men go home to their families."

"You can imagine the influence $9,000,000 has on them," Sam said. "They are not going to call time out and go home. I wish I didn't have to kill them, but right now there is no other way to keep Christine alive. Ben and I will try every way we can. One thing we cannot do is put Ben's life at risk during that split moment when it counts. As with me, he is only alive because he strikes first and does whatever he has to do to stop whoever is on the wrong side. We have to keep that edge. But even then, if a person worries over something for one second when they shouldn't, they can be killed. Ben and I have to go now."

Sam hugged Dana every time as if it could be the last time he would be able to. Then he and Ben left to go after Tanoak and Hinoki.

***

"Hinoki Yoshida?

"Yes."

"I am an agent working with matters concerning the lottery Tanoak is involved in. I know you must have looked at your phone and see that the phone I am calling from belongs to Daniel Bradley. We have his computers and information about the illegal actions you and Tanoak and he are involved in. Of course Daniel is no longer available to assist you.

"Agents are deciding as we speak what actions will be taken against you and your brother. I can see that you are with your brother in a moving vehicle near your house. Put your phone on speaker so he can hear me.

"'Tanoak, my name is Ben, and you cannot hide from me. I have Daniel's computers. I am able to hide your marker and Tanoak's so that you could not be paid for eliminating Tanoak's opponent. As it stands now, you will be charged with murder if you kill Diana Austen and attempted murder if you harm her in any way. And remember what I just said. You cannot hide from us.

"My boss is with me right now, and that should tell you that this is a very important matter. You have lost your position in the lottery. There will be no more money, and you will be lucky if we decide to let you and your brother live. There are other agents ready to come after you if we call them. You were made aware of the rules and broke them. I am going to hand the phone to my boss."

Sam took the phone: "Tanoak, Hinoki, I advise you not to do anything beyond what you have already done. I can turn your markers on at the same time to locate both of you, and they are both on now. But there is another side to this if you are smart enough to listen to me. There is someone who does not want either of you to be killed. I am not at liberty to say who that is.

"I am against it, but for the person who has asked me, I am willing to give you a way out. I can fix it within the lottery so that you keep the money Tanoak has earned and go back to Japan to your families. Give me one excuse, and this option will not be offered. You will both have to meet with me."

"Have patience with me please, Tanoak said. "If you expect me to believe you, it will take more than this. You could have guessed that my brother and I are near our house."

"Okay, turn onto a side street and I will tell you its name. Just this once. If you question me again, this conversation is over, and we will kill your brother as well as you."

"You just turned onto Barnes Street heading east. Tanoak, you are pushing your luck. It would be easier for me to kill you and your brother and be done with this. I am going to put my phone down now. If you change your mind call Daniel's phone. And do it in a hurry. I will not tell you again."

Sam turned the phone off.

***

"What do you think Hinoki?"

"I think they are nobody, only trying to save the life of their friend."

"But you know they can tell where we are," Tanoak said. "We could call the Induction Center and find out if they know about this, but we have broken the rules, and the penalty is death. I do not want to call them."

"You think then we should run like cowards?"

"That has not been suggested. You heard the man talking. He is not treating us that way. It is true he could be lying about not killing us, but I think we have to meet him. We can outrun him for a time but not forever, and we know one thing. With Daniel's phone and computer, he can make me not be able to earn the money from this match. Please call Daniel's phone and see if it goes to him."

"This is Ben. I am glad you decided to call back."

"Please wait. Tanoak wants to talk."

"Ben or the man who is with you, I have no choice but to meet with you. I make one condition if I may. I will fight either of you to the death. You have insulted my honor. My family name carries more honor than any other in my country.

"I understand that as long as you have Daniel's computer I cannot be paid, so I will stop until we fight and not hunt again in this lottery. If you have honor anywhere in your family, as I have from just my brother, you will allow me to fight and settle this."

"Tanoak, this is Ben. I know of your black belt, but you are foolish. You do not know me. The United States Government has trained me to kill. But if it is your wish I agree to fight—if that is what you want. I will kill you and put your brother on an airplane to explain to your mother why you died. He will tell her it was because you were foolish, and there is no honor in being foolish.

"I will tell you where to meet me, and you must come fast to that place. If anyone follows you, I will also kill your brother—with my hands. The same way you will die."

Sam called Frank from his phone.

"Frank, where are you and Christine? Tanoak and his brother will meet Ben and me."

"I am at the park where you left us."

"Okay. Ben is telling them where to meet us."

"Hinoki, this is Ben. From where you are now, I will give you twenty minutes to meet me in a park located at the corner of Fifth Street and Tennison Avenue. Put that in your phone and do not be late."

Thirteen minutes had passed when the blue Porsche Spider pulled along the curb next to the park. The park was partially forested and not far from where Sam had parked was a large maintenance building. Sam had unlocked the door. He and Ben were standing under a canopy of several pines near the building.

"I am Tanoak and this is my brother Hinoki. One of you must be Ben."

Tanoak locked his car and the alarm sounded.

"Tanoak, look at the black truck parked ahead of you facing this way. The man has a rifle. Unlock your car and both of you toss your weapons into it. Do it now, or he will shoot you where you are."

Frank was focused on the driver of the car. Tanoak and Hinoki both placed their handguns in the car.

"Now come up here," Sam said. "The man at the truck is not going to hurt you."

Sam pointed for them to step into the building. Tanoak had not taken his eyes off of Ben but spoke to Sam.

He said, "Please tell me that you are Ben."

Once they were in the building Ben removed his outer shirt and then his tee shirt and placed them carefully on a table in the room. Then he backed away into an open area sixteen feet by fourteen and said to Tanoak, "Make yourself ready and bring your family honor to me. As I said, I will kill you and maybe your brother too."

Tanoak walked toward Ben, his eyes never leaving Ben's.

As he came near he bowed and said, "I do not bow

because I am afraid to fight, but for my son and my wife at home. My heart says fight, but I do not believe I can win. I am ready to die, but wisdom tells me that for my family I must submit. What must Hinoki and I do? I have shamed myself forever in his eyes."

He turned and bowed to Hinoki, "I have brought shame to our family and will gladly die now if you wish."

"Brother," Hinoki said. "I am not as strong as our father. I am glad for the decision you have made. This could not happen again in our lifetimes. There can only be one man like this one, and when we are home we will never see him again. I will never tell anyone of this. You have my oath."

It was obvious Ben was touched by Tanoak's humility. He extended his hand to Tanoak and cautiously Tanoak accepted it.

"This is what happens now," Sam said. "Tanoak, you will sit here in this chair. I mean no disrespect, but you need to be sitting so you don't fall. Hinoki you will watch what happens. I am going to give you a shot that will stop your vital signs for a short time. But I promise it will not kill you. We will all leave here together. Computers at the Induction Center will see that you are dead and at that moment you will be free from this lottery forever. The two of you will go home to your families, and there will be no questions asked. You will have all of the money you made in the past, just not for this contest. We have secured tickets for your flight home, and that flight leaves in three hours.

Frank and Christine were in the building now.

"This is Frank," Sam said, "and his wife, Christine.

"Tanoak, you are going to be dead as far as the Induction Center is concerned. You should know that Christine and one other person did not want you to die. They made us promise if there was any other way we would not kill you, and I think in your country that is a sign of honor. Each of you owe your life to the ones who saved you—but there is no debt to pay.

"Christine will win this contest and because of that, she has offered to pay to send your cars home. You will leave us your keys, and I will give you an approximate arrival time for the transport ship to dock in Japan. Frank and I will ship the cars."

***

Tanoak appeared dead for a matter of seconds and his marker had a red 'X' over it as it is each time a contestant dies. Hinoki was able to see it. Christine's marker showed on monitors at the Induction Center as being with Tanoak at the time of his death.

"Men are also bound—individuals and societies—to take care of their temporal happiness and do all they lawfully can to promote it. But what can be more inconsistent with this duty than submitting to great encroachments upon our liberty? Such submission tends to slavery and complete slavery implies every evil that the malice of man and devils can inflict."

–Simeon Howard (1733-1804)

Thirteen

Sam and Ben took Tanoak and Hinoki to the airport. They both carried I.D. in their hands and walked them onto the airplane. They hoped it was true, but the brothers seemed relieved to be returning home and out from under the lottery. Tanoak did have several million dollars he had already earned.

Tom Hundley was gone. Brian Cooper was gone, Paul Elijah Thomas was gone, Vance was gone, although not a contestant, and the Yoshida brothers were on their way home to Japan. Dana's name had never been mentioned, but they were alive because of her.

Christine had taken Tanoak's car home from the park, and Jeremiah went with Frank to get Hinoki's car from the house where it was parked. The brothers took only the things they could carry to the airplane. Tanoak had been very lucky that day, and Ben too in a way. He did not want to kill Tanoak.

The Induction Center had become more powerful and punitive to contestants during the last year. It was clear that those in their offices saw themselves in just positions to give and take lives. Workers in the Induction Center were calloused as if each and every contest or death had dulled their hearts toward kindness. Once a person was in the lottery, there was only one way out—and Christine's next hunt would begin on Saturday, March 1st in thirty days.

***

Christine and her family had found everything they could on her next opponent. He was a man, and he was old.

Sam had gone with Christine and Frank to give Tom's money to his mother. Dan took them. It was a sad time, but it was a promise Christine had made.

She said to Frank, "It doesn't matter what a mother's children do, she loves them anyway."

Tom's mother had never fully recovered from losing a daughter, Tom's younger sister, to violence. She had been abducted on her way home from school by gang members, and her death was not an easy one. More than that, her attackers had been released when other gang members vowed to burn the city if their companions were not set free. People thought there was no way to recover from the lawlessness that was taking place, but thankfully that began to change in the years after.

The hatred that had been promoted during those years began 'The Hunt for Money' lottery. The government knew how to turn what they could not control into a multi-billion-dollar lottery they could control. The thought of life being valuable did not seem to have meaning. Children had been taught that hating was as much a moral right as loving, that killing was something they would never pay for with their own life, even when brutal rapes and torture were used to kill. Governments believed, some at least, that violence could be reduced on the streets if there was a place where people could do it legally. The Hunt for Money resulted from that thinking.

It was like training children in the war camps of Afghanistan, when young people in America were taught they could get anything they want by burning and looting and killing and that they would be released from jails.

In 2020, during that extraordinary fight for political power, America became more divided than it had ever been. By 2036 people were willing to settle for simply not having their businesses burned, yet they believed they were still living in a free nation. A dark cloud had settled over America.

***

Christine's next contest had the potential to be worse than any the family could have imagined. Sam thought about trying to destroy the lottery and stop 'The Hunt for Money' completely. After all, if that department of government did not exist, there would not be money paid to contestants. The problem was that there were too many agents employed by the lottery. It was impossible to know where they were. Many of them were in different states with legal power to eliminate, without trial, anyone who might break the simplest rule. And whether or not a rule had been broken was a call only they made. Could one think that type of power would not come into play as bets were being placed on contestants. It was as much out of hand as CLA had become.

To put it bluntly, most of the lottery's employees only cared about the money they earned and money they could make by betting on certain contestants. At times they would go farther and influence the outcome of a match. They possessed all of the information provided by each contestant, and unlike times gone by, when employees of a company could not enter a sweepstakes offered by that company, no rules applied to the dangerous men and woman who worked in this government lottery.

"Don, this is Daniel. I am not currently in the area, but the money you gave me assures your victory in the match against Diana Austen. I told you I suspected that they were able to know where you are. Well, now I know they can. This information is worth everything you have paid me and more. We will talk about how much more. You know that I would have been protecting your opponent, but her family refused to pay my fee. Protecting you now is the result of that. I will tell you what you need to do tonight, and you do everything I tell you. You are legal to Kill Diana Austen after 7 AM tomorrow morning. Is your grandson still willing to help?"

"Sadly enough," Don said, "for enough money he would kill his mother. He is no good, but he will do anything for me to get his part of this money."

"Okay, and thank you for the payment. It was a lot of money, but I have more than earned it with the flashlight I made for you. You remember how to use it? The prongs on the butt end will do what I said. You need to park a long way from the house. I am certain they can see your location on a computer screen. Then you must have your grandson get close enough to Diana Austen to touch her with the light and bring her to you. If he can do that in the early hours of the morning, maybe two or three, no one should hear him. I promise you, she will not make a sound. He will have to carry her to his car and bring her to you. Does he know how to break into the house and do it quietly?"

"I am sure he does. That is how he makes a living."

"How are you doing Don? Are you feeling okay? I want you to do exactly what I have said and be sure you do not kill her until after 7 am on Saturday."

"Okay, my grandson will do it for me."

"I have a new phone number." Daniel said, "It will be on your phone."

"I don't think I know how to find it, but my grandson will, and if this all works like you say there will be a bonus in it for you."

It is a pleasure doing business with you, Don, and just for you the bonus does not need to be more than another

$1,000,000. You will have over $13,000,000 after tomorrow because of the information I am giving you, and maybe you will live long enough to get one more hunt in. If so, we will talk about another idea I have. But you cannot lose if you do everything I said. Set this up with your grandson.

Daniel could not stay away from the money and the feeling of power he enjoyed by determining who would live and who would die.

***

The person who would hunt Christine next was a retired marine corporal named Don Dehoughe. He would use the deadly skills he had been taught, along with information from Daniel and the flashlight capable of creating a neurologic attack.

In one way, retired Corporal Don Dehoughe was the worst type of competitor. He was eighty-eight years old, hoping to leave the rewards of his time in the lottery to children and grandchildren. His wife had been gone for many years, and he was now terminally ill. He had nothing to lose. All of those things made him the most dangerous opponent Christine and Sam might face. In that sense, it gave Don the advantage. He had the training to hunt and kill but also was willing to die before cancer cut him down. He did not want his children and grandchildren to forget him, and he was certain a gift of $13,842,000 minus payments to Daniel would put his picture on the wall in every family member's home for years to come.

In his day Corporal Dehoughe had been part of MATS (the Marine Attack Training Squadron.) He still thought like a combat Marine. He was just older now.

***

March came in like a lion. The sun would shine, then to the modest elevation of Cimarron Street and the Conder home three inches of snow would come. But on the first day of this hunt it was pouring rain. Sam and Frank and the boys had searched for information on Corporal Dehoughe. That was the name he had given when he entered the lottery. Prior to the day of this match, Sam had sent his father to find out what he could about Christine's opponent. He was older than John, and most of the men and women who served during that time were gone. But through a friend, John found a man who claimed to have served with a Don.

Mr. Vaughn was in a rest home in Latrobe, Pennsylvania. John and Sam went to see him. The only picture they had of the Corporal was one taken in his early eighties, one he had furnished to the Induction Center.

Mr. Vaughn said it was definitely the retired Corporal.

"He was the meanest man I ever knew," he told John. "When he got to where you were standing, you went to the mat, and I mean right now. I saw one man last a couple of minutes with him. Dehoughe told the guy that he didn't know he wanted to play that serious. Then he swept his legs and gave him a straight right palm in the face, a hard one. The man's neck was broken when he hit the mat. Corporal Don didn't mean to do it, I suppose, but he knocked the guy down that hard.

He talked mostly to John. He said, "He never taught us how to subdue an enemy, only how to kill. When I was young, I could crawl through rice patties on my elbows, kill snakes with one hand, and eat rats. But I wasn't as dangerous as Dehoughe. He always said if you go half-assed into a fight you will lose every time, and he was right. I always killed. I never took a prisoner."

He told them that Don would use surprise to catch Christine off guard. He was old, and everyone knew that most contestants had someone helping them. Sometimes those protectors would be paid more than 1M dollars. There was one thing about Dehoughe's age, he would probably not engage physically. He would hope to shoot Christine, rather than kidnap her. But with his experience, he would come from nowhere to do it. Frank wanted Christine to stay in the house and not go out, but if she did that, there would be trained agents coming after her. They could see where she was at all times.

Dana and Karly were at Frank and Christine's when Sam arrived. Ben was with him. There had not been any action for a while, yet Ben was still living in the apartment they had built onto the barn.

"Frank, you are the luckiest man I know," Sam said. "I came to tell you in person that I retired from my job at NASA today."

Sam had already retired from his position as a personal guard to the President, but now he had retired from NASA.

"That makes me completely retired," he said. "Now you can quit working nights to keep me from breaking into your programs. I talked to Jason and gave my two weeks. He said he knew it was coming and told me Evelyn was ready to fill the position, that I was free to go.

"She is good, Frank. The only thing she doesn't have that makes you lucky, is that she doesn't think like you. I had to learn that."

Christine said, "Good luck. I met her at the party last year and the only thing she talked about was her work. She doesn't have another life, but if I had to guess she knows how men think."

Dana waited till Christine was finished and said, "Sam, I am proud of you. I knew it would be hard for you to quit today."

He said, "Surprisingly it wasn't. Frank is starting to lock me out of his programs well enough that I wasn't looking good. I will concentrate full-time on the lottery now."

"Let me put it this way," Sam said, "I am retired from everything to do with the government, but I will stick with Christine until this is over. We all hate talking about it, but the contest this time offers more risk than the last. We were lucky the Yoshida's submitted so easily. Of course, we had them in a no-win situation and could have ended them either way."

Ben added, "All of you need to keep Christine in this house long enough for me to find Dehoughe. Sam, I think you and Dana and the kids should stay here for the first couple of days. I can do my job better if I know you are here. We are not sure how much Dehoughe knows, but being who he is, he has been watching Christine for as long as he knew she was his next opponent. A man like him plans every move. I don't like to sound bossy, but I want you guys to stay in this house, and that means no school for the first couple of days. Sam tells me most hunts are over in that amount of time, and I want to be on the front line. Sam has saved me more than a few times and now it's my turn.

"It's crazy how Dehoughe is always moving and never in the same place twice. I wonder if it is possible for him to know we can track him? Could be that the way he never stops is part of his training even though that was sixty years ago."

"Dad, I've been watching this guy," Liam said. "He is in the area but not close to us. He has driven by the house a couple of times, but maybe he doesn't want to start this as fast as we think. He is south of us right now, driving farther away. Maybe he forgot where we live."

Sam said, "I won't leave the house, Ben. I'll work like CENTCOM for you. You have to sleep sometime, but I am sure you will get him the first day. You won't have to watch the screen, and I will tell you every move he makes. You can use your phone when you are close and move in on him. He will make a mistake. He has to stop sometime, and everybody makes mistakes."

"As long as he is heading south," Ben said, "I am not going after him—not unless he stops and might be sleeping. If he does, I will tie him up and call you. It isn't likely, but Daniel might have had something we didn't find and be working for this guy. If he is, he will die next time I catch him."

"Liam," Frank said, "if we do see Dehoughe stop for any length of time, like at a store, see if you can get into the cameras quickly enough to see him. I want to see him up close. And if you do, we need to tell Ben as fast as we can.

"Ben needs to know what Don is wearing and what his profile would look like in passing. Jeremiah, Jeff, same for you guys. We have to stop him. I hate to say it like this, but we have to kill him. And we cannot be sure he is not wearing a disguise.

"Also, someone at the top could have a lot of money bet on him. We know what they did to Tom Hundley. If they are taking sides, we need to be aware that they could turn his marker on and off, but probably not. I don't know why they would."

Sam said, "Let's not worry a lot about this. Worry can take a person's edge away. Ben is out there, and he is one of the best. He will get this guy. Even if Christine cannot be there to get the money."

"Well, that settles it then," Jeff said. "If no one wants the 13M I will take it—but not, of course," he said smiling, "if it puts Mom's life at stake."

Dana looked at Jeff and said, "Jeff, I'm glad you are the calm one, because I am scared to death. But with Ben out there and Sam with us I am not going to be afraid."

Jeremiah and Karly were at the ranch. Sam could lock it up tightly, so Dana said they could stay there for the night. Sam told Jeremiah about the electric fence and that he would turn it on, as well as the alarm system. Jeremiah would call if the alarm went off and Sam had already given him the combination to one of the gun safes.

That night and the next day went pretty well. Everyone except Sam had calmed down. It was obvious that Sam did not like being at the house while Ben was out on the road, and he told Ben that.

"Ben, why don't you come in for a few hours, and I will go out."

The answer was what Sam knew it would be, "Sam, I've

got this. It is best for Christine if you are at the house."

Sam knew Ben would not have a problem stopping Don, so he said okay.

"I am tempted to take off after him," Ben said, "He is still down on highway 219 to the south. He is driving around as if he doesn't know where he is. I feel like this is going to be easy, but given the amount of money he is worth, I can't take him out till seven in the morning and not without you being close by with Christine. It will be dark soon. When it gets close to morning, call me. I am within a mile of the house. We will take Christine and go get him. He can't get away from us."

"Okay Ben. Thanks. I know you are not doing this for the money, but Christine plans to give you a nice payday when it's over. It will be enough to buy the place you always wanted."

"I'm going to watch him through the night, "Ben said. "Get some sleep, and in the morning we will end this. You are a legend around guys who have fought with you. We will get this guy.

"Okay, if you need to get a little sleep, call me. Dana and I are sleeping on couches in the living room, and I sure don't mind getting up and watching."

Ben decided that if Dehoughe stopped driving, he might be getting some sleep, and if he did that Ben would go get him and hold him till morning. There was no way to go after him while he was awake without the risk of having to kill him before legal time.

Frank and Christine and the boys went to bed. Frank said he would be awake off and on watching Don's location and told Sam to get some sleep.

"He is right, Honey," Dana said to Sam. "With Ben out there, we should get some sleep. You and Ben can go after him in the morning."

Sam kissed Dana and went to the other couch. He laid down with his laptop and a rifle on the floor. Dehoughe was still south of them near Newberg. Sam slept through most of the night with his cell phone on the arm of the couch, but at 5 AM he was awake. He looked for messages on his phone then went to the guest bathroom to take a shower.

***

Don's grandson watched through a living room curtain as Sam left the living room. If only Frank and Christine would have had a dog, or if Frank would have installed security cameras when Liam suggested it.

The grandson pressed a credit card he had stolen into the edge of the door and the door quietly opened. He left the door opened and moved toward Dana. He touched the prongs of the flashlight against her face. It instantly caused Dana to not be able to move or make a sound. He carried her as fast as he could out the door, closing it gently. It was easier than he thought it would be. He ran with Dana out the walkway and along Cimarron Street to his parked car. With her in the car, he took off as fast as he dared toward where his grandfather was waiting.

Sam was enjoying a hot shower, and everyone else in the house was asleep. The living room door was closed again, and Don Dehoughe's marker showed on Ben's laptop to be moving northward on Highway 219.

Ben's phone rang. It was Sam.

"Ben, Dana is gone. I took a shower, and she is nowhere in the house. Go after Dehoughe no matter where he is. I'm coming. I will be after his location. Just go."

"He has not been here," Ben said, "but he is moving this way. I'm serious. He has never been up here."

"Go get him, Ben. I have to get Christine up. If possible wound Dehoughe and kill him when we are close. Put your vest on. Don't take any chances."

"Frank, Christine, get up—fast."

"What is it, Sam?" Frank landed on the floor and pulled his pants on and bolted out the bedroom door.

"Dana is gone. She is not in the house."

Christine heard Sam and jumped into her clothes. She laid them close before going to bed, knowing she might have to get up fast.

"Did you look on the back deck?" She might be by the creek praying."

"She is gone, Christine. Ben is after Dehoughe. Someone has to be working with him and took Dana. I shouldn't have left her in the living room."

Liam and Jeff were up and in the living room, Jeff in his shorts still pulling his pants on.

Liam said, "We have to call Jeremiah. They have to know."

Sam said, "Frank, you have to come to communicate with Ben and tell me where the turns are. Christine, get anything you need and let's go. Liam, call your mom's phone if you need to tell us anything. Please stay here guys, and tell Jeremiah to bring Karly and get over here."

"Should I tell them their mom is gone?"

"Yes. Be honest." Sam said. "We need them praying for her as soon as possible. Frank, it's time for you guys to think about that."

"Okay."

Frank had said that without even thinking. He had never prayed or acknowledged God at any time in his life, nor had Christine.

Liam said without thinking, "Save her Lord. Please help."

Then he said to his dad, "Go get her Dad. Go."

At that moment he had turned to his dad rather than Sam.

Jeff would ask Liam later if he had ever prayed before and admitted that when he heard him do it he also asked God to help Dana.

"They cannot have more than a fifteen-minute head start," Sam said. And he was out the door, carrying the rifle he had retrieved from under the front of the couch.

"Ben, this is Frank. I am running copilot for Sam. Christine is with us. We are just getting onto 219 heading south. Where are you?"

"I'm on 219. I just passed a road coming in from the west called Blooming."

"We are not that far behind you. Sam is doing… a little over ninety. We should catch up with you."

"Only if I slow down," Ben said. "Do you need to catch up with me or should I keep going?"

"It doesn't look like Dehoughe is going fast," Frank said. "We will catch him easily before seven. He surely won't do anything to her before then."

Frank's phone was on speaker. "Ben, this is Sam. There are things whoever took her could do before seven. I want this man dead. We do not care about seven o'clock or money. Kill them both. There must be someone with him."

"Okay Sam, I am doing well over 100. I will get them."

"Be careful, Ben. I don't need to tell you. He has my wife Ben, and it is almost seven."

Sam was fighting to keep his composure. All the talking he had done with Jeff about not losing one's edge. The next thing he said was to himself, asking God to forgive him.

"Ben, if you haven't passed it," Frank said, "turn left onto Scholls. He is going toward 99W."

The Tualatin River National Wildlife Refuge was only a few miles from Dehoughe's location.

Text from Liam: "Mom, he is heading to 99W toward the wildlife refuge. Are you on him?"

Christine: "Yes. Scary fast. Your dad is watching."

"Karly," Liam said, "they are about to catch him and your mom will be safe."

Jeremiah was sitting in a kitchen chair with his head bowed praying, and Karly, if she was praying, was doing it through a river of tears. Her hands were shaking uncontrollably. Jeremiah grabbed her chair and as if it weighed five pounds with her in it pulled her tight against his side. Without a word said he put his arm around her, fighting his own tears.

"Frank, I have a car ahead of me. There are only two people in it. I could see them in the lights of an oncoming tractor-trailer. The one driving is a big guy, and the other is a woman. That's all I could tell."

"I think we see you," Frank said. "We just met a truck. Touch your brakes—Yes, we are right behind you, Ben! Sam wants to say something."

"Ben, it's getting close to seven. What can we do? Help

me. Should you pass and get him between us?"

"No—No—Hold it," Ben said. "He is slowing down. He is signaling to turn left onto a gravel road."

"I know the road, Ben. I just turned my lights off. I am nearly on your bumper. When he turns you keep going straight, and he might not know I am back here. I will follow him with my lights off. Turn around when he is out of your sight and come back. Be loaded.

"Sorry Ben. Everything you have is loaded. If you can turn around and still see him take the shot."

"Good luck," Ben replied. "Take any shot you get Sam. You are the best. I have never seen you miss. You've got this, Sam. I mean it. Stay calm."

There was no more talk. Christine had seen Dana looking back when Ben's lights were close behind them, and it was Dana for sure.

"If Dana can talk," Christine said, "Dehoughe is hearing her message about God. I hope she doesn't make him mad."

"I seriously doubt if a man with his experience will allow himself to get mad, and right now he needs to hear what she is telling him. He is within minutes of dying."

Text from Jeremiah to Christine: "We can see you right by him. What's going on? Has Sam shot him?"

Text from Christine: "Not yet. They are moving, but we can see your mom. She is okay."

Jeremiah never raised his voice but was fighting not to. "It's almost seven. He could shoot Mom in his car."

"They are leaving the road now. No more talk." Christine silenced her phone.

Fourteen

Corporal Don Dehoughe had been hearing about Dana's faith since his grandson pushed her into his car and shut the door. His grandson, Joel, had wanted to go and watch her be killed, but Don said no and left him at his car. He said he would call when it was over. And fortunately for some, whoever they might be, Don took the flashlight from Joel.

After several comments Joel made to Dana while she was in her pajamas, she was certain she was better off with Don. Don would kill her, that was almost certain, but however he did that it would be a better way to die.

As they drove, Don told Dana that after the first two he killed, he wished he had never bought the ticket. War was one thing, but he knew it wasn't right to kill for money. Dana told him she was Christine's sister and not Christine. She told him he would not get paid for killing her. But, of course he didn't believe what she said. He had sent his grandson to Christine's house. This had to be her, and she looked like the picture he had seen.

Dana told Don why her sister bought the ticket.

"Christine bought the lottery ticket to help my family," she said, "CLA took two of my children after my husband died, and I didn't have enough money to pay them."

"I don't believe you, and I would lie too if I was in your place. The only reason I brought you this far is because it's out of the way, and I cannot kill you before seven. But you have—and Don looked at the clock on the dash of his car—three minutes. I suppose it's possible, that I am struggling with killing you. You talk a good story about God, and I respect that. Although, he has never done anything for me, certainly not given my family millions of dollars like I will be able to do.

"I never amounted to much money wise. My kids followed suit, and my grandkids are even worse. I have given them millions already and they blew every penny. But I told my oldest daughter this time would bring $13,000,000, and that would be the last of it. She knows I am dying. I have been given only a few weeks to live. I have already outlived my friends and lived through the war in Vietnam.

"Here we are Diana. I found this place yesterday."

They were at the end of the road and Don said, "Get out. Let's get this over with."

He told her to crawl over the console and come out his side so she couldn't run. He said if she didn't, he would shoot her right in the car. He stepped out holding a military Colt 1911 in his right hand.

Dana had cried so many times about happy things as well as sad but not now. She knew there was no way out and that she was about to be killed.

Text from Jeff on Christine's phone: "Have you killed him yet? What's going on?"

No answer.

Sam knew that if he did one thing wrong, Dana would be dead. She was in the driver's seat now, on her knees with Corporal Don Dehoughe offering his left hand to help her out of the car. Then a voice rang out from fifty yards away.

"Corporal Dehoughe. My name is Diana Austen. You have my sister and will not get paid if you kill her. Her name is Dana. I am the one you want. I'm coming to you. I know you will make $13,000,000 when you kill me. I know Nancy Lee, and I know Aaden Bradly. You will be guilty of murdering a woman if you kill Dana."

Christine had gotten out of the back seat of Sam's car and was running toward Dehoughe as fast as she could.

Sam was out also but could not squeeze the trigger while Don's gun was pointing at Dana from just inches away, and then he saw Christine in his scope. She was directly in line between him and his target. Sam could only hope Don would not shoot until Dana was out of the car. Dehoughe could see the dome light and was looking right at them, but he couldn't see Sam outside of the car.

Christine made it to within twenty yards of Don's car, and he swung with his .45 towards her.

The sound was deafening. The muzzle flash blinding.

Dana had been screaming at Don not to shoot her sister, but now the deadly sound of gunfire penetrated through the protected wildlife sanctuary in front of them. The sound was amplified in the early morning. Christine was lying on the ground—and Dehoughe had fallen at the same time without ever hearing the shot that killed him.

The mistake Don Dehoughe and Christine had made by entering the lottery had cost Don his life, and he never saw the man who ended it. Dana was out of the car running toward Christine. Sam was already kneeling beside her. At the last second, Christine had realized the path she was running in put her in front of Sam. Sam was rested with his rifle on the roof of the car, and she dived to the ground.

At the sound of the shot, headlights appeared on the highway again. It was Ben. He was coming fast to where they were parked. He knew Sam would win this fight.

Sam had served in Afghanistan as commander of a SEAL team following the 9/11 attack on America. And after those years had been employed by the United States Secret Service. As he looked at the retired Corporal lying on the ground, he realized how sad it was. It was caused only by a willingness to kill for money, but Dehoughe had not died in a bed with his boots off.

Sam felt the burden of so many wars he had been involved in. Most of them involving one man against another as he protected the president and other important persons. Sometimes for causes that he wasn't certain of. What he always did know is that it was the right thing to do. It was his role in life to protect others.

Daylight began to expose the beauty of the wild, forested area where they stood, to everyone except Corporal Dehoughe. A new day would offer choices to do what was right or to do what was wrong. Sam had never felt the forty years of fighting to protect others more than he did now. Christine and Dana had been in a place where they could both have been killed. Dana plunged herself into Sam's arms. There was a trickle of blood running down Christine's forehead. She had landed hard in the gravel as she fell, almost not soon enough to clear Sam's line of sight.

Christine moved closer to Don's lifeless body. It was hard for her to do. Sam knew he had to instantly stop Dehoughe's ability to think or to pull the trigger, and he had done it with precise accuracy.

When they arrived home, John and Julie were there with the kids. They walked into the house, and John went directly to Sam. He put his hand on his shoulder and said, "I'm sorry, Son."

Christine had already called and told them Don was dead.

Julie came with a damp paper towel and began wiping blood from Christine's wound. Frank had a hard time letting go of Christine's hand long enough for Julie and Dana to get close. This lottery was a trying time. A desperate time.

"I love you, Baby. What would I ever do without you?" Frank said.

Then John said to Julie, "Stop cleaning her wound. There is something we need to do. If your doctor can meet you at the hospital, she could write this up as a bullet wound received from an opponent and in the next few weeks it could be said to have caused a life-threatening infection. We need some time. This is making an old man out of me."

Teri would write a statement for Christine to be released from the lottery, even if temporarily. It could get her out of the next match if not two.

Julie called Teri Thornburg's personal phone and Teri asked her to bring Christine directly to her office rather than to emergency. She opened early for them. There were pictures taken of the wound and of blood on Christine's head and face. Teri's report gave detailed information stating that Christine was a contestant in the lottery and described the wound to her head as being from a .45 caliber, round-nosed bullet.

Sam called a friend, and as a local police officer he was able to meet them at Teri's office and file a report for the firearms related wound. The report stated the exact location where Dehoughe had engaged Christine. The record would state that before Christine fatally wounded Don Dehoughe, he had fired one shot which hit angularly, tumbling off of Christine's head. He would write that the ammunition was very old and did not break the frontal bone.

The wound looked authentic. When Christine fell onto the gravel she hit her forehead hard on a rounded rock. It made an impression looking as if a .45 ACP FMJ bullet had grazed her. Teri's report of infection would come later, and Christine would take as much time off as she could.

***

"This is Nancy Lee. Is this Christine?"

"Yes, Hi Nancy."

"Christine, I am looking at a medical report I received three weeks ago. I will be honest. I think you are stalling. Your doctor states that you have cepticemia, or a bacterial presence in your blood that could lead to inflammation in all of your body. I am going to demand that you get an opinion from another doctor. I am not sure I can legally do that but let me tell you something. If I find that you are falsifying information I will send one of our agents to talk with you. Do you understand what I am saying?"

"Nancy, I wish we could be on better terms. This is serious for me as well. What effect do you think an infection could have on my baby?"

"That is not my problem Christine. My problem is that I must arrange contests in this lottery. I have other contestants to think of as well as you—you and a baby that isn't even born yet."

"I guess I can only ask you not to send those agents after me, and you would probably be in a lot of trouble if you did. The rules state clearly that in the case of wounds received during a contest, where one contestant dies and the other lives, the survivor must be allowed time to recover."

"I do not like your tone Christine. You need to be careful with me. In this lottery I have no one above me. My decisions stand, and I will do to you whatever I need to do."

"Nancy, I believe you, and I believe you are a fair person. Otherwise, you would not have risen to the top like you have. Please give me a little more time. I will heal from this and be back."

"I am going to give you until the end of this month, and then I am not sure what I will do. But remember this: you will not know what I decide to do until I do it. If I were you, I would seriously consider getting back in the game. Goodbye Christine."

Nancy hung the phone up. It was her way of getting the last word in. Christine did not know that agents were not about to eliminate her prior to the PPV event. Nancy Lee believed Christine had hired a professional team to protect her and kill for her. Otherwise she would not be alive. Nancy was sure she would have the last laugh when Christine was forced to enter the PPV event. She would be an eight-month pregnant woman in a controlled area where her bodyguards could not go. Nancy was sick and believed that she alone controlled life and death.

***

"I heard you talking to Nancy," Frank said. "It sounds like she is suspicious."

"I'm afraid of her, and I will be honest. I wish Sam or Ben would send her straight to Hell."

"You say that as if you believe there is a Hell. Do you?"

"I don't know. Dana makes a good case for God and Heaven and Hell. She probably doesn't talk to you like that."

"Actually, she does," Frank said, "just never when there is anyone around."

"Well, good for her. That's the way to do it. I will say one thing; she really believes in what she says."

It was just one week until the next hunt. Christine had spent her sixth month in pregnancy away from the lottery. Seven weeks in all since Don Dehoughe was eliminated, and now she received a letter from the Induction Center telling her she would be required to return. The letter said she had already been matched with an opponent. It was unbelievable for the Conder and Morrison families that Christine would be required to face an opponent in now her seventh month of pregnancy but it was happening. They had seen her opponent on the website. Her name was Ivonne Bykov. She was thirty years old and worked on one of nine fishing boats her father owned. Nancy Lee emailed Christine to say she was doing her a favor by scheduling this match. She said Ivonne was less experienced and would be an easy hunt. Had she been speaking rather than writing, you would have heard sarcasm in her voice.

***

"Honey, Nancy said my next hunt was with a hunter who has not been doing this for long. Her name is Ivonne Bykov and she works on a commercial fishing boat. She said our worst problem could be finding each other. She is trying to get me back in the hunt and is offering a huge amount of money this time.

I have a tour along the Inside Passage when this hunt begins, but I think commercial boats stay out in the ocean. She will not have a way to know where I am."

"Sounds like a Russian name. What happens if she has family who helps her like Sam does you?"

"I hadn't thought about that."

***

"Ivonne, this is Daniel. You failed to wire the money we talked about."

"You get your money when my dad comes into port in three days."

"I better, or I will tell Diana Austen where to find you

when the hunt starts. She would pay me well for that, and I am not afraid of your father. You tell him that. I will see that money on or before Thursday or move my loyalty to your opponent. Your job is finding fish Ivonne, mine is finding people. You know very well that Diana Austen killed her last three opponents like they were children, and that's because I helped her."

Daniel had worked for only one year at the Induction Center but left after he and Aaden had an argument. In one contest Aaden bet more than he had on an opponent. Then Daniel used personal information from Aaden's phone calls to change the outcome. They went their separate ways, but Daniel was still meddling and gambling in the lottery. The only difference was that he was on the outside and not the inside. No matter what Nancy or her staff did, Daniel knew who the contestants were and personal information about them. He would then sell his services to both sides, pretending to favor each. He claimed that contestants he helped had never lost. And, of course, and no one could prove otherwise.

***

"Honey," Christine said, "when I leave for the inside passage, see if you can get a few days off. If that Ivonne woman is working on a fishing boat she would not be at ports where I will be, but I would like to have you with me. Maybe Sam or John can find out what boat she is on and where it is. I want to stay a long way away from her."

The reality of Christine's next hunt was beginning to set in. There was a good chance she could be in the Inside Passage with a person who knew every inch of that territory. Frank had been right about Nancy Lee from the beginning, and Christine hoped she would never have to speak to her again. Worse than that, she had a bad feeling about this contest. Not only had Nancy lied in order to sound like she was giving Christine something, but Christine already felt the fear of coming face to face with a woman who fished on the ocean. She pictured her weighing 220 pounds and having 22 inch biceps.

***

"Christine, this is Daniel. I would like to talk to you about something. Do you have a minute?"

"Sure. Frank and I are just talking about how to get me out of this lottery, and we were planning to call you about reloading the glove in case that doesn't happen."

Christine did not let on that she knew what Ben had done to Daniel and that Daniel was supposed to be a long way from this lottery. And Daniel did not know Christine was associated with Ben.

"You used it already?" Daniel knew perfectly well she had. He knew Paul Thomas was dead and that a man associated with him was found dead in the same house with his hands tied behind his back and a plastic garbage bag over his head.

"You work fast," he said. "We could meet somewhere and I would refill the needle. I wear a mask and have special gloves for that now, and I bought a reserve of the toxins from my contacts. It's very expensive. More than it was last time."

Daniel had no intention of refilling her glove with the real toxins.

Christine told Daniel that Westman's Adventure Outlet was not far from where they lived and that meeting in the outer area of the parking lot would work for them. Daniel agreed to meet later that day. Ironically, they would park below the same flashing billboard that had gotten Christine into the trouble she was in.

Refilling the glove looked much easier than Daniel made it sound, and Frank caught himself wondering if he was foolishly trusting a man that neither of them had believed since they met him. But Sam did not want to ask Ben to kill Daniel yet, not before they knew what he was doing.

Daniel said, "Christine, I am glad you guys decided to let me build the glove. There are not many people I would trust with something like this, and it brings me to a question. I have been thinking about helping you in other ways. I shared with you that I have access to the same information my brother has at the Induction Center. I know you have made several million dollars already.

"For me, it is comforting to know you are only

eliminating bad people, who unlike you really want to kill for money. Ivonne Bykov comes from such a family. Her father has put several people into crab pots and dropped them overboard into the Bearing Sea, and without my help I am afraid you could be one of his victims. Ivonne's family would find you easily, but I can turn that around. The problem is—well, I do not want to be offensive, but my knowledge is worth a lot of money. And your life even more.

"I know you will earn $17,914,000 if you survive this contest against the Bykov family. And yes I mean family. I know of her father and brothers. I have done a lot of research. I know it will be worth a lot for you to retain my services again. Her father, Leonid, is a very powerful man. His sons are ruthless killers, and Ivonne has killed four already in this lottery.

"Because of the circumstances I will ask $1,000,000 in advance and in turn will keep you informed almost hourly of where she and her brothers and her father are. You cannot know where they are without me. They will find you, and it would not be pretty to get captured by her brothers. I know where they are right now. I am sorry to be so formal, but I am concerned for your safety. You are about to be hunted by the most dangerous family you can imagine."

"That is a lot of money," Frank said. "We will not make the decision now, but I will call you tomorrow."

Frank was certain he and Sam with Ben and John's help could find the same information Daniel could find. And he trusted Daniel less now than before. Frank was anxious to tell Ben he was back and involved in the lottery again.

As they drove away from the parking lot, the daunting billboard flashed: "Enter The Hunt for Money—$703,649,000—Win—Win—Win…"

Christine had never felt more like this hunt could be her last, and by an extraordinary ability to picture things in her mind she envisioned a marble headstone. It read: "The Lottery Ticket 2035—Here lies Christine Conder—1998-2036."

Frank called Daniel that evening, "Daniel, I feel like you have us in a situation here, but you are asking too much money. Christine has done well so far, and she may even get out of the lottery. She is talking with people there. I'm sorry, but we are not going to pay you to protect us. We do not even know if you can."

"And would that be Nancy she is talking with? You are making a mistake Frank. And I am afraid this one will cost you. Your wife is worth far more than the price I asked, but it is your choice. I do feel obligated to tell you that the Bykov family has offered me the same amount. I hope this will not be the end of our friendship. I was hoping to be on your team."

Daniel did not know anything about the Bykov family, other than that they were fishermen. But there was one thing for sure—Daniel Bradley was a dangerous man, and he would turn on the Conder family.

***

"Liam, where is your mom?" Frank said.

"She is out by the creek. She is feeling pretty bad right now. Sam called today to see if I found anything on Ivonne Bykov. I looked at her kills, and they say she choked a man to death with her bare hands. Sam is going to feel pretty stupid having to kill a woman."

"We cannot believe any of that Son. They also think your mom has killed all of her opponents. They only record what they are told. Ivonne is probably not that tough. Her kills were probably done by some Russian fisherman that can pick up cars."

"You ought to see her," Liam said. "I saved a picture. She is on the deck of a crab boat wrestling about a seven-hundred-pound steel crab pot. Her family owns a business named Bykov Crabbing, and all of their boats have live video on deck. It still amazes me how many businesses don't think about things. The wheelhouse has a camera, and while it watches the controls and gauges, the operator's laptop is sitting right there. All I had to do is get into the camera and over the period of a couple of hours; I saw several passwords they entered. The vessel I was watching is named KSENIA один. The KSENIA boats are numbered one through nine. KSENIA один is operated by

Leonid Bykov and sure enough Ivonne Bykov is on that boat."

"You ought to be up for an award for the way you do this," Frank said.

"Guess what else I got? I have the passwords to what looks like a business bank account and a personal bank account, both in Leonid's name. And this guy has some serious money. Ivonne's only reason to be in the lottery must be so she can buy her own boat, or maybe to prove something to her father."

"You forget those passwords. We are not thieves."

"Yeah. I just think we could control the Bykov family if we locked up their millions and told them to keep their daughter or sister or whoever she is away from my mom."

"Our whole family could get killed is more like it," Frank said.

"That may be true. You and Mom have a lot of money in the bank that you never had before. We need to get Mom out and be happy with what we have. I think there must be some way to use this to our advantage.

Frank said, "Sam should be here any minute. He wants to talk about Mom going on the tour to Alaska."

Frank praised Liam again for finding so much information on the Bykov family. Sam and Dana stayed for dinner, and they talked about what Liam had found. They also discussed the leverage they could have on the Bykov family if they changed the passwords on Leonid's accounts. They would not take any money, but there could be a way to use this.

Frank asked Liam if there would be a way to trace the person or computer that was used to change the passwords. Liam assured him there was not, that he could change them using an untraceable webserver.

"Wait a minute," Sam said. "When Daniel tried to intimidate you for not paying him, he said Ivonne had offered the same amount of money. What if she really refused to pay him, and that is why he came to you? Daniel would be the perfect suspect to the one who locked their accounts."

"You are right," Frank said.

"Dad, I can change those passwords in just minutes. What could it hurt if they cannot track it to us? I think it could work and make them unable to focus on anything else—like Mom. It might even put Daniel on the run."

"Do it, Son. I am afraid of Daniel. He is undoubtedly doing dishonest business with the Bykov's, and they would go after him instead of us, at least for a while.

"And check this out," Liam said. "You can use a VPN and send an email as if it was from Daniel to Ivonne, telling her you will lock her father's accounts if she doesn't pay more money. They would reply to your ghost email, and we would know what they were doing. We will make it sound like he wants more."

"Never do anything against conscience even if the state demands it."

--Albert Einstein (1879-1955)

Fifteen

There was a knock on the door at John and Julie's house. Julie answered, "Daniel, what brings you here today?"

"I need to talk to you and John about something. Is John here?"

"Yes, he is downstairs. Come in. I will get him."

John came into the room and reached for Daniel's hand as he greeted him. Daniel was standing with his side toward John and Julie, pretending to look out of a window beside the door. When he turned to meet John's extended hand he held a silenced handgun. On the end of the barrel was a Silent Air-9 silencer. The handgun's magazine held 17 rounds of subsonic, 147 grain hollow point cartridges.

"John, something has come up in my relationship with Frank and Christine. I know they are not your family but having met your son only one time, I have reason to be afraid of him. I think he is helping Christine, and you are my best way to handle this matter. I went looking and found out who he is. My job is finding people. I could shoot both of you right now and not even arouse the neighbors, but I don't want to do that. I only want you for a short time while I negotiate an offer I made to Frank. When he gives me the money I want, I will leave the country for good. Come with me, and please John do not make me shoot Julie. I will if I have to."

When they got to Daniel's car, he directed Julie to sit in the back, on the passenger side where he could see her. He drove and John was in the opposite front seat. Being a negotiator in his career, John talked to Daniel about stopping what he was doing without serious consequences. He said they were very willing to forgive him because of what he had done to help Christine. But Daniel was focused and John had seen that before. The shutdown to sound reasoning is common in men who do not plan to surrender. Within an hour they were parked in front of River Sound Yachts on the waterfront just east of the Interstate Bridge.

Daniel warned them again, "Do not cause me to shoot you. You know that I will."

John asked Daniel to tell him a little about the problem he was having with Frank and Christine, as if to distance himself, and offered to help if there was something he could do.

He said, "If I ask them to pay you, I am certain they would. They have a lot of money now. A payout here and there is part of this type of business, and the matter would be settled."

Daniel said, "John, I like you, but I am a smart man. I have taken the side of Christine's opponent, although she hasn't paid me yet. But she will. Frank should have paid me, and all of this would be over, but now I have no choice but to help Ivonne Bykov. I will tell her where Christine is, and that brings me to you. You are not a problem to me, but Sam is. I only checked you for weapons because I know you carry one, and I do not want you to shoot me. We are going to go for a ride on my yacht. Then I am going to call Sam. He will come for you, and I will kill him. From what I know of him, he would hunt me for the rest of my life unless I kill him. You are just an old man John, and I am not afraid of you."

"Christine could not live anyway," Daniel continued. "My Brother is planning her elimination as we speak. She will either be killed in the PPV event, or my brother will have her killed before it is over. Would anyone think such a crooked lottery would pay $100,000,000? They will have a check and a real one for the cameras, but there will not be anyone left to receive it.

And for a measly 1M dollars Christine's husband would not allow me to save her and turn this around."

Daniel put the handgun in the front of his pants and slightly pulled his jacket over it, but he kept his hand on the gun.

"Stop John! This is my boat. Please use the ladder and be careful. And don't be stupid. I'm sure you understand that I only need one of you."

John walked up the ladder first then reached back to help Julie. But there was a man standing in the boat's cabin. He was most likely a friend of Daniel's, but John was smart and had to take the chance. He could play this either of two ways and end up dead.

He reached up, as if to scratch his cheek and put his finger to his lips for the man in the cabin to see. He was taking a big chance. Daniel had told John about Ivonne Bykov and his request for money not being met. The man in the cabin was wearing a hat embossed with the name, KSENIA один, and he was holding a short barreled shotgun.

While Julie was on the ladder John said, "Daniel, you haven't told me what you will do to Ivonne if her family doesn't pay you."

Knowing that it would not matter, Daniel chuckled out loud.

He said, "You would be a good partner John. You always think ahead. I would kill her, and it would look like Christine did it. I cannot lose either way. Her father is a stupid fisherman and would never know how it happened."

Daniel took his hand off of the gun and reached for both rails on the ladder. When he stepped onto the deck, a phone rang inside the cabin. Then Ruslin Bykov, Leonid's son, appeared in the cabin door. He was holding the shotgun in one hand and his phone in the other. He motioned Daniel to stand against the rear cabin wall. On the other end of the conversation John had heard a weathered voice say the name Ruslin. The younger man listened then turned the phone off and put it in his pocket.

From John's time in government he spoke Russian fluently. Then in Ruslin's native language, he said, "The Lion Man—He was talking to you on the phone? You heard what this man is planning. He is taking my wife and me to kill us. We know many things about him. He lies to people and takes money from them."

Ruslin's laugh sounded like his father's voice, as if their vocal cords had been frozen in the cruel winds of the Arctic Sea.

He spoke English as well as John spoke Russian and held Daniel's gun now. He had instructed Daniel not to say a single word, and Daniel was sure Ruslin meant it. Daniel stood still and remained silent.

Ruslin said to John in Russian, "I do not know who you are, but God brought you with this man to me for your safety. You and your wife can go. This other man—my father tells me he has taken money from us. My father has been heading this way for more than one week to fish herring in Alaska's Area 1 in the southeast. But he did not know till today what Daniel did. When we meet there Daniel will give our money back."

Ruslin looked at John and said in English, "My father is

the one who named me. He is Leonid, like the lion. I am sorry for Daniel. He will suffer for what he has done, but you are my friend."

John shook hands with the hard, muscled fisherman and asked him to wish his father well. He said, "Please tell your father that John Morrison will be indebted to him forever, until a time when he can pay back."

John went down first and stood firmly at the base of the ladder as Julie came down. He then thought about not having a vehicle and asked Ruslin if he could have the keys to Daniel's car. Daniel produced them instantly and tossed them to John. He was not willing to offer any resistance to a man with a shotgun aimed at his stomach, yet he believed when John and Julie were gone, he would convince Ruslin to let him go. To Daniel lying was a simple matter of doing business.

John did not know Liam had changed two of Leonid's passwords blocking him from the bank accounts, but this family was certain Daniel was the one who locked their money up.

John walked Julie to the car. Along with appreciating the fact that they were alive; he was thinking about what Ruslin said, "God brought you with this man to me."

John had asked for Leonid's phone number so he might thank him in person for sending his son to stop Daniel. When Ruslin took the keys from Daniel, he asked John in Russian if

Daniel had anything else of theirs. He then handed them their cell phones and Daniel's. Daniel had purchased a new phone the same day Ben Bonoski took his, and John would find a new laptop in the car.

There was one thing certain about what had happened. Daniel was the only one responsible for the situation he was in. He would not need his phone or car again.

***

It was getting late when John and Julie arrived at Frank and Christine's. Julie had called Sam, learning he and Dana were at Frank's already. When they arrived, they told everyone about Daniel planning to kill Sam and about Ruslin. They also said they had two things they had not left home with earlier. One was Daniel's phone and the other was Liam's car. That statement was followed by a brief silence.

Liam looked out the front window and saw a 2036 Cadillac CT9-VX in the driveway. Its black, waxed color perfectly reflected the pillars on the porch.

He said, "What's the catch? That's a $140,000 car. Who does it belong to?"

John told his and Julie's story and said Daniel had given him the keys, which wasn't a lie. He did fib a little and said Daniel was certain he would never drive the car again and wanted Liam to have it.

Understanding what had happened Christine said to

Liam, "Just say thank you."

They all walked out to see the car, and Liam said, "Tell me how this car is mine."

John said, "You have earned it, Liam. But first do your homework and see if Daniel has any children who should have it. He told us when we first met that he wasn't married, but you look into that. If there are no children, I know he would want me to get the title from his house and sign it over to you. His signature is on the registration, and I know someone who can sign it better than he did. He looked at Christine."

"Liam," Julie said, "you have done an incredible amount of work to help other people. If Daniel does not come home in a week or two, we will know his terrible life has cost him everything."

***

It was early on a Wednesday morning when Ruslin pulled the beautiful yacht alongside his father's fishing boat in the Gulf of Alaska. They were only a few miles offshore from Sitka. The ceiling was no higher than 100 feet as Leonid lowered a skiff from his fishing boat. He landed and tied off to Daniel's yacht. Once onboard, he could see how his son had treated the thief who would dare to take money from them. Understanding his son's strength and confidence, he knew Daniel's face had not been beaten to such a condition while he was tied to the chair. Ruslin would not beat a man with his hands tied. Daniel was a coward and had never faced men like these. He had been a coward when Ben questioned him, and he should have quit then. He was given every chance.

Leonid went into the cabin and brought out another chair. Then he untied Daniel. He handed him a pen and a small tablet and said, "Write for me the passwords you made for my bank accounts."

Through swollen, bloody lips Daniel said, "I do not know what you are talking about. Doesn't it make sense that I would tell you now, knowing what you can do to me."

"You are a stubborn man," Leonid said. For you to give me the numbers would only be for my convenience. When I get home, my attorneys will open the accounts. In Russia we do not be fooled and put up with things like you do in America."

Leonid spoke to Daniel again, "I am old, but you are free to fight me now. Who knows, maybe you will defeat me and swim to the shore, but it is April, and these waters are very cold. Maybe I will let you try that instead of putting you in a wire cage. We are only a few miles from land. The water is a little above freezing, and you might be strong enough to make it."

Daniel was starting to panic. He said, "You will be caught. They will find my boat and look for me. Your son's fingerprints are on everything."

In a last desperate act, he lunged at Leonid. But took a hard a blow in the stomach with the strength Leonid would use to stop a sliding crab pot on an icy deck in the winter season. Daniel fell to the deck on his knees struggling to breath. Leonid picked up his feet and Ruslin his arms, and they dropped him over the rail. What followed was the most fearful situation a person can know. Daniel still had no air and was not able to scream or even swear. With his clothes on, he swam only ten yards from the boat and turned around. He tried to find any hold on the beautiful yachts polished finish, but the boat would not even help him. His black eyes narrowed with fear and anger at the same time as the cold, green water pulled him to his grave 900 meters below the surface. Crabs would leave his clothes empty as if he had never been in them.

Leonid's crew lifted the skiff, secured it, and with Leonid's instruction turned toward the yacht. The sound of splintering fiberglass echoed against the sharp icebreaking bow of KSENIA один, and what was once a $2,000,000 yacht sank into the nutrient-rich, blue-green water of Alaska's coastline. The life and future of Daniel Bradley was over. He would never be remembered for goals reached or for accomplishments achieved in the life he had been given. He was simply gone.

A voice from behind Ruslin said, "I would have taken that pretty boat."

Ruslin turned to his sister and said, "That is not Dad's

way."

Ivonne answered, "I know. And his way is good."

***

The hunt between Christine Conder and Ivonne Bykov was sweeping through news channels like none had in years. Christine's character was loved, Ivonne's hated. Christine was the sweet, loving wife and mother from Oregon. Ivonne the ruthless, brutal killer from Russia. Odds were 6:1 that Christine would not find Ivonne until some chosen time, chosen by Ivonne, when she would attack from the pale, gray shadows of the Alaskan Gulf to utterly crush Christine with her bare hands. Ivonne was thought of as a type of monster; Christine the caring, compassionate woman who tried to give her lottery ticket back.

Ivonne stood on the deck of KSENIA один now, crying in her father's powerful arms. When she bought the lottery ticket in Seattle, her hope had been to quickly earn enough to buy and restore one of her father's older fishing boats. She wanted to be like her brothers, mastering their destiny as it was, searching the oceans for aquatic gold. This gold, however, could swim and hide from the most seasoned fisherman as storms and ice and loneliness drove even those who loved the sea back to land. There were always a few who could not take it any longer and would never go out again once they were safely home.

Ivonne had known too many who never came home. She had to be strong when her uncles, two of her brothers, one sister, her mother, and countless friends never came home. She would never see them again. There was not even the finality that should come from standing at their grave. From the day when each disappeared they became only a name carved into a massive stone which had been placed on a high cliff overlooking the sea.

As Leonid held his daughter, he fought to hold back his own tears. Ksenia had been his wife and mother to Michail, Adrian, Khristina, Ruslin and Ivonne. She seldom went to sea, but on her last trip a storm hit them so quickly that Leonid was not able to make shelter on the southwest side of the Kamchatka Peninsula. As they ran, they were caught in a 130 mph winds. Those winds tore the Bering Sea from the north into fjords of hammering, assailing, ice-pelting waves. The crew fought ice as it formed on the rails and the deck. With Leonid having no way of knowing it would happen, Ksenia ran out of the wheelhouse onto the deck. She pushed Ivonne into his arms. He had not been able to see Khristina hanging for her life onto a crab pot line as the powerful, determined storm washed her outside of the ships rails. Michail had her arm in one hand. His other gripped their older brother Adrian and Ruslin was running with a section of rope in his hands. As a mother would, Ksenia raced across the deck, not thinking with reason, only panic. She must try to help hold onto her daughter.

When she should have told Leonid to go, she went. Most of the crew had their survival suits on and secured, but Ksenia did not have one on. Ivonne was ten-years-old. As if that storm was the devil's temper unleashed against a God-fearing family the sixty-eight-foot vessel rolled to the starboard side. Leonid held Ivonne in his arms not knowing what else he could do. He watched his wife and three of their children disappear into the white wall of foam that forever separated them from him—and from Ruslin and Ivonne. There had not been time for him to do anything.

Ivonne was holding on to her dad again, this time crying about Daniel disappearing into the freezing, unforgiving water. She knew he was a bad man, but he was still a man who could have done the right things. Ivonne was guilty of mistakes, that was for sure, the greatest being the purchase of a lottery ticket to kill for money. But she felt different now. She was standing in a lion's arms, a lion who was crying with her.

The crew had gone to do their jobs or maybe just to leave Leonid with Ivonne and Ruslin alone. Some of them had been in that storm. The boat turned toward Area 1 and the Inside Passage.

***

"Dad, I will not go onshore when we fish for herring in the bay. I will never hunt for people anymore. No more. It is sure they cannot do anything to me when we are at sea, and they will never come to our home. I hope you will forgive me. I wish I could give the money from my next hunt to the woman named Christine and that she would say I was dead and let me go home."

"If you do not want to hunt anymore, then there is no one who can make you. I will see to that. You are safe here. Go to bed. Our crew would die for you, every one of them. And there is something else. Demyan does not want his father's fishing boat. It has not been to sea for a long time, but your Uncle Timur would want you to have it. I will call and buy it and have it made ready while we fish. The electronics will be old, but we will replace them. The hull is strong. Timur only used the boat a few years. I will buy it for you tomorrow, and it will be better than this boat. Now I know that you really want to fish with Ruslin and me. I will protect you. And your brother, yes, no one will come against you as long as he lives. It is a wonder Daniel came this far after Ruslin heard what he said. You must think of a name for your boat."

"I already know. It will be Ksenia's Daughter."

***

"Larissa, this is Leonid."

"I know. Can you think you would hide your voice from me?" They spoke in Russian. "Why do you call so late? Is all well with your venture to the south?"

"It is time for me to buy Timur's fishing boat. Demyan has told me he does not want to live on the sea as his father did. It is a hard life. He is smarter than me. Maybe smarter than Ivonne too. The boat is for her now. She will not hunt in the lottery anymore."

"You make me cry for joy. Where else is a brother-in-law like you? You will know what to pay for the boat. It is yours. I am only sorry it is not pretty for Ivonne."

The next six days were clear and bright.

On those days a true fisherman says, "Where else should I live?"

The world is bigger out there. There are not many things in the way.

***

Christine was passing through Wrangell Narrows on The Blue Ice Queen with a small group of April travelers. The Blue Queen, as she was called, hired Christine's services through SunDay Travel. Anyone can book a cruise in the Inside Passage but it was Christine's heart for history and her love for people that brought them back again and again. On each cruise she would know one or two people and meet friends they brought with them to learn the history of the amazing inland and offshore ecosystems. They would learn about the communities and strong-willed residents who live there. There is a standing joke between those who live along the shorelines inside and those who live in the small town of Dutch Harbor at the tip of the Aleutian Islands. And that is the joke. A comparison cannot be made.

***

"You have reached the office for the 'Hunt for Money Lottery.' Please leave a message, and we will return your call as soon as possible. If this is an emergency relating to violations, please press 4."

Leonid pressed 4.

"This is Colin Brown. How may I help you?"

"My name is Leonid Bykov. You will know me as the father of your contestant Ivonne Bykov. Ivonne chooses not to participate in the lottery any longer."

"I'm sorry Mr. Bykov, but let me tell you how this lottery works."

Before Colin could speak another word Leonid said, "I should speak to your boss. You are obviously a small person in your business. Give me to one who will make decisions for you."

"I will transfer you to my superintendent. Her name is

Nancy."

"Mr. Bykov, this is Nancy. You have made it to my desk, so I hope what you have to say is important. Tell me what violation you know of."

"A woman is about to be killed, and she is not one of your contestants."

"That is not a problem we can deal with. You should hang up and dial 911."

"You do not understand me. I am Ivonne Bykov's father. If she is not released from your lottery, you are the person who will be killed. Please trace my call. I am in the Gulf of Alaska now but will be in the Bering Sea in a few more days. If you can hear me well, it will not be me who kills you. I have hundreds of friends in your country who will take care of this for me for very little cost."

Leonid's voice sounded like the lion who had lived in him since childhood. A man who could face below freezing ice storms in 60 knot winds from the north.

"I will look on my daughter's computer in one hour. If she has no announcement of being released from the lottery, there will be no place you can hide. You will be killed immediately, and your government would do nothing. You are not important. And my daughter's competitor will be the same. Christine Conder will not hunt or be hunted anymore. She is out of the lottery as my daughter is. She is with a baby. What kind of a woman are you? I will tell you. A dead one if I do not see both of these things happen. My daughter will tell me. Do not let me find different. I have a friend near where you live, and he knows every day what I will want to know about you. And I owe him my own life."

Leonid hung his phone up. In less than one hour a statement was made on the lottery's website: "The match between Ivonne Bykov and Diana Austen has been canceled. They have been replaced with two mystery contestants you have not yet seen. They are thought to be the most interesting contestants of the year. Watch for details as we put this match together."

Leonid called John, "John my friend. My daughter tells me the lottery has let her go and your friend with the name Christine also. You will tell me if that is not so. I am finished with herring in a few days and will go home for the snow crab season, but I will send men to help you if Christine is not left alone. I will come with my daughter to visit you in the spring. I will soon ship down more crab and salmon than your family and all of your friends can eat."

Leonid sat down with Ivonne and the crew to a meal of the finest rib steak money could buy, potatoes and onions both grown in Canada's Matanuska Valley and pies baked by the chef. On KSENIA один no one sat down to the evening meal without the chef. He prepared the food but that was all.

Members of the crew who were not needed on deck were waiters. Yet there were times when they were setting or pulling crab pots that they would eat as they could, sometimes working through bitter-cold nights.

Ruslin prayed, "God, thank you for the abundance we have. Thank you for these men who work for what You give us. Thank you for our catch. You are good to us. Thank you that my little sister has become smarter and that she is still with us. And thank you that the man who wanted to kill her is on the bottom of Your great sea now. He was not a good man. We will protect our family's and our friends with our own lives as You would have us do. Thank you for my father. He guides us into plenty as you guide him. In the name of your own Son, Amen."

***

There was relief and a false sense of security in the Conder home and in Dana's home with news that Christine had been released from the lottery. Christine's table was heaped with fresh snow crab Ivonne had brought to meet her new friend. She stayed at the Conder home for two weeks getting to know the family, and John and Julie, and Sam and Dana. She told them her father was very sorry he could not come but he wanted her to tell them they were his own family now. It was because John and Julie had saved his daughter from Daniel.

John was not sure how they had done that, but he and Julie were very willing to accept the Bykov family. Sam told Ivonne that he would take his father soon and go wherever they had to go if he could meet Leonid and Ruslin. Of all the things Sam and John had done together, they had never been on a crab boat in the Bering Sea. And the very mention of doing that meant that Julie would not want to go. She had been seasick one time and that would last her for a lifetime.

While Ivonne was there Nights were restful and days were filled with sightseeing. But she was not impressed with the busy life and tall, city buildings. She did like Liam's car and the story that came with it. She shared many of her stories with them and her sorrow about Daniel's death. She talked about the mistake she had made to buy the lottery ticket. She told them how she felt different now; how she would have jumped into the sea to save Daniel and give him another chance, but she believed her father; that Daniel was not a good man.

It was on a Saturday when Christine took Ivonne to the airport. Ivonne would fly to the Amderma Airport in Russia, landing near the Northern Sea Route and board KSENIA один with her father and brother in the bay sheltered inside of Novaya Zemlya, the northeasterly lying finger of land separating the Barents Sea from the Kara Sea, each being part of the continually-frigid Arctic Ocean.

Christine and Ivonne shared the longest hug, and Ivonne

left with her luggage for the check-in terminal at Portland International Airport. They had formed an inseparable bond from what they had been through together.

On the trip back to her house, Christine anticipated the joy and relaxed life of being free from the lottery. She planned to work less and spend more time at home getting ready for Hannah.

Sixteen

Ruslin called John: "Privyet John, this is Ruslin. Ivonne should be here now. Did she stay longer and not tell me?"

"No, Christine took her to the airport. There may have been a delay in her flight, but she did not call us if there was."

"Will you check that for me? I have called her phone, and she does not answer."

"Ruslin, I will call you as soon as I find out where she is. Sam will be able to tell. He can see different contestants on his computer. I will call him now."

"Sam, there is a problem. Ruslin Just called. Ivonne did not make it to where he is waiting. Can you see where she is? I need your help to find her."

"I will look and call you back."

"Dad, she is not showing up in my program. That can only mean someone turned her marker off—or she is dead. We were apparently not watching the program during that time to see her number go out. If the Induction Center deleted her number, and she is alive, it can only mean someone in there is hiding her. Maybe one person does not want others in the system to know where she is. And I am not able to turn her marker back on when it isn't visible.

Christine had taken Ivonne to the airport, but when they checked the flight record she had not boarded the airplane.

"Meet me at the airport Sam, and get Frank and Christine there if you can. It would be good if Christine would bring a picture of Ivonne taken in the clothes she was wearing that day. I had Ivonne's phone traced, and it is on the airplane she is supposed to be on."

"Do we know anyone on that airplane?"

"No, Son. That was the first thing I checked."

"I'm on my way." Sam said. "I will call Frank. Hopefully we will get to the airport near the same hour when she would have left and have the same people working."

"Bring your I.D., Son. No one knows you retired."

"I have it."

"Ruslin, this is John. Is your father in a place where his phone will work?"

"I am on the phone with him now. I will bring you in."

Ruslin tapped 'Add Call.'

"Leonid, are you there?"

"Yes, John. Ruslin tells me Ivonne does not answer her phone, but that he has left messages. When she changed airplanes, I think she would have seen those and called him."

"Leonid, I am afraid," John said. "Her phone is on the airplane, and she did not get on. We are headed for the airport now and will have a picture of her with us. I am sure someone working will remember seeing her. Sam has clearance that will get him anywhere we need to go in the airport. We have a person who will check the airport security cameras too. Sam told me you had a threatening conversation in order to get Ivonne and Christine out of the lottery. Who did you talk to? That person could be who took Ivonne. They would know her location."

Leonid told John he had talked to a woman named Nancy.

John said to Leonid and Ruslin, "I have to go now, but I will call you as soon as we know anything."

"Dad and I will leave as soon as possible to come there," Ruslin said. "Our crew will work. We will catch a flight within a couple of hours.

***

At the airport John said to Christine: "Leonid talked to someone named Nancy and threatened her to get you and Ivonne out of the lottery."

John was visibly shaking. It had been years since he felt this type of adrenalin.

"I know Nancy," Christine said. "She is in charge of the place where people sign in to the lottery. At least on the west coast, and I hope someday she gets what is coming to her. If Leonid was forceful with her, she had it coming. She is a terrible person, and we can be sure she hates him now."

Sam said, "We have to find Nancy, and I would rather it not be inside the building with her staff. I don't want to kill all of them until I know who supports her and who works there out of fear. I need a picture of her, license plate number, address, anything we can find."

"Frank," Sam said, "you should get Liam into the airport security cameras. They will have seen Ivonne. We know the day and hour she was here. Someone had to have taken her phone and slipped it into another person's luggage as they were boarding the airplane."

"Dan, this is Sam again. Call me as soon as you can. I need a fast ride to San Francisco. And if you can, I need some toys. I am at PDX and didn't bring much with me. Anything you have will work fine."

Minutes later: "Sam, I am in the air, but there is another pilot on the ground in Portland. He can help with anything you need. It's getting old sitting in this cockpit every day, and I would love to send my next few clients to a friend. All I have to do is tell them the airplane is making noise, and they are glad to give me some time."

"Thanks Dan. Can I take some things on the other airplane, and is he like you? Might he have something?"

"You can, and he is never far from his own type of security. He is one of our old friends. I will call him, and he will be waiting for you in the same place near PDX. Will Ben be with you?

"Yes, Ben is on his way to the airport. The pilot—it's not Jackson is it. We got shot down every time we went up with him."

"Yes, it's Jackson, but he stopped drinking years ago. He is reliable Sam or I would not send you to him. I have to go. Call me in an hour. I haven't done anything exciting for years."

"Dan, I thank you for the offer, but you are safer where you are. It will not be safe where Ben and I are going. I'm afraid he and I will be in a bad situation. Someone in the Induction Center has kidnapped a very good friend, a young woman. She could be dead now, but we don't know. I think they are holding her to get at her father. You met Christine at my wedding. The woman who is missing is a friend of hers. Her name is Ivonne. Her father and brother are on their way here from a crab boat in Alaska, and I wish they weren't. I am going to have to keep them alive now as well as find the woman we are looking for. And once we start this, they will have every field agent employed hunting for us. I have no idea who those agents are. That is the hard part Dan. We could get caught by surprise."

"Sam, if we did not have so much history together, I would tell you what I think of you right now. We have been there for each other hundreds of times, been shot each at the same time, both lived through it, and now you think I'm an old man needing to stay in a safe place? What in the hell does staying safe do for men like us? Maybe you get to die of old age."

"I am over California right now," Dan said. "I am going to land this airplane and wait for you. I will transfer my passengers then call Jackson and tell him where to bring you guys.

"Depending on your plans I have enough toys to get started. If there are things you need from home, Jackson would go back to Portland once he drops you off. You know him as well as I do. He will do anything to help and the more dangerous the better."

"Dan, you are a brother, and I do want you with me. I'm sorry I said it the way I did, but I have a good memory and you have been through a lot in your lifetime. It will get serious here. How many times do you want to catch bullets saving me?"

Dan was always lighthearted in the face of danger.

He said to Sam, "I will say six more, and then I am done."

***

"Ben thanks for coming. I called Dan, and Jackson is on the ground waiting for us. He will fly you and me to an airport near the Induction Center. I only wish I had asked you to bring some things."

"I have a few in the trunk. When you called, I opened your safe and brought what I knew you would want."

"I should have known. You never go anyplace unprepared. Did you bring the .338?"

"I brought that and all of your armor I could find. And a couple M16s with so many loaded magazines, I had to make two trips."

Sam said, "We will take it all and trust Dan to have a place to leave what we can't carry."

Sam turned to Frank and said, "Frank, Ben, and I are leaving for San Francisco. I am not needed here. Keep in touch and tell me everything you find, and I will let you know what we get into. Watch once in a while to see if Ivonne's number comes back on. I will check when I can. And there is one other thing. At some point, I might need Liam to kill some cameras. When can you call him and be sure he is ready to do that?"

Christine said, "Sam, Liam just sent me a picture of Nancy and a government license plate number associated with her. Her home address too."

Christine sent the information to Sam's phone and to Ben's.

"Be careful, Son," Julie said to Sam. "I love you and need you."

"You too, Ben." She kissed both of them on the cheek.

On the way to board Jackson's airplane Ben called his mom. "Hi Mom. I know I haven't called for a while, but I love you. Would you tell Dad too if he is around?"

"He is here, Ben. I'll…"

"No, you tell him for me. I am leaving on an important mission. I don't know for sure when I will be back, but I just wanted to say I love you. I've got to go now. Goodbye Mom. I will call later."

Sam called Dana, "Hey Love, Ben and I are leaving now. I don't know if Ivonne is alive, but we need to find her. Liam saw two lottery employees take her from the airport, and we think they are holding her to bring her father. I guess he threatened someone in a high place within the lottery, and it seems reasonable that they are hoping to eliminate that threat. I love you. Ben and I will be home soon."

"The kids and I will pray for you and Ben. We will pray for the other guys too. Not for their safety but for them to miraculously know what they are doing is wrong. I love you."

"I love you too. Please tell Jeremiah and Karly I love them."

With that Dana's voice began to crack. "You come home and tell them yourself—but I will tell them now. Give Ben our love too."

Sam and Ben boarded Jackson's airplane, and they were on their way to find Ivonne.

"Sam, I wish I was with you. Without your clearances they would not let us look at anything after you left. Christine says it was Colin Brown and Nancy Lee who took Ivonne.

They took her out to a black suburban parked at the curb. In an outside camera Liam could see that it had a government license plate. It is A993012. A friend is finding that plate right now. We are sure it belongs to the lottery, but it may be assigned to Nancy Lee. When they got to the vehicle Nancy got in the driver's seat."

John called again and confirmed what he thought. The vehicle was assigned to Nancy Lee. Dan called Sam and said he was waiting in the lobby where they landed last time and that he had some toys in his truck. His passengers had been moved to another charter.

Sam and Ben arrived in California and thanked Jackson for the fast trip. Sam tried to pay him, but Jackson said he and Dan had talked, and he was not going to take money for helping this time.

They met Dan in the lobby and began to make plans. Nancy Lee's home address would make it easy to find her, and Ben insisted that he go into the house first. It was already past quitting time at the Induction Center.

In a rich neighborhood, Ben got out and broke the gate-rod on a well-built, stylish security gate. He stomped the rod so hard, putting 278 pounds into it, that the rod pulled out of the end of the hydraulic tube. Ben thought it was a small cylinder for such a heavy gate. He opened the gate and Dan drove through.

Knowing they would not be expected, Dan parked along the curb behind Nancy's black suburban. In a matter of luck that would surely never be duplicated Nancy Lee was still in the suburban. She had been leaned over picking something up from the passenger floorboard and sat up right in front of them. When she got out of the vehicle it was Nancy Lee for sure. She smiled and waved at the men in the truck and started toward the house. After Liam seeing her and Colin take Ivonne from the airport, none of the three men had to guess if she was guilty. That would make what they were going to do easier.

Ben was out of the four-door truck like a teenager. On the way out he said, "Colin could be in there. Back me up."

Even though they were words that did not need to be said, rehearsal and repetition were key to men trained in dangerous operations.

When Nancy saw him coming she started to run, but he caught her before she made it to the porch. He put his left hand on the back of her neck and said, "Do not fight me, or I will kill you. Let's go in the house. Is Colin in there?"

"No, he is not."

When they got to the front door Ben tested it, and it was not locked, a sure sign that someone was inside.

Knowing he had to keep Nancy alive, he took one step to the hinge-side of the door, and Sam kicked the door opened hard enough to know if someone was behind it. With the M16 in his hands, he swept the room left to right. It was clear.

Nancy screamed, "Shoot."

Ben's grip on the back of Nancy's neck was hurting her and the Glock 10 mm was in his right hand. Dan had run through a gate to the right side of the house to watch the back door. He was standing tight against the house, so the door would open away from him. Then as he guessed, when Sam and Ben came through the front door, Colin ran out the back.

Dan was a big man, not as big as Ben, but his uppercut was coming to full power when it reached Colin's chin. Colin fell unconscious to the ground. Dan dragged him into the house to where Nancy was sitting on the floor having her wrists handcuffed to her ankles.

When Colin could talk, Sam said, "Colin Brown, if you lie to me about anything, I will kill you right now. I don't like men like you."

Colin blurted out, "I think you know who I am. I have the power to have all of you killed with just a phone call. I am a United States government employee."

"Colin," Sam said, "You better give me the right answer, because we do not need you otherwise. Where is Ivonne Bykov being held. You and Nancy took her from Portland International Airport earlier today. We want her right now. Do you think she is worth what will happen if you don't tell me?"

Colin looked at Nancy. She was siting straight up with her

knees bent up against her chest and a hand towel stuffed into her mouth.

"Take the towel out of her mouth," Colin said. "She knows where Ivonne is."

"I need to go to the bathroom," Sam said. "Dan, would one of you guys take Colin into a bedroom and lay him on the bed? And make sure he stays there. From what he just said, I don't think we need him anymore."

Sam went to the bathroom by way of the kitchen and guessed within two doors where the garbage bags were kept.

He could hear Colin begging as Dan's fist put him to sleep for the second time. His crying and begging stopped instantly. Dan swung his feet up and laid him on the bed.

Sam came back, still adjusting his zipper and had two garbage bags hanging out of his pocket.

He said, "Where did you put Colin? I need to go see him."

Nancy saw the two garbage bags in Sam's pocket as he walked away. After a minute he came from the bedroom, and there was only one garbage bag in his pocket.

He said to Nancy, "You have been very rude to Christine Conder, and she is pregnant. Now tell me where you have put Ivonne Bykov."

"You can kill me. I will not tell you anything, so go ahead and put that bag over my head. It won't take long, and you will never find Ivonne. Her father will find out how she died because of what you did."

"You really think you are tougher than Colin don't you? You are not a very big woman and your toilet holds a lot of water. I was sure you would do this the hard way. I'm going to ask you one more time where you are keeping Ivonne. I don't believe you have killed her. I think you want to trade her for her father."

Ben picked Nancy up by the waist and headed toward the bathroom. Dan stayed in the living room.

"I hope you die," Nancy screamed.

Sam had not flushed the toilet and those were the last words out of her mouth for several seconds. Ben lifted her face out of the toilet after she had gasped in the yellow urine and water.

Sam waited until he thought she could talk and said, "Where is Ivonne?

Still choking she said, "I will never tell you!"

"You will tell me. Waterboarding has been proven for centuries to work."

Ben lowered her into the toilet and held her there. This time he had to bounce her pretty hard to get the water out. It was a full ten minutes before vile words began to spill out of her mouth again.

When her hair went into the water next time she

screamed, "Stop!"

Being upside down was all that had saved her.

Calmly Sam said, "Where is Ivonne?"

"In my purse." And she began choking so bad she couldn't talk.

She finally said, "There is a receipt for a motel room two miles from here. She is in number 5."

Ben dropped her in the bathtub, still with her ankles handcuffed to her wrists. Sam went to Nancy's purse and dumped the contents onto the table. Along with the receipt for the motel room and the key, a snub-nosed 38 caliber pistol fell onto the table.

"I wonder how many people she has shot with that?" Dan said, as he reached for the receipt and the key.

"Come with me, Ben. Sam will keep an eye on Nancy."

***

Dan and Ben arrived at room number 5, and Ben pulled the 'Do Not Disturb' tag off of the doorknob. Dan unlocked the door. Ivonne was nowhere to be seen in the room. The bathroom door was shut, so Ben asked if anyone was in there and knocked on the door.

He said, "I am a friend of Christine Conder's. Sam and another friend are with me. If you are here Ivonne, Nancy and Colin are dead, and we are here to get you."

At that there was noise in a small closet. Dan opened the

door. The closet was 36-inches wide and 24-inches deep with a wooden dowel for hanging clothes near the top. Ivonne's hands were tied behind her back and her ankles were tied tightly. A wire hanger has been untwisted and twisted again around her neck and around the dowel. It was tight on her neck, and her mouth was taped shut with heavy duct tape, the sticky stuff that does not come off easily. Nancy had put it tightly over Ivonne's mouth. She wrapped it around her hair and back to cover her mouth again. obviously believing Ivonne would never have to worry about getting it loose from her hair.

Ben untwisted the wire from around her neck and picked Ivonne up as if holding a child in his arms. He sat her on the bed. Her wrists and ankles were wrapped with wire hangers, and they were also twisted tight. It was a blessing for Ivonne that they found her so soon.

Ivonne left the bed as fast as she could and went into the bathroom.

Dan said, "We will be outside."

They walked out and shut the door loud enough for Ivonne to hear it."

Ben called Sam and told him how they had found Ivonne. If Ben would have been Jeff, Sam might have scolded him for the words he used to describe Nancy. But at times Sam was not a saint either. As his blood pressure rose he felt the same way Ben felt.

"We are coming to get you now." Ben said.

"Thanks Ben. I think I will get some exercise and start walking. And we don't need to worry. Liam shut down all of the cameras in the neighborhood before we arrived."

"I thought so," Ben said. "When I got out to open the gate I heard you talking to him."

"You never forget anything, do you?"

"Sometimes. Not things that interest me."

There was no talk about Nancy and Colin on the trip home. Ben and Dan didn't heed to ask and would have done the same thing after what she did to Ivonne.

"The sacred rights of mankind are not to be rummaged for among old parchments or musty records. They are written as with a sunbeam in the whole volume of human nature—by the hand of the divinity itself and can never be erased or obscured by mortal power."

–Alexander Hamilton

Seventeen

Leonid called John from the airplane: "John, this is Leonid. Ruslin and I will land at the airport in Portland in one hour."

'Okay, Julie and I will pick you up. She will make a sign with my name on it. You will see it in the window of our car. I will call you a few minutes before we drive along the curb. Wave me down when you see us, or I might see Ruslin first."

John would have guessed that Leonid was Ruslin's father. They looked like they had just come in from the Kara Sea and not combed their hair or changed clothes.

Reaching his hand toward Leonid first, John said, "I would not need to ask. You are the lion. I am John, and my wife Julie is in the car. And here is Ruslin, he extended his hand, "Julie and I owe him our lives."

"Now it is both of you again that I owe for the life of my daughter," Leonid said.

"Leonid, you stop that," John said.

Leonid smiled at John's boldness.

"Julie and I would both be dead if Ruslin had not handled our situation with Daniel like he did. We are the ones in debt to you for raising such a fine son."

"Ruslin and I were very relieved when you told us your own son and two of his friends have Ivonne safely away from the people who would harm her. We will not argue anymore."

"Okay," John said, "but you know I am old. It is the young men who are bringing your daughter home."

***

When they were at Frank and Christine's house, Sam said, "Leonid, Ruslin, I feel like I know you both. I am Sam. This is Ben, and another friend who helped bring Ivonne home is Dan. He sends his best but had to return to California. We have been very blessed to talk with your daughter on the trip home. She is bonded to you as much as any daughter or son I have ever known. It was an honor for us to bring her to you. My mom told me that we will all have dinner together, and it smells good. You must know that Ivonne and Christine are like sisters? We will forgive them for crying when they are together now. Your family is loved here.

"You must meet my wife Dana, and our children Karly and Jeremiah. I fell in love with their mom and both of them at the same time. It is a story I will tell you sometime."

Ivonne and Christine were holding hands talking. Dana and Karly went to them, and Karly slipped inside of Ivonne's arms and leaned against her.

The fresh crab and fish Leonid had sent earlier would not be outdone, but Oregon grows, arguably, the finest beef in the world. A large uncut prime rib sat next to a full brisket on the table. It was a table which had been custom built for Christine. It was a heavy, wood-built table much like Sam's, Dana's now. Five-inch planks formed the top and were cracked from age. It had been built that way. The cracks were filled with bright, turquoise epoxy.

The meat had rested twenty minutes but was still hot from the barbeque. Surrounding the meat sat all of the trimmings a hard-working fishing family would enjoy.

After dinner, it was decided that Ivonne would stay the night at Frank and Christine's. Leonid and Ruslin would go with Sam and Dana to the ranch. Karly wanted them to see Dusty, and Ivonne would see him the next day. She was anxious. She had never felt a horse's soft nose, and Karly was excited for her to do that. Christine would come over the next day and bring Ivonne.

They would leave that morning at 10 AM for an 11:50 flight leaving Portland and would arrive back at the Amderma Airport in Russia to rejoin the crew aboard KSENIA один. The fishing season was underway.

***

Now that Nancy and Colin were no longer there, no one could be sure what might happen with the matter of Christine and Ivonne being released from the lottery. Aaden might find in Nancy's computer that she had officially released both of them and let it go at that, or she may have written a second letter retracting what she said in the first.

Sam told Ben that he wished they would have allowed Colin to call for help. They might have been able to kill some of the field agents, but it presented a risk he wasn't willing to take. Before he and Dana were married, maybe, but not now. He could not know how many agents would come, and even if he lived, his eagerness to kill them could have caused Ben or Dan be killed in the fight.

Newspapers and television news channels focused for days on the murders of Nancy Lee and Colin Brown. The lottery was a story followed by millions of people. What would never be known is that their deaths were similar to Vance's. The three of them had suffocated with garbage bags over their heads. When Sam walked away from Nancy's house both of the bags were in his pocket and the handcuffs were on his belt. He later put the bags in a dumpster at the airport before leaving for home. Nancy and Colin were found lying on a bed beside each other, both dead. It was a fitting ending for two people who had been responsible for so many deaths.

***

June came and news reporters were again talking about the lottery and the PPV event that was scheduled in the Ochoco National Forest on the tenth of June. The same contestants were made legends by some reporters and condemned by others and Christine's fame had not been forgotten. One of the major networks aired a piece concerning what they called a heavily contested letter left by Nancy Lee.

Aaden Bradley had taken Nancy's job as manager. He spoke live on two news stations about the mysterious disappearance of his brother and about the letter his former boss had written releasing Christine Conder and Ivonne Bykov from the lottery. He did not have the courtesy to use Christine's given name, Diana Austen. He insisted there was foul play in both matters. He claimed to have his brothers phone and computers in his possession and said it was only a matter of time till he found the person responsible for his brother's disappearance. He said that Christine Conder and Ivonne Bykov would be brought back into the lottery.

He promised loyal followers that he would learn the truth and justice would be done. It was clear that Aaden had become more powerful in the lottery. Ben had brought Daniel's computers and phones to Sam.

Not more than a few days passed and Aaden said that a second letter had been written by Nancy Lee. He vowed that to honor her founding of the PPV Christine Conder and Ivonne Bykov would be brought back into the lottery—one way or another.

The letter was of course a forgery. Aaden said in front of millions of viewers that Christine was pregnant but that according to strictly enforced rules being pregnant would not affect her contract with 'The Hunt for Money.' He promised that agents would be used if necessary to bring the contestants back.

No one knew for sure how many field agents the lottery had. There might have been one or two. There might have been twenty. It was possible that the mention of them was nothing more than a tactic to promote fear among contestants and excitement among the public. But Sam was getting closer to finding the answer to that question.

Christine called Sam and told him what Aaden had said during both interviews.

***

Ben and Sam were home and Ben said, "There is a way to end the lottery forever. Between us we can call fifty friends who are trained and dedicated. It is time to erase this thing and all that it stands for, but there is one downside. If we charge into this and get killed, Christine and Ivonne will die. You know we can kill Aaden as easily as the Bykov's did his brother, but it's bigger than that. The government needs to decide this lottery was never a good idea. If they believe that, they would not try to solve the riddle of who destroyed it."

"You are right, Ben. We need to get Dad talking with people at the top, and I need you to keep me on track. I am ready to charge into this. It is too close to home, and think how many families have been destroyed?"

"Those who lead investigations into bombings, or whatever has to happen here," Sam said, "determine what the news reporters know and therefore what the people know. We would need people in those positions to polish over what has to happen.

"Ben, I am glad you're on my side. If we could make our case high enough, we could call an air strike at night on the Induction Center. All we would need is for the right people to deny being involved and case closed."

Sam smiled for the first time in more than an hour.

"We are talking about something which has needed to be done since its beginning," Ben said. "When it's over I am going to take a vacation and then go home and get back to my regular work. I am going to bed now and make a list of reliable, trustworthy friends who might help us. I know you have a wife and kids to spend the evening with, but do the same when you can. We will compare notes. Sam, today has been a good day. Ivonne is safe, and I am sure Leonid will keep her out to sea for a while."

"Goodnight Ben. It's early, but I'm tired too. And I need some time with Dana and the kids. Be in for breakfast about eight."

"Goodnight Sam. One day we will look back on this and will have done a great service for our country. I have never been more ready."

When Ben got to the barn, Karly was brushing Dusty.

She said, "Ben, can I ask you something?"

He said, "Anything in the world."

"You are a man, and I want to know what you would like me to call you if you married my mom. Right now while I am twelve."

Ben was all of a sudden not the negotiator he thought he was. "Wow Karly. That is too big of a question for me. I have never had a girl like you. But I think if I was your dad I might be so happy I would cry. I know your real dad is gone, so it is true that Sam is your dad now. And I know Sam. He is the greatest guy next to your own dad that you will ever know. Do you promise not to tell anyone if I give you my answer?"

"I promise."

"If I was Sam, I would want you to call me Dad. I think you should ask him the same way you did me. You should take ahold of his hand and say, 'Is it okay if I call you Dad?' I know he will say yes."

"Okay, I am going to ask him tonight. Do you talk to your dad a lot?"

"We don't talk very much. My dad drinks a lot; too much. And he is always mad about something. He used to be mad at me, but then I left and haven't seen him for a long time."

"I'm sorry you don't see him. Can we pray for him now?"

Ben didn't know what to say. He said, "Yes, but I don't know how very well. Would you do it?"

Karly reached for Ben's hand. He was reluctant for a moment but offered his big, strong hand to hers.

"Dear God," she said, "Ben's dad needs You. I don't know where he is, but please tell him that Ben loves him. And somehow tell him that he shouldn't drink so much. You will know what to tell him. Thank You. In Jesus' name, Amen—and bless Ben's mom too."

"That's all there is to it," Karly said. God loves your dad and He will help him."

Ben said, "Thank you Karly. Maybe we can do this again."

She told Ben she would pray for his dad when she went to bed. Ben didn't know that meant praying for his dad with Sam and Dana.

***

"Good morning Ben." Jeremiah and Karly were already gone to school. "Can Dana and I talk to you about something. It's important?"

"Sure. Am I getting kicked out of the barn?"

"No. You are not getting kicked out of the barn. Last night when Dana and I prayed with Karly she prayed for your dad. Dana and I want you to go see your parents, and we want to pay for the trip. It seems that we are not paying you much to stay here and protect all of us. I'm serious Ben. We can't be sure what is coming in this lottery thing. You need to go see your mom and dad. Will you do that?"

"Sam, I am not sure I want to see my dad. The last time I was home we had words, and I left it that way."

"Don't worry about that Ben. We want you to go and try to make that right."

There was silence for a minute.

"Okay, I will go home."

"And do what Ben?"

"I will see my dad."

"Okay." Sam put his hand out to close the deal.

Dana said, "You are a good friend Ben. I think you are like a big brother, or an uncle to Karly. Jeremiah is a little harder to get to know but he thinks the world of you. We will always have a place for you here. That room in the barn is yours. So can I arrange the flight, or will your friends come and get you in the helicopter?"

"No, that was a onetime deal for Sam's retirement and wedding. I will not plan on that happening again."

"Okay, you guys talk business, and I will get you a flight."

"Honey, let me call Dan first. He could have time to take Ben home and bring him back when he is ready."

Sam called John and asked if he would come out to the house. He and Ben and his dad talked for hours about who they might know and how far up the ladder they could get.

John had done a good job keeping in touch over the years since he retired. He had contacts in important places, particularly in the Air Force. He and Julie had shared meals many times with friends while John was in the service and many of those relationships continued after he retired. They knew the children of those families, and some had made careers in the armed forces.

They made a list of contacts, and for a young man Ben's list was impressive. Under the roof of that ranch house there was a burning desire to end the lottery. Ivonne was safe, at least for a time, and Aaden Bradley would have been to leave Christine alone. Dana continued to be a soft, compassionate voice in Sam's head. He asked John and Ben what they might do to spare the lives of as many of the lottery's employees as possible.

It was obvious that destroying the Induction Center at night would spare the most people, not that there was anyone innocent. They made their living from people hunting people. They would find out if records were kept anyplace other than in the building. They did not know how they would find that out but they would. They had to know if there was a janitor or anyone working at night. How much area cleared did they have around the building? Who did they know who knew explosives well enough to only do what was necessary? Were there other

Induction Centers in the United States? These questions had to be answered.

They hoped the field agents, if there really were any, would be like bees—when the nest was gone they would go away and forget the lottery. But that is not entirely how bees are. They will leave the destroyed nest but build another somewhere else.

Sam wondered who in government authorized such a terrible lottery in the first place? That is where they had to start. As they sat around the table not one of them could think of an easy or gentle approach that would end 'The Hunt for Money' forever. It would have to be stopped permanently. No facilities and no people left working there would be the only way.

From these three men would begin the most powerful movement against a corrupt government that would be seen until the final destruction of America when politics would once again be used as a weapon of war. The next time it was used, a lack of unity among Americans would bring bloodshed that would be difficult to recover from—if ever.

It was decided. Ben would go home to see his mom and dad. If he contacted any of the people he knew, it would be in the quiet of whatever room he stayed in, not around his family.

John knew who he wanted to call. He would start at the top, while Sam would begin to work out the details of what would happen on the ground.

The PPV was only two weeks away, and every contestant chosen had been contacted except Christine.

Eighteen

At 1:40 in the afternoon, the day after Sam met with John and Ben, the doorbell rang at Frank and Christine's house. Frank was at work, and the boys were in school. Christine followed protocol. The family had discussed how she would not leave the house without a bodyguard. And if she answered the door, she would have the glove on her hand and her handgun held behind her back. At times Ben would stay over, and this morning was one of those times. He was at the breakfast table and the curtains in the living room were drawn. They had guessed the man who took Dana during the Dehoughe match must have watched Sam leave the room, and they would not allow that to happen again.

Cameras had been installed. Liam, Jeff, and Frank linked their phones to the cameras. Christine's, Sam's, and Ben's were linked also. Ben bolted from the table when his phone alerted him to two people dressed alike standing at the front door. He could see on his phone that they were not holding weapons, but he was.

Christine opened the door and said, "Yes?"

There was a woman close to the door and a man behind her.

The woman held a picture of Christine and said, "You are wanted at the Induction Center. Nothing serious at this time, but for your safety we need to talk to you."

Christine said, "Please come in."

She moved away from the door, and the two agents stepped inside. Dana moved toward the woman and slapped her on the arm with her glove. The man reached for a concealed handgun just as Ben's fist met the side of his head. He was dragged the rest of the way into the house, disarmed and handcuffed in seconds. And the front door was closed. Ben sat the woman, who had wet herself, on a mat Christine brought to place in front of one couch on the floor, and Ben handcuffed her wrists to her ankles with her own handcuffs. He then disarmed her and emptied her purse onto a coffee table in front of the couch. He brought the man's billfold, handgun, and I.D. and laid them among the contents, then unloaded their weapons and called Sam's phone. Christine called Frank. This would be the time when Frank quit his job. His boss, even though a friend, was running low on patience. Christine had received to date $29,846,597.00. Frank did not need to work away from home.

Ben guessed the vehicle they came in was a rental car. It would employ Real-Time GPS but would not be linked to the lottery.

'You are in so much trouble," the woman said to Christine and Ben when she could talk again. "You have no idea what could happen to both of you now. But I promise to not report this if you release me and listen to what I have to say."

Ben knelt down and put his hand on her face and turned her toward him. "You will do exactly as I tell you, or I will kill you, and I will kill your companion. Please say you understand me."

"I understand you."

Both of their cell phones were on the coffee table.

"Sometime soon," Ben said, "one of your people from the Induction Center will call to see why you have been here so long. If they call your friend, I hope he has come to so he can talk to them. But he might be dead. I will check him when we are through talking. I can usually tell when a person's neck breaks."

Ben looked at the man on the floor, "He is breathing, so he is alive for now."

Her eyes widened as she understood that Ben had killed before.

"I am going to write on a piece of paper what you will say when they call. You will say exactly what is written, as believably as you can, or I will kill you. I am going to trust that you still understand me."

"I do."

This is what you will say: "We are on schedule. We are talking to Christine now and will finish what we came for. You will see us leave soon."

Ben said, "If you make it sound like you are reading I will kill you along with whoever they send."

Sam arrived at the house first and then Frank.

Ben said without using Sam's name, "Take over please. You know what we have here."

Tim was now sitting with his hands behind his back against the wall near the door. He was free to say anything he wanted and had not said a word. There was only a blank stare in his eyes.

Sam said to Frank and Ben: "I want you guys to take their car to a parking lot somewhere close and leave it. Go through it thoroughly for anything that belongs to them."

Christine went to the pool building and returned with two pairs of nitrile gloves. Frank and Ben took them and went to the car. Christine smiled when Ben held one close to his hand. They opened all four doors along with the trunk and the hood and went through everything.

Sam began with the woman, "Who are you, and I do not mean your name. If you do not tell me the truth and cooperate with everything I say I will kill you. Is there anyone from the lottery close to here now?

"No. We flew from California, and it is just the two of us."

"Okay, thank you. What is your position with the lottery?"

"We are field agents who bring persons to justice when they break the rules."

"Have you or that man ever killed people? Believe me. I can make a phone call and find out. Aaden Bradley will tell me anything I need to know. I know things about him and as long as he cooperates with me I leave him alone. Have you killed people?"

"Yes."

"Both of you?"

"Yes."

"How many agents does the lottery employ, and where are they now? If you lie to me, I will tie some type of a weight on you and drown you in the swimming pool that is just outside that door. From watching others, I think it is a terrible way to die. Now answer me."

"There are eight others. We are spaced across the country and fly to wherever we are sent. Tim and I live here permanently."

"I might actually let you live. You are good at this, but if I want to find the others how do I do that?"

If you could see monitors like Aaden does, you could see

our code numbers on the monitors. None of us can hide from him."

"If I could see that? How are their numbers different from contestants?"

"I am A9. Tim is A10. Agents are the only numbers beginning with A. Tim and I hate the two other agents. They have killed families. There is no law that the lottery answers to, and we are protected by the government."

"Who has Tim killed?"

"Only one man, and he was holding hostages."

"How many people have you killed?"

"One man."

"What was he doing"

"He was with the man Tim killed." Both of them had killed people who were not in the lottery. Then they made the mistake of threatening employees of the lottery."

"Christine would you please bring my phone to me? I left it on the two laptops in the bedroom."

Christine brought Daniel's phone to Sam. He entered Daniel's password and went to contacts, then to Aaden's phone number. He showed the phone to the woman sitting on the floor. Then in turn he showed her Mark's number and Colin's and Nancy's.

"I do not believe you about the lottery only having four agents across the entire nation. I think I need to call and verify what you are telling me."

Sam held the phone as if to dial it.

"Please don't call Aaden. We let someone go recently and Aaden said he would have us killed if it happened again. He sent us here as a test to kill Christine, but we were not going to do it. Aaden told us she and Ivonne Bykov had threatened employees of the lottery. We hoped when we explained this to Christine that we might get a contact who would help us get into Russia until someone kills Aaden. It is only a matter of time and someone will kill him. He has ordered the elimination of innocent people in the past. But it is also only a matter of time until he kills us.

"If you call him, we are dead. I have nothing to lose by telling you this—as long as he doesn't catch me."

Christine said, "I believe her."

Sam said, "Tell me how much you would have received for killing Christine and maybe I will believe you."

"Only our wages."

"How much do you make in a year?"

"$72,000."

"And you kill people for that?"

"Not good people. We never have. Tim and I have only worked for three years and have worked together during that time, but Aaden is suspicious of us. We have killed only the two men I told you about. If a contestant has too much money coming, or if Aaden has money bet against a contestant, agents will sometimes kill them during the contest period and make it look like someone else did it.

"That is why we were told to kill Christine. Aaden is afraid of her. He is afraid of the way her opponents are killed. Also, he could see that Ivonne has been with Christine at this house. He knows they spent time together, and he is afraid of Ivonne's father."

"What am I going to do with you in case you are lying?"

"I can tell you what to do, and it will help all of us. I do not know who you are, but I feel like you are more powerful than those at the Induction Center. They do not have many employees. Ten field agents and only a few in the office. They operate on fear. But whatever you plan, if you need me to, I will call Aaden. I will tell him we were captured and that Christine is here alone guarding us. That you missed taking my phone and I am able to call. He will send the other two agents to kill her and us at the same time. But he would never send more than two for a thing like this. I would tell him an exact time when her husband will be at work and she will be here. They would kill Christine's husband if he was here."

Emma continued, "Nancy and Aaden both hate, or hated in Nancy's case, Christine and Ivonne. Nancy was the one who found out that Ivonne booked a flight on the day she and Colin took her. They had a contact in the airport. Nancy knew

Ivonne was at Christine's address and guessed she would be going home. She had Colin check the flight records. He is her puppet. Take our phones and hold us here, and two agents will arrive on the next flight.

"Once you work for the lottery, there is no way to leave other than to a shallow grave. Aaden did allow his brother to leave, but we think he had him killed later. Tim and I just want out, except Tim doesn't look so good right now. I hope he is okay. He is a very nice man and has a family. They would miss him."

Ben and Frank were back and Sam asked Ben if he had the key for Emma's handcuffs. Sam looked at the badges, one in Emma's purse and one in Tim's pocket. It was obvious they did not want to be identified before getting into the house. Sam was also having a hard time not believing that Emma was telling the truth.

"Emma, go talk to Tim. See if you can bring him around. I think he was hit pretty hard by the big guy."

Christine offered to get each of them a glass of water or a soda. Emma said Tim was a coke drinker but she would like water.

"Tim, are you okay?"

For the first time his eyes moved, and he looked at Emma.

"Can you talk to me?"

Faintly he said, "There is pain in the back of my head and my neck."

Christine rolled a bath towel and put it around Tim's neck, tying it loosely in the front.

"Is this tight enough?" she said

Tim felt relief as he rested his neck against the towel, and Ben apologized for hitting him so hard. He told Tim it looked like he was going for his gun, and Tim said he was because he thought Emma had been killed.

Christine asked Sam if she could take Emma to her bedroom and find her something to wear. Sam said only if Frank went with them. Emma did not blame them for being careful and said she was good with that. Frank could turn his back, and it would be okay. Christine had a pair of loose jeans she hoped would fit and some panties that were still in a package. She asked if Emma wanted to shower or just wash up, and Emma said for now washing would be good.

***

Sam spoke to Tim: "Tim, are you okay? I want to know if you and Emma were given the shot that allows the lottery to see where you are and when you die?"

"Yes. They watch us pretty close."

"What do you know about the other field agents?"

"They are mostly bodyguards for Aaden now, but some are scattered across the country. They used to protect Nancy and Colin and Mark, but someone got to Nancy and Colin. They were found dead at Nancy's home. There isn't really much call for going into the field to eliminate contestants, but a lot of dangerous contestant's hate Aaden and hated Nancy even more.

"Emma and I are not trusted and both believe we are days from Aaden sending agents after us. That is why we hoped to be able to get into Russia for a while. That is one of the countries where lottery employees cannot go.

"But I asked how will we get them to come here?"

"I am sorry. I never got to the question. We heard that Ivonne Bykov's father threatened Nancy, and that is why she took Ivonne from the airport. It is the first time Nancy did something like this herself. She hated Ivonne's family so bad that it got in the way of good judgement. And that got her killed. She hoped to trade Ivonne's life for her father's, but the Bykov family did exactly what they said they would do to her.

"No worry with Aaden. He will not go after anyone. He is terrified of the Bykov family and will send agents to kill them if they ever come back. If you threaten to kill Aaden, he will trace your call, and other agents will be on the next airplane. I don't have much money, but would give it all to you to kill them—Aaden too if it is possible. Then I could keep my family here."

"I like you Tim. I hope you don't cross me. What caused

you to work for the lottery?"

"It is hard to get a job when you have been in prison for embezzlement. I work in computers, or did, and find ways to get money that isn't mine. I am done with that now, but knowing how to do it is something companies are afraid of. I cannot even get a job at a gas station or car lot. A friend told me that being a field agent for the lottery was easy. He said you never kill anyone unless they are bad, and you only go out a few times a year. The rest of the time you get paid to eat donuts and drink coffee. And that is mostly true."

"There is one thing I encourage you to be careful of," Tim said. "If Aaden were to suddenly have no field agents, the lottery has enough money to hire an army."

"Who would do the hiring?"

"I don't know. I think there was no one higher than Nancy and Aaden has that place now. I can tell you that the Induction Center does not handle money. Checks to contestants are made by accountants, and our checks come from the same place. On my phone you can see a picture of my last check."

"Checks are made by 'Charles Bondin, Incorporated,' Sam said. "That makes sense. The lottery is operated under contract allowing the government to shield itself from accountability. I have one more question. What do you know about a pay per view event that is scheduled to happen later this month?"

"Emma will know about that. She was onsite with contractors when they installed the cameras."

Emma said, "I was there as a contact between the contractors and Nancy. I know the event perimeter will only be definable by GPS. It will be up to the contestants to stay within the wilderness area. If they leave, they will lose any credits they have earned by eliminations and will be eliminated themselves by agents. Tim and I are supposed to be there with the other agents. I suppose this could change that."

"Okay," Sam said.

He left the room to ask Frank a question. They went out and stood by the creek. "Do you know if you can turn Christine's number off and if any of the lottery employees would be able to turn it back on?"

"Yes they could. We are all in the same program. It would be no different than if I turned it back on."

"It's possible, but I would have to be careful and call on a bit of luck to know they were not in the program at the same time. If they were, they could see what I was doing. They would not know who was doing it but would know someone was making changes."

"We need to do it tonight after they go home," Sam said. "Can you build a block into the program like you did around your own password? If you could do that, after you turn

Christine's number off, they would not be able to turn it back on? Emma could report that she and Tim finished what they were sent for. Do you think they would know the difference between a number which canceled because of death and one that was turned off?"

Frank said, "No. When a contestant dies, the default setting is to turn that number off. I would have to build a wall between her number and the rest of the program, but I could do it. For example, they should not have reason to turn Tanoak's number on again, but if they did they would see him moving in Japan and would know they were cheated out of the money for his elimination. But if they cluttered their monitors with numbers that died we would still see them. If I can do this, I could block Tanoak's and Hinoki's also. We would be the only ones able to turn them back on."

Sam and Frank returned to the room where the others were.

"Emma," Sam said. "I think we have a plan that would not give Aaden reason to send agents after you, but we will have to keep both of you here while we think more about it. I will ask you not to communicate with anyone in the next couple of days. Tim, it will be hard, but that means no contact with your family."

"We will do anything to come out of this alive." Tim said.

Sam answered, "At times we all have to take chances, and

we are taking a big one trusting both of you. Tonight we are going to make it look as if you killed Christine, and you will report to Aaden that you did. He will check, and her number will have died on his monitor. I have a pill that she will take, and for a short time her vital signs will stop. There are people who supply me with things that would scare you."

"It will not work." Emma said. "Nothing has ever fooled the program that collects and feeds information to the Induction Center."

Sam said, "Emma, that is what they tell you and want you to think. Trust me. It will work. They want you to believe they can catch you at anything and that no one can hurt them."

Sam would never reveal that a pill would not be given to Christine. As they were speaking, Frank was creating the wall that would block Christine's code from access. She would go to her bedroom under the idea of taking the pill and only Frank would be with her. He would then block access to her number.

"Emma," Sam said, "we have to know if it worked. Can you see lottery contestants on your phones?"

"Yes we can."

"I want you to show me."

"This is unbelievable," Emma said.

Tim had to look, "Christine's number shows her as dead. It worked. Watch—her number will disappear within a minute or so."

"When could you report that you killed her?" Ben asked.

"There is a hot line we call. Aaden will not allow field agents to contact him directly, but the message will go straight to his phone. Then he will expect us to come back. What will we do about that?"

"I don't know," Sam said. "We will have to figure that out. Offer suggestions if you have any."

“Those that can give up essential liberty to gain a little temporary safety deserve neither liberty nor safety.”

–Benjamin Franklin

Nineteen

That night couches in the living room were arranged facing each other and touching. One of Tim's wrists was handcuffed to Emma's ankle, and Sam reminded them that the house was surrounded by cameras. They decided not to kill them, but Sam assured them if they tried to escape that would change. The Induction Center was closed when Emma called Aaden. On the recording, she told him they had killed Christine.

Tim slept head one way and Emma the other. Ben stayed the night and slept in the living room with them. If one of them had to go to the bathroom, he would take the handcuffs off and let them go. Tim would want nothing to do with causing Ben to hit him again. He was better, but his neck and head still hurt. Sam went home and would come back the next day—Ben had a plan he hoped Sam, Frank, and Christine would agree to.

After talking the next day with Emma and Tim, Sam decided to trust them, but no one could think of a way to kill the other field agents without Aaden knowing it. If he knew it, he might hire twenty to replace them.

There were several ideas, and Ben offered to kill Aaden

regardless of what else might happen. With that done, Aaden would not be able to call the other agents, but Mark might call them if Aaden failed to answer his phone or come to work.

Emma said she would not like Mark to be hurt but that he had been part of using Sardac to immobilize contestants. By doing so he was certainly a part of one or more contestant's deaths. But he had a family, and she believed he could never kill anyone personally. She did hope that Aaden and the other eight agents could be killed. She and Tim believed if that happened, and the lottery's records could be destroyed, that the lottery would end. She said Sam could figure out how to anonymously tell the government not to start the lottery again or worse would happen.

No secrets had been revealed to Tim or Emma. They would not be trusted with some things.

***

The next day Liam asked his mom and dad and Sam into his room. Ben had been waiting for a chance to talk to Sam but he was assigned to Tim and Emma and would have to wait his turn.

"Check this out," Liam said. "In Daniel's computers I found details showing how he collected a portion of the serum which had been injected into Tanoak and injected it into Hinoki. He used a syringe and extracted some of the serum. And get this: He created the first serum used in the lottery when he worked there. If Daniel's notes are accurate, I cannot believe how simple it is to make the serum. According to his notes, he believed the serum stayed near the surface of the skin—exactly where it had been injected. He was obviously an engineer in more than mechanical products."

"If this is true," Frank said, "Julie's friend Dr. Thorneburg could remove the serum from your mom and Ivonne. And with our program, we would know if it worked."

Ben was with Tim and Emma in the living room. It was Saturday, but Dana, Jeremiah, and Karly had not come to the house with Sam. He did not want Tim and Emma to know who they were.

"Sam, can I talk to you alone?"

"Sure Ben. Let's go out to the creek."

Ben looked troubled on the way, and Sam wondered if keeping Tim and Emma alive was bothering him. Ben was very good at his job and taking life was not the same to him as it had become for Sam, especially after he married Dana.

Ben chose his words carefully: "Sam, now that the Induction Center thinks Christine is dead, I would like to replace her in the PPV. We are at the doorstep of destroying this lottery along with Aaden and the field agents but please let me say this: There is a $100,000,000 guaranteed purse for the winner in the PPV plus a $50,000 bonus for each contestant eliminated by the final winner. If Frank could put me in there,

I would fight for that money in Christine's place. I will never have another chance like this."

Sam did not answer quickly. His had a lot of respect for Ben after all he had done for them, but he knew being in the PPV event might be more dangerous than most things Ben did in his normal line of work.

"I am not sure I can answer that Ben, but it is an incredible amount of money. It just wouldn't be right to use our ability to see the locations of other contestants then kill them that way. Saving Christine's life has been different. She didn't want to be in the lottery, and Aaden forced her. I also don't want to live without you Ben. We have been through a lot together. That and some of the contestants who will be in the PPV are probably good people with families, just wanting the money as you do."

"If Frank could get me in I would not ask for the advantage. I have the skills to win as fairly as if I had bought Christine's ticket. I believe a check for $100,000,000 is worth me taking the chance. Race car drivers take a chance every time they get in their car, and every time you went after professional killers in your job you knew the chance you were taking."

"Ben, it would not surprise me if we could erase Christine's past and enter you as a mystery contestant Nancy Lee saved until now. There is one problem and that is Aaden. He may have gone through all of her records by now and know there is no record of her talking to you."

Ben said, "Frank could write a password protected letter as if Nancy wrote it and show me as the mystery contestant she planned to use after Christine was eliminated. With Christine supposedly dead now, it would make sense. Frank could include a picture of me with the letter. Then an anonymous phone call could tell Aaden the caller had killed Nancy and Colin. He could say he had followed the lottery since it first began and that before Nancy died he got a password out of her to reveal new information Aaden didn't have access to.

"I want this, Sam. Frank is the only one who could make a letter and create the protected file. Talk him into trading me this. I was here to save Christine if the agents had been going to kill her."

"Ben, you have become like a brother to me. I don't know If I could live with myself for putting you into this with eleven people who have risen to where they are by killing. What if one of them gets you, and I have to think about that."

"That's not going to happen. And you know I am not greedy. I would share the money with all of you."

"Ben, we will talk to Frank and Christine together if you have to do this."

***

After much talk it was decided that Tim and Emma should go back. Aaden believed they had killed Christine and that would keep them in safe standing for a while. With the PPV coming, Aaden needed enough agents to watch the perimeter of the Mill Creek wilderness, and 17,400 acres would be a lot to watch. They agreed to go back on one condition. They asked that Ben or Sam promise to kill Aaden after the PPV, and before Sam could say a word, Ben said he would gladly do it.

Tim and Emma did not know yet that Ben might be one of the contestants, but it was agreed between Frank and Ben, that Frank would enter the letter into a password protected file and make the phone call to Aaden. He would pay cash for a pre-paid phone and destroy it after making the call.

Frank made the call from a gated road leading onto forestland where there were no cameras. The phone was a cheap investment that would only be used once. Liam momentarily killed the cameras at the store where Frank bought the phone.

When Frank was home, he installed the letter into Nancy's personal file and that afternoon called Aaden. He first reached Mark, but when he told him he knew who killed Nancy Lee Mark quickly sent him to Aaden. Frank played the game well. He admitted that he had killed Nancy and Colin and described how Aaden could access the letter Nancy had left. Mark was frantically trying to have the call traced, but, of course, he would not be successful.

Later that day, Ben called Mark. He told him of hearing on the news that Nancy Lee had been killed and asked Mark if he was aware of his arrangement with Nancy and promise to be entered into the PPV as a mystery contestant if any scheduled contestant should not be able to make the event. Mark brought Aaden into the call.

Mark and Aaden had seen Nancy's letter and the picture of Ben. In Frank's forged letter, Nancy commented on taking the picture herself. Of course, the properties of the picture had been deleted. Ben had worn his jeans and no shirt for the photograph. His hard, muscled body was impressive to say the least. He was the man Aaden would put his money on.

Aaden ask about Ben's background and reason they should accept him. After talking about his military history as a SEAL, they asked him to come for an interview. Their true intention was to see if Ben really was the man in the photograph attached to Nancy's letter. Christine had been their promotional contestant, and they needed a more dynamic prospect now to bring advertisers to the table.

During the interview, Ben did not reference his real job as a body guard directly to the President, but he did have a second military I.D. created and a driver's license with the name Anthony Strangmann. The last name was Christine's idea. Its meaning was from old English meaning Strongman.

At the Induction Center, things went well. Ben received

the serum and was given the number S106. When he left the building, Dan was waiting for him in the parking lot for the flight home.

It might have been possible for Ben to go back to Frank and Christine's home, or Sam's, but after landing in Portland, he drove to an apartment Christine rented before he left. With the serum injected, he would not be able to go to their homes again, at least till the PPV was over. Tara Thornburg had removed the serum from Christine, and they called Ivonne. She would come when she could and go to see Tara. In the meantime, Frank had removed their names from the records.

***

The day finally came, and Ben received a call from the Induction Center. He was to report with all of his gear to the Wildcat Campground east of Prineville, Oregon. Portable buildings had been set up for the contestants. It was hard for Ben to imagine that they would stay in the same campground during the nights and hunt to kill each other during the days.

With their injected markers, it was certain there would be no foul play without fear of the agents eliminating anyone who would attempt to harm another outside of the boundary. Christine had called Tim and Emma's phones. When Ben arrived at the Wildcat Campground, they would greet him as if they were strangers.

Field agents were instructed to meet with each contestant

prior to the contest and discuss the rules. The event would last until there was one contestant remaining or for three days. The number of contestants living at the end of three days would be required to share the money among themselves. It was not likely that even two or three contestants would want to share $100,000,000. They would work hard to eliminate every competitor.

Rules stated that contestants must engage. If field agents determined that a contestant was hiding and not hunting, they were authorized to eliminate them from the contest. And with the program, they could see every contestant's location. Contestants were allowed one hour during a day when their marker could be motionless. That was all. If agents were able to see that two or more contestants were together for more than one hour without one or more being eliminated, those contestants would each forfeit the cost of one elimination, or $50,000. Contestants were allowed, however, to claim an elimination they had not caused. They only needed to arrive nearest the fallen opponent first.

Contestants would have approximately twenty-five minutes to arrive at the site of an elimination before they would not be able to receive credit for the victim's death.

There would be twelve contestants starting on day one: Ben Bonoaski or Anthony Strangmann as he had registered, Randy Mason, Jim Bader, Alex Harmon, Robin Mitchell,

Kenneth Armendez, Tara Andrews, Juliana Johannson, Linnea Saddlemen, Colby Blackwell, Orlando Ruffin, and Chang Nisbet.

Ben would have an advantage with his training and background. His main weapon would be a Mark 13 Model 7 Marine sniper rifle chambered for the 300 Winchester Magnum cartridge. He was extremely skilled with that rifle. In his duffle bag, he also had the EL Range 10x42 binocular by Swarovski, a satellite phone, a ghillie suite perfectly colored to match the predominately pine forest at 1500 meters' in elevation, a Leupold RX-2800 laser range finder, and a thermal clip-on for a Night Force ATACR 7-35x56 rifle scope. The thermal imaging system would detect anything that put out heat. Even if a person was hiding in the daylight hours, he would see their heat signature. There were still patches of snow, and the ground was relatively cold. That would help.

This event would be different than contests in the regular lottery where hunters are killed in a variety of ways. This event would require long range shooting skills and a more than good sense about moving and hiding.

Randy Mason was a writer. He published a few books, mostly fiction, but had never really been successful. At 35 years old he had worked his way up to meet this challenge for $100,000,000. He went with a friend to learn how to shoot at a local gun club with a maximum 300-yard range. He would carry a 270 in a Tikka T3x. As nice as the 270 cartridge is for hunting, Randy had no idea of the distance that would be shot in this event.

Jim Bader did know. He was 52, a game warden from Idaho and a serious whitetail hunter. He had taken bucks out to 900 yards. Jim would carry a Model 70 Winchester rifle in the 300 Winchester magnum cartridge with a 4.5-14 Leupold Mark 4 scope. He could read sign well and understood how wind, temperature, and elevation each relates to accuracy.

Alex Harmon had never decided what he wanted to do and the lottery looked like an easy way to make money. He would certainly have the chance for that now. At 21, he had never been away from Beverly Hills, California. He borrowed a 243 Short Mag from a friend in Oregon and told his friend he didn't need practice to win the PPV. It wasn't known if he had even fired the rifle prior to arriving at Wildcat Campground. He had eliminated just three contestants before now, but a friend knew someone who could get him to where he was today. It would turn out to be an event Alex should not have attended.

Robin Mitchell was a lot like Jim Bader. He was a successful big game hunter. At 61, he had made his way here by using skills in both surprise and shooting. He came with a custom built 338-06 rifle and six boxes of hand-loaded cartridges.

Kenneth Armendez was 22 years old and a car salesman before winning a chance to compete in 'The Hunt for Money' lottery. He had eliminated six opponents, easily earning his way to this event. But he must have thought it would be thick timber with underbrush. He came only with a Marlin lever action in the 45-70 caliber and a Glock Mod 40. The 45-70 and 10mm cartridges are great for close range shooting but not in the Mill Creek Wilderness competing against long range rifles and people who know how to shoot.

Tara Andrews was another story. She and her husband owned a 130,000 acre cattle ranch in Montana. It had belonged to Tara's parents, and she grew up shooting predators on the ranch. She was 47-years old, 5 foot 9 inches tall and looked very confident. As only a few of the contestants would do, she would keep her rifle hidden, only exposing it after the helicopter set her down in one of twelve landing places in the wilderness. She carried a custom rifle. It was an original Sako Finbear made in 1961, an L61R that her father had built. It had a full 30-inch custom Shilen barrel and was chambered for the 300 Remington Ultra Mag cartridge. Tara had brought 200 rounds of hand-loaded ammunition, knowing that she would use very little of it. She would shoot 180 grain Barnes, TSX bullets at 3415 feet per second. Her scope was etched for those ballistics, and she had taken coyotes at more than 1000 yards with the rifle.

Juliana Johannson should not have come. She did not get there by impressively eliminating opponents, but as Sam did for Christine, her brothers had killed six contestants in six months—but they could not be with her now. Juliana was a model for a clothing company. She was proud of herself and not a nice person. She had never been out of the city. Her brothers sent her with a Savage Arms Axis II XP Pink Camo 243 Winchester Rifle. A nice rifle, but she didn't know how to use it. The only clothes she brought were light hiking shoes and what looked like clothing she would wear in an office.

Linnea Saddlemen was a jolly, older woman from South Carolina. The way she talked about killing, made it sound like she had no care whatsoever for another person's life. But she was well-kept and looked strong. As with Juliana and others, she had purchased the winning ticket herself, but was not the one who had eliminated six contestants. She was a long-haul truck driver, and four of her victims had died with their hands tied and the front tire of an eighteen-wheeler on their chest—and she bragged about that. She used it on the website as a fear tactic. No one knew if it was true or not.

Colby Blackwell was more dangerous. He was 27-years old and two years out of the police academy in Detroit. He was training to be a sniper on the SWAT team but on this trip carried a nearly unfired 300 Winchester Magnum. He concealed it as some did but he was not familiar with the rifle.

Time would tell if Colby could shoot long range competitively.

Orlando Ruffin was 24-years old, a black guy, and the nicest guy you would ever meet. Those in the camp would know him as extremely sincere and caring. He wished other contestants well if they talked in passing. Whatever made him buy the ticket no one knew. But apparently he had done well eliminating contestants on his way to this event. In his high school year book, he was chosen as the nicest guy in his class, yet now he was hunting for money.

Chang Nisbet spoke English but not well. He had purchased a lottery ticket while in the United States on business then returned from China when he was called by the Induction Center. If intelligence was the only skill needed to win, Chang would be dangerous. It could play a big part, but he was not experienced at hunting or shooting.

One could wonder what so many of these contestants thought they were getting into. How could they not have studied the Mill Creek Wilderness and the surrounding Ochoco Forest to know there is so much opened ground? Some areas are predominately grass, maybe scattered with pines, juniper's or rocks. Hiding and hunting is difficult in country like that.

"In the beginning of a change, the patriot is a scarce man, and brave, and hated and scorned. When his cause succeeds, the timid join him, for then it costs nothing to be a patriot."

–Mark Twain (1835-1910)

Twenty

It was in the Wildcat Campground the afternoon before the event would start when Tim and Emma introduced themselves to Ben. There were eight other agents, and not one of them was caring or polite. To fit in with the others, Tim and Emma tried to be the same. Agents were free to do anything they wanted to the contestants. They were eager to tell them what would happen if they broke any rule.

Ben was storing the face of each agent into his mind. He did not ever want to forget them and wouldn't. Each contestant would carry a GPS to be certain they stayed inside the boundary. Those were furnished by the lottery and set to one radio channel which would contact any of the Induction Center staff.

Aaden Bradly and Mark had set up a modest command center a good distance outside of the boundary and away from contestants. They were a little less than one mile from the westernmost lobe of the wilderness and south of Whiskey Spring in a meadow southeast of the Quarry. From there they would watch the contest live by camera and instruct agents if anything were to go wrong.

At one hour after daylight, the sound of two helicopters

broke the silence that is otherwise well known in the Ochoco National Forest. What would happen next had been discussed. Each helo would take three contestants from the base camp at Wildcat Campground. They would do that twice and the contestants had no say about where they would be dropped off. Landing sites had been located and practiced by the pilots. They would set down, look to whichever of the contestants they might and say get out here. The next contestant might be let out a quarter of a mile away or two miles away.

In the briefing, they had been told that hunting ended at 5 pm sharp. The pilots would not fly until after that time, and contestants were ordered to be close to a landing site. The sites were well marked so that even if a contestant was miles from where they had been dropped off, they would have seen one of the landing sites. If any contestant was shot after 5 pm, it would not be a legal elimination. If the shooter was known, they would be eliminated from the competition.

Ben was dropped off on a small butte south of Moccasin Prairie only a mile and a half northwest of where five agents were set up on Whistler Point. The steep Desolation Canyon was a half mile to his west. As luck would have it, Tara Andrews was let out on the Twin Pillars Trail near the two pillars. She was directly southeast of Ben and carried the most accurate rifle in the competition other than Ben's, but she was two miles from Desolation Canyon and not in shape to get to where Ben was. As soon as Ben hit the ground, he took his rifle from the pack and traveled fast down the south side of the 1700 m butte where he had been dropped off. He moved until he was out of sight from the overlook on Whistler Point and set his pack on the ground. The next thing out was his ghillie suit. With that, he became invisible in the forest as well as on the opened ground. There were standing dead trees remaining from both the Hash Rock fire and the Desolation fire, but the regeneration of trees and shrubs offered excellent cover to move in and hide. Tara would not be able to see him and was much too far away.

Because of Ben's training, he had the wisdom to sit in the early morning and listen to each helo as they set out the other contestants. With an Avenza Map on his phone, he set red pins as near as possible to every location where he heard the helicopters set down. He knew close to where the other contestants were, but of the five set out in the first transport he did not know who had been dropped off in each place. That morning he had been seated in the helo with Tara Andrews and Colby Blackwell. Colby was positioned first on Forked Horn Butte, then Tara to his north and then Ben east of the canyon.

From the pins Ben had set on his map, he knew contestants were mostly set on high elevation points where the trees were not as thick. He had studied the wilderness extensively using Google Earth and learned that areas in the southwest below Twin Pillars and Belknap trails were more heavily stocked with timber and brush. Two contestants had been placed along the Wildcat trail where it turns north and runs for several miles toward Whistler Spring.

Ben heard a shot to his south. He was sure it was north of the East Fork of Mill Creek and would, therefore, put the shooter less than a mile from him. Ben began moving in that direction. His plan was to stay relatively low and watch the high points. Most proficient shooters would want to be high where they could see a long distance, and that would be to Ben's advantage. He would be hard to see. He would glass every high point as he moved. He knew there would be a hunter moving somewhere south of him to get close to the fallen opponent, if they were not already there. And instantly he saw movement. With his range finding binoculars, Ben saw Juliana Johannson on the ground and Chang Nesbit moving toward her. Chang was out farther than Ben's range finding binoculars would work, but he brought out his Leupold laser rangefinder. Chang was 1645 yards out and within four hundred yards of Juliana.

Ben would have to shoot before Chang was close enough to Juliana to register her elimination. If he stopped Chang before he reached her, he would have $50,000 times two, and it was only a little past sunrise. Ben moved almost silently for a big man. Unconsciously he traveled from one point of cover to the next, glassing high points as he went, moving deliberately but slowly to not be noticed as something that had moved in the forest. He was now at 1406 yards and Chang was getting close to Juliana. Ben's pack came off, went to the ground, and he laid his rifle over it. Not high enough. He unfolded the rifles bipod. Leaving the legs short, he set them firmly on the pack. His breathing slowed and the report from his rifle echoed easily to both lookouts where agents were sitting. They had already started their morning with mixed drinks and bets on the contestants they thought would win that day.

Juliana was dead, and Chang was dead. None of the agents could see Ben, other than his marker, and he had recorded two eliminations.

Ben heard two other shots. They were west and southwest of his position. There was not time for anyone other than Tara Andrews and Colby Blackwell to be in that area. It was too far for Ben to go, but he was certain there would only be one of them on the west side of Desolation Canyon now, and if it was Colby he could cross the canyon. They had been a little more than two miles apart on reasonably good ground. He guessed Colby had gone after Tara Andrews, and that would have been dangerous. A person moving runs the risk of being seen.

Ben had two pins on his map where the Wildcat trail

bends north. Chang could have been one of two set off there, but it was more likely he had been set on a butte near the south end of Desolation Canyon. Ben moved towards the two buttes near the bend in Wildcat trail. Deliberately and surprisingly quiet. His mind was clear of all things other than what he was doing—that is a skill that few people have.

He traveled through creeks and low country to get close to the buttes. The one nearest the bend in the trail was 1758 meters in elevation. Ben never moved more than a few yards without looking in every direction. That included his back-trail and he was almost impossible to see when standing still.

***

At John and Julie's house the phone rang. It was Leonid.

"John, this is Leonid. Ruslin and Ivonne are with me. We are scheduled to land in Portland tomorrow at 7:14 in the morning. I am sorry for not calling sooner. I should have gotten Ivonne a different phone number when we left last time but didn't think of it. She got a call from Aaden Bradley almost a week ago. He said she has a contract with him and he would have his agents kill her if she did not report within the week. We will not spend our lives hiding. Our plan is to leave her with Christine. Then Ruslin and me will find Aaden and end this."

"I have a doctor's appointment in the morning," John said, "but will call Sam. He will pick you guys up or Christine will."

"Okay John. Thank you. I hope your appointment is nothing serious."

"Just a little, Leonid. I had a heart attack several days ago, but I am okay. I just turned 82, and I am too young for this stuff."

"John, I do not want you to worry about what we will do. Maybe Sam will know how to find Aaden for us."

"Sam told me the lottery people have gone to manage a pay per view event east of here in Oregon. I'm sure Aaden is there. Sam said it is televised, and Aaden likes to be in front of cameras. I can tell you this: Sam becomes more upset by the day with what is happening. You will talk to him when he picks you up."

"Leonid, this is Sam. Dad said you are coming into Portland and he told me why. I am sorry you have to go through this. I will be there to pick you up."

At Sam and Dana's house, Ruslin told Sam he would kill Aaden as soon as they could find him. Sam said it would have to be done more carefully than that. They did not want the law snooping around before certain things were accomplished.

Ruslin's reply was that he and his dad do not allow people to threaten their family, and Sam appreciated their conviction.

Dana called Sam to say she and Karly would take Ivonne when they got there and go to Christine's, allowing him to stay and make plans with Leonid and Ruslin. She said Christine was sending Frank over to sit in on the meeting and discuss what he could do to help.

***

"Leonid, Ruslin, without knowing it, your timing is perfect. I would not ask you to get involved in whatever we have to do to stop this lottery, but it seems that you have no choice now. In the past, I have been afraid of what their field agents could do. I don't know who they are, and that would make it impossible to stop them if they came after Christine or Ivonne.

"With the pay per view now, we have them all in one place, and this is our best chance to stop them. There is one thing that I must say. You and Ruslin are fisherman, not trained for gun fights like this might be. I have contacts who are at the PPV event, and they will know where all of the agents are."

"Sam, you do not know us. In our country we must be strong to survive. Ruslin and I will go alone if we cannot go with you, and that is my word."

"Sam," Ruslin said, "I mean no disrespect, but you do not know things my father and I have done."

"In fishing, you do not shoot rifles at long ranges," Sam said. "I have experience, and my friend in the event also has experience. I do not mean this against you, but if I let you go with me, you have to listen to my plan."

"We would have it no other way," Leonid said.

"Okay men, let's talk then. If we hope to destroy the lottery, we have to destroy a place called the Induction Center where all of their records are kept. And we have to be at a pay per view event at the same time. If we are at either place first, people could be warned at the other. And from what I have learned, we will have to kill nine employees. Eight field agents and Aaden Bradley."

Sam told Leonid and Ruslin about Tim and Emma, that they were on site to do whatever they could, which would include killing three field agents in their camp. That would leave five on the other side of the wilderness. Interestingly enough there were no cameras set to watch the agents. The helicopter pilots would have to be stopped but not killed. They were probably under contract. Mark, an employee of the lottery, would not be killed by request from Tim and Emma. Sam would give pictures of them and Mark to Leonid and Ruslin.

With help from Tim and Emma, Sam knew exactly where to find Aaden and the other agents. He had not been able to talk his friend Dan out of getting into the action. It was decided that Leonid and Ruslin would take care of the Induction Center, and Dan would fly them from there to Prineville. Frank insisted on going to the PPV, but Sam said no. He said he needed to stay with the family at home. Sam said while this was going on, they should all be in one house, and Frank would be armed at all times.

***

In the Mill Creek Wilderness, Ben was within a snipers range of the westernmost butte near the bend in the Wildcat trail. He was sitting with a bushy, young Ponderosa pine behind him. He had snipped enough limbs to be sitting back inside of the tree. His back and on both sides were hidden by limbs, and his ghillie suit made him invisible from the front. His pack was on the ground beside his leg and on it was a forked stick he cut from one of the limbs he had removed. It could serve as a monopod if he needed it.

Ben glassed the highest butte steadily. Then he was sure something moved. He raised his rifle and saw movement on the butte. To his disbelief, Linnea Saddlemen, the cruel truck driver from South Carolina was setting a camping chair in a new position facing eastward toward the second butte.

He ranged her at just under 1100 yards. Ben could make the shot but wondered about the climb. He would have to reach Linnea within twenty minutes. He decided to move closer. He moved slowly out from the pine tree and put his pack on after carefully scanning the timber in every direction. After five minutes, he had not seen movement and moved forward 70 yards to a thick bush. He checked to his sides and back again.

Ben moved the same way several more times and was as close as he could get without losing view of Saddlemen and the top of the butte. She was 2000 feet above him in elevation and 740 yards as the path of a bullet travels. He could easily make the climb. His concern would be constantly moving with very little cover up the face of the butte. Even in the ghillie suit, movement is detectable. He moved from the bush to a small Douglas-fir and found a good position to rest over its limbs. With the rifle secure and his right elbow rested he held on Linnae's neck. It was a steep uphill shot, and his bullet would drop very little. The rifle was sighted in at 300 yards and shot tight groups at that distance.

Ben used every resting point available. He was sitting on the ground with his left knee drawn up tight to his body. His left elbow rested on it. His left hand was under a small but sturdy limb with his fingers reaching up on each side of the forearm of the rifle. His right elbow rested on a balanced set of two limbs. With his finger on the trigger he let his breath out and held it. The trigger was set at 1.7 pounds. Too light for combat but not for a sniper. The 180 grain, boat-tailed bullet left the barrel with no awareness of its destination. It tore through linnae's ribs and heart, exiting the far side of her chest. Ben had never killed a woman, but this woman was here by choice and would have killed him if she could.

Before moving he turned to face again in all directions,

including one last look to the top of the butte. It was an easy climb in the amount of time he had. He would stop more than once to look below—and to not wind himself so badly he couldn't shoot if someone came to the sound of his rifle. Ben was nearly to the top when he saw a contestant on a paced run toward the butte. It was Alex Harmon. He was young and in good shape. Ben would lose sight of him as he finished his climb to the top but once there he would have a clear view from the other side.

Ben went first to Linnae and then to the far side where he could see down. There were more trees along the Wildcat Trail than he had hoped for, but he could see Alex moving. The young man was now a target. Ben ranged him at 1100 yards. He was downhill and there was a slight crosswind blowing from the south. The shot was possible but Ben waited.

With Ben's rifle laid over his pack, Alex closed the distance; 1000 yards, 900 yards, 800 yards. Alex never looked up once. Not that he could have seen Ben, but it caused Ben to wonder how these people got to where they were in the lottery. They had obviously never hunted in a wild, natural environment, away from cities and asphalt parking lots. This was not one of those places where you might find your opponent in a grocery store or distracted by other people while you moved closer.

Ben lowered his binoculars and brought the rifle against

his shoulder. He checked the wind in the wispy tops of smaller trees along the trail. His trigger eased back to one pound, then to one-half, then to the precipice of the sear. The shot Alex would never hear was gone.

Linnea had no gear that Ben needed, and he began his decent to where Alex lay dead on the trail.

Ben had seen a designated pickup location in an opening near the trail where he first saw Alex. It was afternoon, and he had earned $200,000 in eliminations. He decided to rest near the pickup site. He would stay 100 yards out and stay hidden in the ghillie suit until he could hear the helicopter. Then he would bundle everything along with his rifle in the long duffle bag that was laced to his day pack. Ben knew how to travel and carry what he needed.

Each contestant he eliminated was in his opinion undeserving of the experienced competitors he thought would be there. He didn't know about Colby Blackwell. From his position, he had not known if Colby was down or if it was Tara Andrews. Colby had followed the higher, flatter ground from Forked Horn Butte north toward where he knew Tara or Ben had been set out. Even at that elevation he crossed five creeks, Brogan Creek being the last he crossed. From there, he hit the Twin Pillars Trail where it turned northwest along the north side of Brogan Creek. And where it turned again, to the northeast this time, Tara saw him walking. He was where the trail zigzags several times. Tara was waiting as a predator would. She was sitting comfortably with her father's rifle nestled into her pack, ready to shoot without movement of her body. Colby had come to her as if he had no experience hunting, unknowledgeable of the life-determining requirement to blend in with natural surroundings.

There was a solemn feeling in the small, portable buildings at Wildcat Camp Ground that evening as the helicopters continued to fly. The bodies of those who had been killed were being lifted out and taken to the command center near Whisky Spring where Aaden and Mark waited.

People had seen the action on PPV channels as cameras captured all but Juliana and Chang's death. Juliana who would be expected to follow the trails had not, and Chang had spotted her.

Later that night, Ben was surprised to hear a knock on his door.

"Ben, I am Tara. There are only seven of us left, and I only got one. I think you did pretty well for the first day."

"Have you talked to the others?"

"Yes. Everyone but you and Jim Bader came to dinner in the mess hall. It wasn't a great dinner, but it was free, and there was food we could take for tomorrow. You must have everything you need."

"Tara, I'm not much for talking. I wish you well, but I

would just as soon not know you."

"I see that in you. Watch out for me Ben. I can shoot a long, long way."

"Probably farther than I can."

"Somehow I doubt that. I am sure one of us will know after tomorrow?"

"Good night Tara."

"Good night Ben."

It was a common sound for Ben to hear the helo coming the next morning. With only seven contestants left, they would take three again in one and four in the other.

Ben carried his day pack and duffle bag deliberately to the farthest helo. He had learned something overnight that he didn't know before. Orlando Ruffin followed, Ben and Tara came next.

Kenneth Armendez, Randy Mason, Jim Bader, and Robin Mitchell flew on the other helicopter.

"Good morning Ben. Good morning Tara. My name is Orlando. This is pretty scary isn't it?"

Tara answered and started a conversation with Orlando. Ben wrote something on an energy bar wrapper. The first stop was in the northeastern portion of the wilderness one mile east of the Wildcat Trail and one and a half miles from the northern boundary of the wilderness. The pilot told Tara to get out there. On the way to the next landing site, Ben moved to the seat beside Orlando.

"Orlando, listen to me. From wherever you are let out, unless you are really serious about this, you need to hide. Or if you are close enough to a boundary line, run outside of the boundary and hide. You have no reason to believe me, but something is going to happen today. If you live through the day you might live to have grandchildren."

The helo sat down on a high point directly south of the agent's day camp on Whistler Point. The pilot motioned to Orlando to get out. Orlando would be to the east of Desolation Canyon.

Ben said, "Remember what I said Orlando. Hide till this is over or get outside of the boundary. The agents will not go after you. Believe me."

Orlando looked Ben in the eyes for several seconds before getting out.

"I will," he said.

"Go down the south side of the butte and get into the big canyon. Follow it up to the boundary or hide on the steep ground."

With only Ben left in the helicopter, he went to the front seat opposite the pilot and extended his hand to Sam's longtime friend Jackson. He put the paper he had written for Orlando in his pocket and put a headset on.

Jackson said, "What a kick, huh? People out here getting

paid millions to kill each other. Sam and Dan and I did it back in the day and hardly got paid anything."

"Sam called last night and told me which bird you were in, but he said I would get shot down if I went up with you." Ben laughed. "He told me his dad got you up here as a replacement and that today is the big day."

Jackson flipped a switch and disconnected his radio from the control center. Ben turned his radio off.

Jackson said. "Did Sam tell you everything?"

"No. He was with Leonid and his son and told me I would be briefed when you got here."

"Sam left this morning to drive up. He said you would know Frank's truck. Leonid and Ruslin left yesterday for San Francisco. It's going to be better than the fourth of July. Frank bought a used thousand-gallon tanker truck and filled it with a mixture of gas and diesel, whatever he could get. This evening they are going to drill a three-inch hole through the wall of the Induction Center building and back the truck up to it. Then run a hose into the building and turn the valve on. Sam made a floating detonator with a timer. They will push it through the hole first. Sam told Leonid to break the keypad at the door so no one can get in, and Dan will be waiting for them. Sam said his nephew is going to kill the cameras around there. The truck was bought with cash and there will not be any fingerprints on it. Not that much will be left after it blows. The detonator will not go off until the tank is empty.

"Dan and the Bykov's should be here any time. Sam figured there could be four to five inches of fuel on the floor, seeping under doorways and everywhere. Everything in that building is going to melt. The bottom of the main entry door will be sealed."

Ben said to Jackson: "Sam told me that early today he will be here. He will meet the others in Prineville and call us. Then they will park at a quarry near the control center and walk in. When we deliver your package, Sam and the other guys will break the door down and Kill Aaden.

There are two agents on the south side who have radio communication with us. They will kill three agents that are with them and 'Project Elimination' will be underway."

"Did Sam tell you about the fate of the five on the north side?" Jackson said.

"He told me you were in charge of that."

"See that container that looks like a beer keg right behind you."

"Don't tell me. Something you made? Sam warned me about you."

"That's funny, but you get to do the honors. Those agents to the north will think we are bringing them a keg of beer when they see this thing falling. It shouldn't burn the wilderness down this time of year, but we cannot deliver it until

Sam is at the command center."

"Jackson, I wish I knew you better. Don't lower me too close. I need my hair and eyebrows to stay where they are and this bird to stay in the air. How many times have you been down?"

"Only three."

"The philosophy of the school room in one generation will be the philosophy of government in the next.

–Abraham Lincoln

Twenty-One

Ben, this is Sam"

"Hey Sam. Are you here? We are ready when you are."

"We are at the quarry unloading a few things."

"I'll bet you are."

Sam asked Ben, "What time does your watch say?"

"11:03 and ten seconds."

"Okay. We need to walk in. It's not far, but I hope they don't have a dog tied out. If we have to kill them Aaden won't be here to pay you."

Jackson could hear the conversation. He and Ben were back on the ground at Wildcat camp.

Jackson said to give him a minute and for everyone to stay quiet. He switched his communication back on between the helo and the control center.

"Aaden, you there?"

"Go ahead pilot."

"Did you or Mark bring a dog? I heard one barking east of you. Could be a wolf or a couple of them."

"No dog here."

"If you and Mark walk out from the building toward the east you will hear them."

Sam, Dan, Leonid, and Ruslin were almost there when Aaden and Mark came out of the building. They walked a short way toward the wilderness hoping to hear the wolves.

For the last hundred yards Sam and the others were able to walk quietly in the meadow where the control center was located. They went into the building. There were two rifles leaning against a wall by the door, but Aaden and Mark undoubtedly carried handguns.

Sam told Ben to stay quiet till he called again. Then it would be time to deliver Jackson's keg to the north side.

Sam turned his radio off. Aaden and Mark were fifty yards from the building listening to hear a wolf. Having not heard one, they returned to the building—Sam was sitting in Aaden's chair. Leonid and Ruslin were one at each side of the door holding rifles, and Dan was holding his own standing near Sam.

"Who are you?" Aaden said. "Do you know who I am?"

But he and Mark quickly understood the situation they were in.

Sam raised his radio and said, "Ben, go ahead."

On the same radio he said, "Tim, it's time to go."

As the three agents with Tim and Emma turned from their mixed drinks to the sound of Tim's private radio, Tim shot two of them and Emma one.

Within seconds, a deafening explosion echoed

throughout the wilderness, its sound easily penetrating the walls of the control center.

Sam said to Aaden, "Do you know what that was?"

"If I had to guess, there are government employees dead out there, and you will spend life in prison for whatever you are doing. We have no money here."

Leonid walked over and laid Aaden's gun and his own on the desk by Sam.

"Aaden, I would have known you anywhere," he said, "because I threw your brother into the sea in Alaska. He sank like a rock, but now you have called my daughter Ivonne and threatened to kill her. You are not smart enough to be in this business and neither was Daniel."

Mark was not armed. Ruslin told him to take a chair and sit down close to Sam.

Then Ruslin said to Aaden: "I want to know if you are smarter than Daniel. My dad offered Daniel a chance to go free by fighting him, and he tried it. For my dad he was no more than a child."

Ruslin smiled for only a second, then looked at Aaden with exactly the same look Daniel had seen when they met on his Yacht.

"I don't see that in your eyes," Ruslin said. "At least Daniel tried to fight. You are a coward, and it is only a matter of how we kill you that will matter."

Ruslin stood facing Aaden.

Sam said, "Aaden, we don't like you. And there is no one here to help you, so if you do not do exactly what I tell you to do, you will die a horrible death."

Just then Jackson set the helicopter down near the building, and Ben went inside.

Ben's ghillie suit was off, leaving him in just a tee shirt again. The neck was either too tight and cutting his circulation off or his neck looked like that all the time.

"Aaden," Sam said, "I want a check for $100,000,000 dollars. You are going to contact Charles Bondin and tell them to make that check and send it to you here in Prineville. On the way through town, I bought a mailbox. And by the way, you should meet Ben. He is the horrible thing I said might happen to you."

Ben was just inside the door.

"You will not have to do that," Aaden said.

"Tell me how are you going to give me that amount of money?"

"I have a check I would have presented to the winner on national TV when the event is finished."

"The event is finished," Sam said.

Aaden went to a tote with food sitting on the lid and removed the lid. It was filled to the top with beer, ice, and a few bottles of very expensive whisky. He spilled the contents onto the floor. With the heavy tote on its side its floor looked like a safe with a combination lock. Aaden opened the door and removed the check along with $600,000 in cash.

He said to Sam, "There is enough cash there to pay one winner if he or she would have eliminated every contestant themselves. You should know that I have access to a lot of money. More than this. I can make each one of you very wealthy."

Aaden handed Sam a certified check from Charles Bondin, Inc. made out for $100,000,000.

He said, "You sign it and I will witness the signature."

They both signed.

Ruslin said, "There is one more thing now. You promised to kill my sister, and I cannot allow you to threaten her again."

At that Aaden turned to run for the door—but Ben was standing in front of it. He hit Aaden so hard in the forehead with his right hand that you could hear Aaden's skull break.

Mark sat back in his chair and said, "Is that going to happen to me?"

Sam said, "That depends," and outside the building the helicopter sat down again.

"It depends," he said, "on what two other people choose to do with you."

Jackson had gone back to get Emma and Tim.

You could see the fear in Mark's eyes before Emma and

Tim came into the building, not knowing who it might be.

Mark said, "I thought all of the agents were dead."

"All but these two," Sam said.

"Tim, Emma, do you think my family and these other men can ever be safe if I leave Mark alive? I will kill him right now if not."

Emma said, "Thank you Sam."

"Mark," she said, "these men have not killed you, because you are not like the others. And because you are Tim's friend and mine. And because you have a family that needs you."

Emma turned to Sam again, "Mark only works a few hours during a week. He was the Induction Center's computer genius and knows everything about the lottery. The rest of the time he is home. His wife was paralyzed in a car wreck when their children were five and seven, and Mark took this job because it pays the same as Tim's and mine but allows him to take care of June and help raise their daughter and son.

"Mark," Sam said, "do you think Ben could kill you if I asked him to?"

"Yes Sir. I have no doubt."

"Before we go any farther, don't call me sir, or I will have him do it. My name is Sam. And see these two men are honest fishermen. And Aaden promised to kill Leonid's daughter, the youngest in his family. You can't let a man like that live. This other man is Dan. You do not ever want to cross any of us. Do you agree with me? Give me more than a two-word answer. I have heard by a reliable source that you are a genius."

"Sam, I promise you, as a sworn oath to my family and my need to be there for them. I am your friend and loyal to what I think you have probably done. If I am as smart as you say, I think you have gone farther than I know in destroying this lottery. I have prayed for someone like you. You wouldn't know, but once you work for the lottery you learn things about them and live in fear of what they can do to you, and sometimes to your family. You would not know a woman named Nancy Lee, but when I said once that I was going to quit because they wanted me to do more than work in the books, she said it would be sad if my wife had another car wreck. My wife isn't able to drive, but that ended my hope of leaving."

"I did meet Nancy once," Sam said. "Mark, you said you are my friend. If that's true, it means barbeques and things like that if I let you live. Are you able to walk away from this building and never mention to anyone what happened here?

"Yes Sir—I mean Sam."

"Are there any cameras around this building?"

"None. The lottery only wants to see people in the wilderness get shot."

"What PPV? I thought you didn't remember that you were here."

"It will be a new life for my family. I only need to find another job that will allow me to be home."

"I have a check for $100,000,000 in my hand. I think we could help you till you find another job."

***

"Jackson, this is Paul. Are you by your radio?"

Jackson heard Paul on Emma's radio that was linked to the helicopter. "Go ahead Paul."

"I'm sorry, but I am half way back to the hanger. Someone set some explosives off in the wilderness, and I didn't sign up for that. I didn't like this whole thing anyway. Sorry Jackson. Good luck. Be careful."

"Thank you for letting me know. I don't blame you Paul. I will find out what the explosion was and pick up any remaining contestants."

***

Every contestant had a receiver with one channel to hear messages from the pilots and agents.

"Contestants, this comes as an immediate order," Sam said on Emma's radio. "Stop hunting. This is an order from the top. The event has been canceled. Any elimination now will not be paid, and you will answer for any illegal action. Go to your nearest pickup site and a pilot will come."

Jackson and Ben flew the area to the northeastern point

and back twice. Tara Andrews, Jim Bader, and Orlando Ruffin were the only ones left. Orlando had hidden on the steep side of Desolation Canyon. When Jackson's beer keg went off at a mile and a half as the crow flies from Orlando, he guessed it was part of what Ben told him about. He hid under an overhanging rock shelf until hearing Sam on the radio.

Mark watched one of the monitors. No one was moving in the wilderness. It was as still there as it had been before the contest started, and everyone was accounted for. Before the day was over, Jackson and Ben would bring all who had not survived into the meadow at the control center, and a team under contract would pick them up.

Each surviving contestant was paid a fair amount for what they had earned. Jim Bader who had not eliminated anyone the first day was a surprise. During this morning, he had eliminated every remaining contestant except Orlando and Tara, but Tara had a tourniquet on her left arm. She had taken a bullet from Jim Bader's rifle through her right arm just below the shoulder. She held Bader at a distance by shooting her rifle with one hand. If the transmission had not been heard to stop, Tara would probably have added one more to Bader's eliminations that day.

Ben had changed during the hunt. He was not the coldblooded killer he might have thought he was. He and Sam found a place to talk, and Ben confessed how wrong it had been to do this for money. He said it was so different than doing it during war or for protection of another person. He knew those who were brought there might have been threatened by Aaden and should not have died.

From what he had heard of Linnae's past hunts he said to Sam, "Except her."

Jim Bader would be paid $50,000 each for Robin Mitchell, Kenneth Armendez, and Randy Mason.

Tara Andrews would be paid $50,000 for Colby Blackwell. Sam told each contestant they could have the tracking serum removed from their arm.

Away from the others, he gave Orlando $100,000 and told him that was for believing him, to go home and never do anything like this again. Orlando assured him that he wouldn't.

Sam and Ben took charge of the money. They gave Mark $2,000,000 in exchange for a promise that they would be invited to a barbeque sometime later. Sam said his family would want to meet June and the kids.

Ben was generous concerning the money and understood that he had not competed for the full amount. He accepted $200,000 from the cash box for eliminations. Sam told him he hoped some of the money could go toward a good cause and asked if $10,000,000 would be enough for Ben's time spent in the hunt. Ben said it was more than enough. Sam shared with him that Dana and Christine had an idea to put some of the governments money toward helping kids.

$88,000,000 was left. Of course there were bills to pay. The helicopter invoice would be settled, and Jackson would receive $500,000 for his part. They were down to $87,500,000.

Ben felt that Sam was the real winner of the event for the long fight he had been in to protect Christine and end the lottery. Sam said it would be a family vote as to what they should do. Leonid and Ruslin refused to take any money. They said the Lord had provided well for them and that they owed all of the money for Ivonne's safe return home. They were a strong, loyal family and had become lifetime friends.

Sam kept all of the equipment that had belonged to Aaden, and Mark earned his money going through the computers. When he was told that the Induction Center and everything in it was completely destroyed by fire, he told Sam he was certain no other records existed. Ruslin had written with a black marker on the door of the building to protect firemen: BUILDING FILLED WITH FUEL / DO NOT OPEN DOOR!

***

On the way through Prineville Sam reported to the police station that the event in the Mill Creek wilderness had been cancelled. He told them contractors would be there to clean up and asked them to allow a couple of days before going out to inspect the area.

Aaden's body would not be collected with the contestants who died. Jackson and Ben airlifted him to the steep, western wall of Desolation Canyon and dropped him into a deep fracture in a rock formation. As it would be for his brother Daniel, no one would ever find him. Mark knew that Aaden did not have a family. The disappearance of both brothers seemed a fitting end for the way their lives had been lived—without care or compassion for anyone.

The family paid John and Julie $1M for helping during the time Christine could not get released from the lottery and for the fact that they were nearly killed by Daniel Bradley. Frank and Christine insisted that Sam and Dana receive exactly $29,846,597 to match what Christine had earned while Sam kept her alive. He had not accepted anything from them until that day.

The remaining $57,653,403.00 was put into a fund to help children who had been harmed emotionally or physically by CLA. Dana asked Christine to help her and the David Foundation was created. Tax-exempt donations began to pour in as families became aware. One large outlet mall in San Francisco replaced their illuminated billboard from 'The Hunt for Money' lottery to the Foundation's logo, a small girl standing in an empty, whitewashed room, with the words: 'Please Help Me.' Her hand was reaching upward, but there was no one there.

At Westman's Adventure Outlet where Christine purchased the lottery ticket the same sign flashed: "Support the David Foundation—Give What You Can to Help Children—$72,431,356.00—Thank You for Your Gift." And the dollar amount grew every day. The Foundation's generosity could not keep up with donations coming in. At least from Christine's point of view, it seemed like compassion was becoming part of life again.

***

"Honey," Sam said one day, "I think it is time for you and Christine to get help operating the Foundation. Now that I am not working, I need more of your undivided attention, and I know the right person. Sam called Mark. It had been one year since the destruction of the Induction Center and the closing of the lottery. Mark was working from home as a tax consultant, but with the offer to do something where he could make a difference in the lives of children and families, he asked Sam when he could start. Sam said it would only be possible if he closed his other business or put it on hold till he knew if this was right for him. Other than that, Sam said the following day would be the right day to begin learning about the Foundation.

Sam and Dana met Mark's wife and their children after the PPV ended. They had shared barbeques together at Mark's and at Sam and Dana's ranch. Mark found that he was a new man after getting away from the stress of working for Nancy and then Aaden. He could not remember one headline questioning the disappearance of Aaden Bradley.

Hannah was one-year-old and an absolute darling. She had big blue eyes and blonde hair like her mom, aunt, and grandmother on Christine's side. Liam and Jeremiah both had girlfriends. Jeremiah and Charlotte were still together and seemed a perfect match. Liam had met Elizabeth Weber at a car show where he entered his 1976 Ford truck. She was a truck-girl from the moment she saw his old restored truck with the Cummins engine.

Jeff continued to work in the gym with Sam, and at sixty-two Sam was making jokes about the weights getting heavier. In the pool Jeff could swim to one end and back while Sam swam to just one end, and that coming from a retired Navy SEAL. But age catches us all.

At the threat of being a copycat, Sam and Dana had built a pool at the ranch similar to Frank and Christine's. It was larger and had a more powerful stream flowing into the main pool. Where it entered, rather than being a waterfall, it was a swift stream that challenged almost anyone to swim against it. It turned out that Christine could hold herself in the current longer than anyone in the family. The power of the stream was adjustable.

Sam and Dana had remodeled and made the house Dana's. There was not body armor and bullets on the table anymore, and with reconstruction, the house was almost twice as big as it was. There was a second story now with an attached log garage. The main home was 3,890 square feet, and Sam had been careful to have the contractors use the same size of logs as those used originally. When the project was finished, you could not tell there had been an addition to the older log home.

***

It was spring sometime in the morning, and the sun's rays were shining through Dana's kitchen windows. They were thick, tempered glass windows, purposely designed to play tricks with the sun's natural lighting. She told Karly to squint her eyes and look into the sun's rays. They both stood like teenage girls squinting their eyes, looking at the brilliant rays as they came through huge, wood-framed windows. The old windows with steel flat-bar were gone.

Then Dana said to Karly, "I'm going to have a baby."

Karly was almost fourteen. There in those magical rays of sunlight she hugged her mom for the longest time.

"Have you told Dad? I have never had a baby in our house and Dad has really never had a baby."

"No. I just found out. I wanted to tell you first, and we will tell the guys tonight at dinner. Should we go over and see Aunt Christine. We will make her promise to not tell."

Sam and Frank were at John and Julie's house visiting John. He was in bed after having a second heart attack. He always said he wanted to die at home reading his Bible to Julie. That time was close. Leonid, Ruslin, and Ivonne were scheduled to be there in the morning. John didn't know how bad his health was but the doctors had told Julie.

As they talked, it was obvious that John did not have long. The last heart attack had been serious. Sam went to another room and called Dana. He told her not to hold dinner, that he would stay through the night at his mom's house.

Dana said, "I wanted to tell you tonight Honey, but you have to tell your dad. I'm pregnant. We are going to have a baby. Tears began to fill Sam's eyes. He knew his dad would never see his only grandchild. He wiped the tears away and told himself that men don't cry.

Back in his dad's room Julie whispered to him, "It will not be long, Son. I can feel it. I have had such a good life with your father, and you are just like him."

At that, Sam wiped his tears again. He sat on the edge of the bed and picked up his dad's Bible.

As he held it in his hands he said, "Dad, I have something to tell you. Dana and I are going to have a baby. She is pregnant now. You and Mom are going to have a grandchild."

John put his hand on Sam's arm.

Sam said, "This child will know you Dad. I will talk about

all of the things you and I have done together."

Then he said, "I have your Bible opened to where you were reading last. I want to read to Mom for you and because I am your son it will be as if you are reading to her."

He began to read what his dad had underlined:

"And he showed me a pure river of water of life, clear as crystal, proceeding from the throne of God and of the Lamb. In the middle of its street and on either side of the river was the tree of life, which bore twelve fruits, each tree yielding its fruit every month. The leaves of the tree were for the healing of the nations. And there shall be no more curse, but the throne of God and of the Lamb shall be in it, and His servants shall serve Him. They shall see His face, and His name shall be on their foreheads. There shall be no night there. They need no lamp nor light of the sun, for the Lord God gives them light. And they shall reign forever and ever. Then he said to me, "These words are faithful and true."

Julie stepped toward Sam and put her hand on his shoulder.

She said, "He is gone from here, Sam. Will you please give me a few minutes with him?"

Sam and Frank went into the living room. Sam sat in his father's chair, the chair where Daniel had shown them how the glove would work. John was always the one who looked out for others. If anything might have happened, he wanted it to happen to him. He and Frank could hear Julie softly crying.

"I'm sorry Sam. This must be very hard on you and your mom." Frank said. "John was an amazing man."

"I am okay, and you are right Frank. He spent his life doing good for everyone around him. Sometimes that meant getting rid of people who killed and hurt others, but that was okay. It was his job. We are all good at different things. I hope I have been like him and for the same reasons."

"Sam, if it were not for the sacrifices you made, I would not have my wife now. You are just like your dad. I saw your dad's Bible opened before you picked it up. Those words you read must have been what he read last? It made me wonder about some things. I have never taken time to consider the things that made your dad such a strong man. He really believed in what you read didn't he?"

"He did Frank, and I wish I had spent more of my life believing as strongly as he did. I gave up so many years of love and being loved for what I thought I needed to do with my life. I suppose because I was good at getting rid of bad guys—just like Dad was. I need to go home for a while and see my wife, and you need to go see yours. I will take care of what I can here, then come back and stay with Mom tonight."

"Sam, tell me if there is anything I can do to help. Your dad and you have given me a lot to think about.

***

Christine was standing on the front porch as Jeff walked out to catch the school bus. She was holding Hannah. As Jeff stepped up into the bus, he turned back and waved at Hannah.

She waved and said, "Bye."

In spite of all odds the Conder family had not only survived the trials of a lottery that should never have been, but their family had grown. It was October again. Christine and Dana would once again have babies who would grow up together. Hannah would be less than two years older than Sam and Dana's baby. His name was Johnathon Samuel Morrison, and they called him John.

Karly was in college studying to be an attorney. Jeremiah had married Charlotte and served as the senior pastor at a local church. Liam and Jeff both enlisted in the United States Navy. Liam specialized in 'Characterization of Satellite Remote Sensing Systems,' and Jeff became a Navy SEAL. As it always is, each of the kids were busy with their own lives, but they had formed a bond throughout the time of the lottery that would never be forgotten. And there was no question that they would come together again if troubled times called.

***

KSENIA'S DAUGHTER would be seen from time to time fishing herring in the icy waters where Ivonne had cried in her father's arms over the death of Daniel Bradley. She would be caught in those inescapable storms on the high seas that have taken so many lives. Occasionally she would shut the engines down and drift silently over the same waters where her mother and sister and brothers had disappeared from her. Over the door where she entered the wheelhouse the name 'Uncle Timur' was carved into a weathered board that had been fixed to the aluminum cabin.

***

January 19th, 2045: "Hi Dad, my team is leaving for a mission. I can't say where but will call when I can. Is Mom home?

"No, but I will tell her you called."

"Thanks. I called Sam's to wish him a good day on his birthday and Dana said he is in the hospital but wouldn't say why. What happened?"

"Liam and I spent a couple of hours with him today, then Liam had to fly back to the ship.

"I will be honest Son. Dana told me she didn't want you to know right now. She said you need to concentrate on what's ahead, but Sam was shot. There was a note in his shirt pocket that said, 'Sam killed my family. This is just the beginning!'

"Son, I am sorry for doing all of the talking. Sam will be okay. The bullet came through the side window and cut through his scalp right above what they call the Coronal suture. You can imagine the bleeding from a wound like that. He was unconscious and must have looked like he was dead. John was playing outside and heard the shot, and lucky for Sam, Dana was there within a minute and got him to the hospital. Jeremiah and Charlotte will stay at the ranch until we find out who shot Sam. And Ben is on his way, so don't worry about us here. Sam told me he learned from Mark when the pay-per-view ended that Colin Brown had a son who was nine-years-old when Colin and Nancy were killed. He would be nineteen or twenty now and Sam believes it could be him. I am not sure what leads him to think that, but I never doubt Sam.

"Your mom went to visit Dana this morning. You must have called before she got there."

"I called just a few minutes before calling you. I wanted to ask Sam a couple of questions. Dana didn't say anything about Mom being there, and I am sure she would have. Did Dana know she was coming?"

"I don't know if she called ahead, but she should have been there, Son. I'm worried. Your mom would have called me if she changed her mind…"

Made in the USA
Middletown, DE
24 June 2021